CHINESE WALLS

A Novel

•

DAUGHTERS OF HUI

A Fiction Collection

2nd Edition

1st edition *Chinese Walls,* Asia 2000 Ltd., Hong Kong, 1994.

1st edition *Daughters of Hui,* Asia 2000 Ltd., Hong Kong, 1996.

CHINESE WALLS

A Novel

•

DAUGHTERS OF HUI

A Fiction Collection

XU XI

with a preface by Dr. Michael Anthony Ingham
Department of English, Lingnan University

CHAMELEON PRESS LTD.
Suite 23A Success Commercial Building, 245 - 251 Hennessy Road,
Wanchai, Hong Kong, S.A.R., China
www.chameleonpress.com

This is a work of fiction. The names, characters, places, and incidents either are the product of the author's imagination or are used fictitiously. Their resemblance, if any, to actual events or real-life counterparts, is purely co-incidental.

A CHAMELEON PRESS BOOK
CHINESE WALLS • DAUGHTERS OF HUI (2nd Edition)

Distributed in the U.S. & Canada by **WEATHERHILL**
41 Monroe Turnpike, Trumbull, CT 06611 • www.weatherhill.com
tel 800.437.7840 • fax 800.557.5601

Agent for all rights **Harold Matson Company**, New York, NY

Cover design by **Bill McGuire** and **Julia Brown**

Typeset in Adobe Garamond and Optima
Printed in Hong Kong by Elite Printing Co., Ltd.
ISBN 962-86319-1-8

CONTENTS

PREFACE TO THE SECOND EDITION
Chinese Walls • Daughters of Hui

by DR. MICHAEL ANTHONY INGHAM
Department of English, Lingnan University

1 Rationale for the Present Edition

It's not hard to discern that identity is a major thematic concern in Hong Kong/US novelist Xu Xi's *oeuvre.* Her first novel, *Chinese Walls* was published under the moniker, Sussy Chako, after which she reverted to her Indonesian name, Komala, before finally settling on her simple but engaging Chinese name Xu Xi, under which by-line all her recent work, including the critically acclaimed *The Unwalled City* (2001) and *History's Fiction* (2001) has been published.

The change of publisher from Asia 2000 to Chameleon Press is not the sole reason for the appearance of the present portmanteau edition of her first two major works, *Chinese Walls* (1994) and *Daughters of Hui* (1996). With burgeoning interest in her work both in Hong Kong and the United States, partly on the back of her reading tours and commitment to literature in education, this fresh publication of her earlier work fulfils a need for both the initiated and the uninitiated reader. Despite the fact that works like *The Unwalled City* and *History's Fiction* speak for themselves as literary artifacts, it is illuminating to trace the nexus of inter-textual and cross-cultural threads, which permeate her shorter and longer fiction, and gain insight into her characters, situations and preoccupations through recursive features which appear across her writing.

Bearing in mind the growing academic and international interest in English-medium Asian authors, it is high time that these two provocative and distinctive reflections on love and sexuality, cultural, family and gender values, Hong Kong life in the lead-up to 1997, the *wah kiu* and the diasporic experience, among many other things, are once more available in the familiar bookshops, (Swindon's, Dymock's, Bookazine *et al).* Speaking personally, it has been frustrating trying to obtain copies of these works for tertiary level courses of Asian Voices in English in the past few years. Just as she became recognized as a local writer of substance and talent with something worth saying in an original voice, it became difficult to locate her early work. Now that problem has been remedied.

Xu Xi has been a tireless champion of Hong Kong writing in English, not from an ideologically pro-Western motivation, but purely for the pragmatic reason that English has become her narrative L1 (first language). Whilst it may not be particularly politically correct in post-handover Hong Kong to assert the values of linguistic and cultural pluralism among ethnically Chinese denizens of this hybrid Chinese city, the fact remains that it is often possible to tackle taboo subjects and employ a critical idiom in a literary *lingua franca* without the deep cultural connotations, inhibitions and linguistic hierarchies consonant with the use of standard Chinese. As she herself asserts in her article, *Writing the Literature of Non-Denial*, 'It didn't work to write British sometimes and American at others. My fiction was jammed between two national Englishes...The day I read [Maxine Hong Kingston's] *The Woman Warrior* I heard the first truly clear echoes of myself. Her novelistic consciousness was uttered in English, but informed by Cantonese...My English is enriched by Chinese....'[1] Thus Xu Xi's use of English as her primary medium is both a practical necessity and an assertion of her bi-cultural identity. Her work is not an approximation or a translation of a literary experience, rather the direct expression of the experience itself. In that respect it is distinctly at variance with the voice of many best-selling Chinese memoir-novel writers, who transpose their experience into English as the result of a commercial and not an aesthetic imperative.

When *Chinese Walls* first appeared in Hong Kong in 1994 it was perhaps difficult to market this debut novel simply on the strength of its real subject matter, a dysfunctional family and a painful emotional odyssey on the part of the protagonist. By packaging the work as a sultry, orientalist romance, as strongly implied by the original cover photo of a mysterious Asian woman, concealing half her face with an open fan, the publisher's promotion placed the novel firmly within a well-established genre of fiction that does little more than reinforce stereotypes about pouting oriental beauties and their interaction with rich, debonair and often duplicitous

[1] Writing the Literature of Non-Denial. (420-2) in *World Englishes,* No.3, November 2000. Blackwell, Oxford, UK & Boston, USA.

men, thus somewhat akin to a James Bond yarn. Fortunately, many reviewers saw through this ploy and chose not to judge the book by its anomalous cover.

It is perhaps a reflection of Hong Kong's imported popular culture, whether American globalised mainstream or Japanese kitsch, that authentic local voices are sometimes stifled, or simply neglected. In the case of Xu Xi and her uncomfortably sharp exposé of the oddly Victorian double standards in the local Chinese psyche with regard to issues of sex and sexuality, it is unsurprising that some would have found her voice grating and discordant – particularly amidst the striving for political and cultural fusion in the 1997 re-integration into the motherland. An uncompromising or idiosyncratic writer, however, may often feel obliged to write against the grain of public, or at least officially public, sentiment, knowing that as a writer, the only ultimate truth is the truth to oneself, as Polonius sagaciously, if uncharacteristically, observed.

Daughters of Hui, a 1996 quartet of stories, the first of novella length, reaffirmed the early promise of her story, *The Yellow Line*, broadcast on the BBC World Service in 1981, and her first novel. They also maintained her reputation for a somewhat controversially polemical choice, not only of theme and topic, but also of angle and viewpoint, including a pointed reference to the 1989 Tiananmen massacre. It enjoyed a positive reception from reviewers and enhanced the perception of her progress as a genuinely Hong Kong writer, in spite of the predominantly overseas setting of the stories in the collection. *Hong Kong Rose*, which followed, and the more recent *The Unwalled City* have restored the balance by concentrating on a predominantly Hong Kong milieu. Interestingly, though, Hong Kong as a place is ubiquitous at the implicit and subconscious level of *Daughters of Hui*, a locus of diasporic nostalgia, tinged with underlying feelings of doubt, disquiet and repression. The dream-like eroticism of the collection's tone and mood is evoked by an altogether more feminist and less orientalist cover design than that of *Chinese Walls*. Four naked women, two standing and two sitting or crouching are drawn, rather than photographed, in poses suggesting self-absorption, self-sufficiency and sexual autonomy from the male. Unlike the *Chinese Walls* cover, there is no seductive posturing for the benefit of an implied male gaze, rather a frank physical self-expression. In fact, this book couldn't be judged too much by its cover either, since its various heroines are mostly aspiring to a state of empowered *nirvana*, as opposed to already enjoying it.

2 Every Wall that ever was…

At this point it may be apposite to say more about the themes and techniques of both *Chinese Walls* and *Daughters of Hui*. The episodic and thematically recursive, spiral structure of *Chinese Walls* is overlaid by a seemingly linear first-person narrative from childhood through adolescence to womanhood in the consciousness of a *wah kiu* Hong Kong woman, who refers to herself as 'a freak, neither Chinese nor Western.' Clearly it derives to some extent from the experience of the author, although it is far from the mode of the autobiographical memoir. What strikes the reader is its lack of sensationalism in the style bearing in mind the subject matter, relating as it does Ai Lin's sexual and emotional odyssey, ranging from her incest with her brother Philip, perverse surrogate sex with her American boyfriend, Derek, marriage and divorce from husband Vince and a sexual relationship with Vince's brother, Don. Described in these terms it would seem to have pre-empted Wei Hui's *succès de scandale*, *Shanghai Baby*, for sheer taboo-breaking shock value.

The reality, however, is more prosaic. Xu Xi is much less concerned with titillating the reader, but with portraying the more universally human tensions of gender difference, emotional insecurity, moral guilt and the psychological scars inflicted by a dysfunctional background, the crisis of cultural identity and belonging in a diasporic community, the fragility of the psyche, whether male or female, the craving for affection and the visceral need for a place to call home. These, much more than sex and female libido, are the recurrent themes of Xu Xi's fiction. It is true that the novel is constructed in accordance with the working title, *The Men in My Life*, which reminds one immediately of Mae West's celebrated *bon mot* to the effect that it's not the men in her life that's important, but the life in her men! However, the men in Ai Lin's life include her father as well as her two brothers, Philip and Paul, her husband Vince and her brother-in-law, Don, to whom she is becoming more emotionally and intellectually attached at the close of the novel, not to mention the obsessive and troubled Derek. Whatever Freudian interpretation the reader may place on these diverse relationships, they form the backbone, not only of the novel, but also of Ai Lin's insecure life. From her acute sense of loss as the male bastions of her life crumble and fall, one by one, Philip dying of AIDS, Paul adopting a hermit lifestyle and her marriage in self-inflicted disarray, Ai Lin starts tentatively to look for herself and learns to recognize her own voice. This theme is elaborated more fully in Xu Xi's subsequent work, in which writing and self-expression play a meta-fictional role, which is central to the lives of many of her female creations.

Interestingly the protagonist's neurotically Catholic mother, a beautifully depicted character, (as is the skillfully drawn cameo of her father's rock-collecting *mama-san* friend, Lulu) is not, unlike her male family members, permitted her own story in the novelistic schema of things. The resulting imbalance can be seen as characteristic of the novel as a whole, oriented as it is towards Ai Lin's interactions with the men in her life. The light brush strokes used to sketch other female characters, including the teenage prostitute with orange hair in the opening chapter, *Chung King Mansion*, underscore the novel's ambience of the female as subaltern in a male-dominated world.

Ai-Lin's Eurasian school-friend, Helena Choy, equally dark-skinned but more amply proportioned than her, born of a Portuguese mother and Chinese doctor father, provides an interesting cultural counter-balance to the narrator. Helena introduces her to another Portuguese Eurasian, Ricardo da Silva, bilingual, bicultural, heterosexual and 'incredibly handsome.' Philip's incestuous jealousy causes a potentially deep and meaningful relationship to be strangled in infancy. However the more open-minded and sophisticated Ricardo reminds the reader of a common theme in much of Xu Xi's work, namely the value of minority Asian and Eurasian intercultural influence and interaction within the dominant Cantonese and English mental landscape. While the role of the Portuguese in Macau has been well documented, Portuguese-Eurasian presence in Hong Kong is much less written about. Later in *Daughters of Hui* we meet characters such as Rosemary's feisty Chinese-Jamaican colleague, Celia Wong, who, likewise, simply do not fit into a neat conventional schema of East-West binary opposition.

As a portrait of an innocent Hong Kong 1960s childhood, an angst-ridden '70s adolescence and young adulthood in the U.S. to an emergent self-estimation and recognition of self-worth back in Hong Kong in the 1980s, *Chinese Walls* conveys the emotional roller-coaster of socio-cultural and psycho-sexual insecurity, the elation of sexual fulfillment, the suicidal despair of failure and loss. Ai Lin's cry-for-help attempted suicide and her stay in hospital under the supervision of the clinically Freudian Dr Felicia Cheung, as narrated in the insightful chapter, *Loving Jade*, establishes a revealing pseudo-dialogue between Ai-Lin and her psychiatrist. The sexual fantasies of Ai-Lin and the men in her life are played out, her repressed consciousness given free expression and gradually a process of psychic healing is embarked on. Understanding of people as they are, especially the men in her life, forgiveness and self-acceptance are the lessons the protagonist learns in this pivotal chapter of the novel.

Despite its surface unity of narrative voice and apparent narrative continuity, *Chinese Walls* is paradoxically dislocated in form and technique, a sequence of loosely linked, spiraling, quasi-short fiction pieces, which can and have been taken out of their novel framework and published separately. Indeed many of them work well as self-contained stories, and the author's predilection and flair for the short fiction form is evident within the novel's loose but coherent construction. Formally and technically she stands out from the crowd of Chinese writers in English. Like Arundhati Roy her form and content are indivisible and consciously worked, and it this felicitous conjunction of the two that characterises her writing. Whether representing the consciousness of the child,

Ai-Lin, through deceptively simple yet questioning language in the opening chapter or switching to the obsessive and abrupt syntax, and bitter irony of the suicidally depressive in *Loving Jade*, the formal variety and versatility and the stylistic fusion of form with content, confers qualities of resilience, robustness and authenticity on the text.

It is writing free from decorative pretentiousness, in which the terse, straight-ahead narrative style is effortlessly molded to the mood, character and moment of a particular strand of the macro-narrative. Subtle shifts of tense and skilful blending of direct, indirect and free-indirect speech, often contained within a stream-of-consciousness closed structure, give the reader the opportunity to interpret the vital links between present and past seemingly in advance of the narrator herself. This distancing effect creates a sense of irony, but at the same time of empathy, between protagonist and reader. Ultimately, the first-person narrator achieves a sense of wry irony concerning her own 'pilgrim's progress.' In that respect we can see *Chinese Walls* as a kind of small-scale *Bildungsroman* – or novel of self-formation and realization – a form that has strong precedents in world literature.

Another way of reading *Chinese Walls* is as confessional literature, a cathartic purgation of the ambivalent, formative experiences of Ai-Lin's life. However, here is no Augustinian conversion. The subtlety of Xu Xi's treatment of the theme of illicit love and sex is ultimately in its acceptance of the narrator's total experience, including the repressed, Oedipal love between her brother Paul and his mother and the physically comforting but erotically stimulating sexual relations between herself and older brother, Philip. Like Arundhati Roy's emotionally damaged sister and brother, Rahel and Estha in *The God of Small Things*, 'they broke the

Love Laws that laid down who should be loved. And how. And how much.'

3 Confucius and other Tyrants

'Twere profanation of our joys
To tell the laity our love

These lines from John Donne's poem, Valediction, preface the final story in Xu Xi's collection *Daughters of Hui*, and provide an evocative connection with the illicit love narrated in *Chinese Walls*, as well as to the quotation above from *The God of Small Things*. The same sense of cultural and emotional dislocation is mapped in the interior landscape of *Daughters of Hui*. The linking device of the opening novella, *Danny's Snake*, and the three accompanying short stories is that the female protagonists share the surname, Hui. All five Hui women (there are two Huis in the story *The Stone Window* – one a *doppelganger* of the other) also share a sense of marginalisation from their Hong Kong heritage, as well as a fear of commitment, familiar themes in the Xu Xi artistic gallery.

Rosemary (Rosa-M) in *Danny's Snake* is, as she becomes aware, both attracted and repelled by Danny and his snake, the latter connoting Christian temptation and fall symbolism. Her fidelity and commitment to absent fellow-immigrant husband, Man-Kit (Manky), is sorely tested, but the reader feels that by the time Manky returns from visiting his dying father in Hong Kong, she has learned more about herself and come to understand and accept her and Manky's joint destiny. Of all these Hui women, Rosemary seems to be the only one who is prepared to contemplate the societal role of motherhood. Now that Manky is back with her in the relatively non-threatening (for Rosa-M) cultural terrain of the United States, she can consider making love to him, 'perhaps without her diaphragm.'

Providing the authenticating and anxiety-inducing background to the story is what is now referred to somewhat euphemistically as 'the Tiananmen Incident.' Rosemary's sense of isolation and mixed feelings about her home are attenuated by her powerlessness and distance, so that she finds it painful to discuss the unfolding drama and tragedy. Her numbed feelings and reluctant voice contrast poignantly with the spontaneous chorus of unified protest, as sketched out for her by her husband on the telephone from Hong Kong. Even her middle-class, normally apathetic sisters-in-law marched!

The other Hui women in this collection are viewed in a more solipsistic light. Like Rosemary, the first-person, anonymous narrator of *Loving Graham* plays the seduction games, but much more promiscuously and amorally than the more self-conscious and less worldly-wise Rosemary. It is perhaps tempting but erroneous to assume that the 'I' voice of *Loving Graham* approximates more closely to the personal experience of the author, and that the relatively insecure third-person narrative of *Danny's Snake* is less personal and therefore more relevant to a woman that is 'other', as opposed to 'self.' Admittedly, the stronger, more assertive and motherly Celia, half Jamaican and half Chinese, provides a foil to Xu Xi's vacillating heroine. Rosa-M is simply a more complex character, whose experiences are viewed from a more omniscient and open perspective, unlike the confessional but selective voice of the *Loving Graham* narrator.

Often with the conclusions and codas to Xu Xi's tales of love and the search for the self comes a surprisingly unsurprising revelation. In *Loving Graham*, for example, we realize that the subtext of the stream-of-consciousness, Parker-esque narrative lies in the notion of romantic love, undercutting the mantra of feminist empowerment in which sex functions as a means to an end, which we had assumed to be the point of the story. In other words the pleasure of the text as a whole is in the variety and freedom from stereotype we find in her combination of first-and third-person 'heroines'. The same cannot perhaps be said of the debonair and polished male characters in the stories, some of whom seem almost identikit in description. However it is equally true that a few of her male characters, especially Manky and the enigmatically handsome, sax-playing Danny, and to some extent Ralph Carder in *The Stone Window*, are much more developed and three-dimensional. Manky's tale is beautifully told from his own perspective in the later *History's Fiction.*

The Stone Window in contrast to *Danny's Snake* opts for a male perspective, but like the other story is told in the third person with a limited, non-omniscient perspective that works well for its subject matter and mood. Love and art are fused in a semi-mythical Greek island setting. We don't really get under the skin of the mysterious Hui women, both of whom the male protagonist pursues. He woos the elusive pictorial artist Philomena, and when she abruptly disappears he meets the fledgling writer Hui Sai Yee through fate or coincidence at a gallery exhibiting one of Philomena's distinctive paintings. The narrative jump-cuts between the four distinct episodes, or one might even describe them as musical movements, enhance the reader's sense of exotic hyper-reality. If one thinks about it this is a neatly deconstructive reversal of the familiar process – an 'oriental' writer exoticising an occidental locale, steeped in myth and mystery. Here the female personas are linked to mythical, Goddess-like archetypes, while the would-be male hero of legend fails, just like his own *doppelganger*, the pot-bellied Greek, in his latter-day quest, and is left with an abiding sense of loss and melancholy. *The Stone Window*, which permits only an interior brilliant illumination without external recognition or vision, provides a fitting trope for the elusive futility of our attempt to discern the meaning of our experience through an exterior, rational frame of reference.

The motifs of loss and redemption, of time present in time past, of written and pictorial art resurface in *Valediction*, the final piece in *Daughters of Hui*, and probably one of the finest and most compelling prose works by the author to date. 'London. 1989. Winter.' And a 3-line suicide note from the narrator's elder sister. The remembrance of things past which constitutes the one-sided interior conversation of the story, again in stream-of-consciousness mode, deals with the successes and failures in life and love of the two sisters, but ends on a note of cautious and role-reversing affirmation. The failed suicide younger sibling recalls the events of their parallel lives and exorcises the feelings of guilt imposed on her by her upbringing ('Confucius and other tyrants'), and finally pays tribute to the memory of her dearly beloved, supposedly stoic and emotionally stable big sister. 'Dear *Ga je*. Until we meet. All my love. *Muihmui*.'

The intimacy of her tone here contrasts with her scathing indictment of the irreconcilable prejudices and hypocrisies of the age-old East-West dichotomy. Fierce critique of cultural preconceptions and hegemonic western attitudes is in fact at the heart of both *Daughters of Hui* and *Chinese Walls*, although Xu Xi never sermonizes or preaches in her fiction, so the reader would not perceive her as an overtly political writer.

'How the western world fails us for our most intimate expressions, our sense of family, our understanding of love.' (*Valediction*). Hence the use of *ga je* and *muihmui* and the omission of westernized names in the narrative.

Xu Xi's own linguistic-cultural 'schizophrenia' (a term she employs about herself in the article *Writing the Literature of Non-Denial*) stalks her writing like a hungry wolf. It is this terse, restless, but unpretentious quality of her prose, alternating with sudden bites of acerbically ironic observation of the absurdity of life – ('Was I an accident? They'll never say and we'll never know. So it's the guessing game, the favorite pastime of Chinese life.' *Valediction*) – that gives her writing such edge. And when a softer voice is heard in her writing, expressing sincere affection, as in this particular story, it is all the more affecting and authentic given the absence of sentimentality in her natural style.

She has remarked of her own method, 'What I discovered was that I needed a different kind of English to speak across the actual language of my characters and for the Hong Kong world I rendered.'[2] This method was honed in the watershed fiction of these two works. Both *Chinese Walls* and *Daughters of Hui* bear eloquent testimony to her ability to create a separate and authentic linguistic and cultural space for her characters to inhabit. Her voice, like that of Hong Kong English-medium poets, Louise Ho and Agnes Lam, can be seen to represent the alterity and idiosyncrasy of Hong Kong culture, in the way that *daan taats*[3] or Hong Kong-style 'English' pubs do. In this increasing globalised city let us hope that they all continue to flourish!

[2] Writing the Literature of Non-Denial. (420-2) in *World Englishes*, No.3, November 2000. Blackwell, Oxford, UK & Boston, USA.

[3] *Daan taat* - a type of custard tart extremely popular and particular to Hong Kong and Macau.

CHINESE WALLS

NOVEL

for Greg

The Master said, "Men are close to one another by nature.
They diverge as a result of repeated practice."

Book XVII, *The Analects*
Confucius
translation D.C. Lau

1

Chung King Mansion

On my ninth birthday, my mother sits me down in front of her dressing table mirror and brushes my hair. She tells me a story of Indonesia, the country of her birth.

"Before the war when I was still a little girl, no bigger than you are today, Ai-Lin, my parents had a big house in Tjilatjap. My brothers took me down to the beach and told me to be careful of the crocodiles." She stops and laughs. "Maybe one day you will meet your uncles. They were funny, naughty boys, full of energy and life."

I try to imagine this big country Indonesia where my mother was a girl and rode horses on the beach. My mother speaks to me only in English nowadays, a funny, musical accent that's a bit like Chinese and a bit like Indonesian. She used to speak Indonesian to me, and even Mandarin, but stopped because Dad wants all the children to speak good English like him.

From the window of my parents' bedroom, I can see clear across the harbor to Hong Kong side. It's Saturday morning. I like it when my birthday falls on a weekend and I don't have to go to school.

My mother continues. "My daddy was a very rich man, one of the richest in Tjilatjap. He used to say that the reason he was rich was because he worked hard, and because he was Chinese. Which is why, Ai-Lin, you must always be proud of being a Chinese no matter where you are. Because Chinese people are smart and successful, and don't ever forget that."

Yesterday, my brother Philip got slapped by Mum because he said Chinese people were dirty and afraid of the British, and that Hong Kong would always be a colony, and why couldn't the Chinese be like the Indonesians who fought for their independence against the Dutch.

My mother brushes harder and faster now.

"My daddy was important as well as rich. In Tjilatjap, he was one of the few men that the Dutch administrator would consult on local matters. Your grandfather was never afraid of the Dutch, like some of the other Chinese, or the Indonesians. He was a tall man, and he stood tall. He knew what was right."

In the mirror, I see my mother's eyes shining. I like to see her smile because then she is the most beautiful woman in the world. My father is away in Indonesia today, on an important business trip. But he left me a new dress as my birthday present, and Mum gave me an extra kiss which she said was from Dad.

And then, my mother's hand slackens, and she holds my long hair in both her hands. "I was so happy in Indonesia," she says. "One day, I'll go back there for good."

I hang up my new dress and get ready to go to the comic book stand. Paul and Philip have both given me money for my birthday and told me to choose my own comics. I want to buy the new Supergirl. Philip asks why I don't wear my new dress and I tell him, quite sternly since I think he ought to know better, that it would be silly to wear such a nice dress just to go down the street. Philip laughs and says I'm such a prim and proper little lady, and then tickles me until I laugh and cry at the same time. Paul tells Philip to leave me alone.

I take the back lifts down my building because I want to go out the side entrance through the Ambassador Hotel arcade. Nathan Road is already quite busy, even though it's only ten o'clock. My mother doesn't like living in Tsimshatsui; she says this area is too noisy and crowded and wants my father to buy a house in Kowloon Tong or Yau Yat Chuen where there are trees and real houses. But I like Tsimshatsui and our flat which has two floors and an interior connecting staircase. From our verandah on the seventeenth floor, I can watch the Kowloon-Canton railway trains pull into the station, and the grey U.S. battleships dock in the harbor. The sweep of the island's hills are like a picture frame for the buildings dotting the hillside and the waterfront. At night, the neon lights go on. My favorite is the one on top of the low building in the middle - three red Japanese characters which Dad says is an advertisement for monosodium glutimate. It isn't lonely in Tsimshatsui, or quiet and scary.

The comic book stand is down a side street a few streets away from my building. I go past Chung King Mansion's dingy, cavernous mouth. Two American sailors are going into the building. Their white uniforms gleam like the teeth on the toothpaste commercial on TV. Aren't they afraid of getting their uniforms dirty in there?

I find the new Supergirl issue I want, and buy an extra Batman comic for Philip. Philip pretends he's too old for comics - he's only thirteen - but I've seen him reading them when he thought no one was looking. Boys are so silly, even big boys like my brothers.

The comics tucked under my arm, I run back along Nathan Road towards Middle Road where my building is. As I near Chung King Mansion, I slow down. Coming down the steps of that building is the strangest looking person. She has orange hair, and wears a short *cheongsam* with a stiff high collar and very high heels. There's something unreal about her, like she's a doll that's come to life. I watch her slow, uncertain progress down the steps, as if she hasn't learnt how to walk in heels. My mother says it's very important for a lady to know how to walk properly in high heels, with her legs straight, taking firm but graceful steps. When I grow up I will learn how to walk correctly in heels.

But this woman on the steps obviously hasn't learnt.

"Paul," I ask that evening, "have you ever been inside Chung King Mansion?"

My big brother looks up from his school books and his glasses slide down his nose. "Why are you asking?"

"Well, have you?" I know if I persist, he will eventually tell me. Paul is the best brother in the world.

He pushes up his glasses. "Yes."

"Is it dangerous in there?"

"Sometimes. Now can I finish my homework?"

I think about this a moment and then give him a kiss on the cheek, which is the way I thank him, and go upstairs to find Philip.

Philip is at the piano in the bedroom of course, which is where he always is instead of doing his homework. He doesn't like to be bothered when he's practising, but I can tell that he's just fooling around and not really playing. So I sit on the bench next to him.

"How come some Chinese women have orange hair?"

He stops playing and looks at me. "Have you been dreaming?"

"You know, like the ladies outside Chung King Mansion."

"Oh them." My brother looks embarrassed. "They want to look Eurasian."

"But why?"

Philip makes an impatient face and I can see he doesn't want to tell me. My best friend Helena Choy is Eurasian, but she has black hair like me and doesn't look one bit like the Chung King ladies at all.

My mother's voice sails up from the living room. "Philip, can you go get my prescription?"

"Can't Paul go?"

"He's doing his homework, which is more than you're doing. Now go."

I tug my brother's arm. "Can I go too?"

Philip grabs the back of my neck. "Okay, come along."

My mother frowns a little when she sees me with Philip at the door. She always says that young girls shouldn't go out too late, especially when the sailors are out. I've never been quite sure what she means by that, but whenever I've asked, she replies that I'll find out when I've grown up. But she lets me go, because it's my birthday, and warns Philip, "Don't you two dilly dally."

I dance alongside Philip, clutching his arm. We go down in the front lifts and walk out onto Middle Road. Across the road, I see some older kids going into the bowling alley. Paul says bowling isn't a real sport, and a waste of money. But then, he thinks everything is a waste of money. I'm going into the bowling alley someday, when I'm older.

"Want to go over the hump?" Philip asks and I nod excitedly. The "hump" is the path next to the Royal Observatory that lets us out right in the middle of Mody Road. My mother calls it the hump because it curves uphill and down again like the hump on a camel's back. Dad says that silly. But I like the name because it's our family's private name for it, which somehow makes the path our own secret, special way.

At the end of the hump, there are low buildings, only three or four storeys high, on a small cul-de-sac. Its mouth is flanked by two huge trees, which my mother says have been there forever. "Concrete jungles are built around the real jungle," she says. "In Indonesia, there's too much foliage and jungle for the buildings. There, unlike Hong Kong, nature is stronger than the vain egos of men." My mother says strange things sometimes. She doesn't like buildings. I like the low buildings, but the trees and the hill of the Royal Observatory block their view. Not like my building, with its wonderful wide open view of the Hong Kong harbor, which Dad says is one of the most scenic harbors in the world, matched only by San Francisco and Rio de Janeiro. I'm going to both those harbors when I grow up to see for myself.

At the pharmacy, the store clerk says to me in Cantonese, "*Muih muih yuht lai yuht daaih aah.* Little sister is getting bigger and bigger." He has a nice smile. Philip takes the wrapped package of medicine. "It's her birthday," he says pointing to me, and the man tugs my ponytail and asks how old I am and I tell him. The man speaks funny Cantonese, and Mum says that's because he's from Fukien, like us. I thought we were from Indonesia but Mum says our family was originally from Fukien, which doesn't make much sense to me. But I don't speak funny Cantonese, and neither do my brothers. It's only our parents who do.

"Want to go home the long way?" Philip asks, and I nod. Mum would have gone over the hump, because it's faster. She's always in a hurry.

The long way is up Mody Road towards Nathan Road, and back to Middle Road. We make a circle. At the junction of Nathan and Mody, Tsimshatsui comes alive like a huge electric circus.

It's sailor night. I see hordes of them all over the place. There was a new battleship this morning docked in the middle of the harbor, flying a Stars and Stripes. My mother says it has to do with the war and R&R. I don't know what she means. I thought the war she always talks about with the Japanese in Indonesia was over before I was born.

"Sailors walk funny," Philip whispers to me as we pass a group of them. "That's because their pants are too tight and their bell bottoms flap around under their knees."

"They look like ducks," I say, and Philip starts making silly quacking noises.

As we near Chung King Mansion, I see her again. Orange hair, orange nails, wearing a shiny, satiny short *cheongsam* that fits her so tightly I think it will burst. She's standing at the top of the stairs like a princess waiting to go to the ball. Her voice is bright and cheerful as she laughs and talks with the other ladies. "It's her," I tell Philip, trying to point discreetly. But by the time he pays attention to me and looks, she's disappeared back into the building.

That night, I dream about my orange lady. She is standing at the foot of the stairs wearing an orange gown like Cinderella's fairy godmother in my picture book. "*Muih muih, yahp lai.* Little sister, come in." I start to follow her, but a group of American sailors rush past and knock me down. Her hollow laugh, like the voice of a ghost, floats into the air as she drifts back into the darkness of Chung King Mansion.

I've been nine almost a whole week now and I think I like being nine. I feel like I'm a lot closer to being grown up than when I was eight. My mother tells me things all the time now that Dad's away a lot. She cries when Dad's away. She says men are not to be trusted, because they have too much pride and have to feel important. Also, men don't understand love. In life, she says, these are things I must never forget.

She's right. Those American sailors who've been roaming the streets of Tsimshatsui all week are always talking loudly about love. They let lots of girls run after them, because they're proud. I know. I've seen them. Everyone knows you don't shout about love all over the place. That's what Mum says.

It's Friday evening and Mum needs her medicine again. She always gets sick when she talks too much. I've told her I'll go to the pharmacy because both the boys are still out. At first, she doesn't want to allow me, but in the end she lets me because I'm grown up and responsible enough now to go quickly there and back, she says.

I go past Chung King Mansion and look for my orange lady. I haven't told Mum about her because, well because Mum's not well and doesn't have time to listen to my silly stories.

She isn't there either on my way out or on my way back. As usual, there are a group of ladies in brightly colored *cheongsams* around.

At dinner, I ask, "Why are there so many ladies around the entrance to Chung King Mansion?"

Philip chortles. "They're not 'ladies' Ai-Lin, well not exactly."

"Do you know any of them?"

This time, Paul suppresses a laugh. "He better not."

Suddenly, my mother bangs her spoon hard. "You boys are getting more like your father every day. There's nothing to laugh at!"

"We were only . . ." begins Paul in a conciliatory tone.

"Be quiet!"

No one speaks for a few minutes. I don't understand why Mum is so upset. And I still didn't get an answer to my question. So I try again. "But who are they, those ladies?"

Mum raises her voice. "That's enough questions from you. These things don't concern you until you're grown up!"

I bend my head over my dinner and don't say another word. It seems I'm only grown up when my mother says so.

Mum needs the clasp on her pearl brooch fixed.

To get to Linda Yue's jewellery shop, I cross Nathan Road and go down Peking Road past the topless bar with pictures of half naked women that Philip snickers at.

Mrs. Yue is wearing a cheongsam, which is all she ever wears. Her shop is fragrant with flowers and perfume.

"Good girl," she says, when I hand her the brooch. "Your mama must trust you a lot if she lets you go out alone."

Mrs. Yue speaks funny Cantonese too, like almost everyone my parents know or do business with. She and her husband are Shanghainese, and are members of the Jockey Club, which is how we know them. Their daughter is in my class. Mum buys all her jewellery from her because of our connection. Everything grown up seems to be connected.

"Here," she hands me a bunch of violets. "Bring to your mother," she says in English.

"Thank you aunty," I reply. I know what Mum will do. She'll make a face and say - what does she give me these cheap flowers for? - so I'll keep them. I like these small violet bouquets with their deep green circular leaf base. Sometimes, when I go to the flower market with Mum, the man she buys from gives me a bunch. My mother doesn't like violets. She says they're what men give to vulgar women at the theatre in Europe and sugar daddies give to girls. I'm not sure what she means by that because I've never been to Europe.

Outside the shop, I see the junks in the distance along Canton Road waterfront. Paul is the only one who's allowed to go all the way down to Canton Road, because my parents say it's dangerous there. I sneaked down there once with Philip, but couldn't see what the big deal was about. It was just an ordinary street, kind of dirty, but with *daih paih dong* hawker food stalls. Philip bought me a bamboo stick with fish balls and pig skin. It was yummy, but Mum would have punished us if she'd known.

I pass the bar and see my orange lady. She's talking to some of the bargirls. Dad calls them taxi girls, because he says sailors hail them like a taxi which sounds funny to me. I don't think my orange lady is really their friend. She looks rather special and different. For one thing, I never see her smoking a cigarette, which all the other girls seem to do. And she seems to be important - even now in the afternoon when there are hardly any sailors around, she is talking, laughing, in the centre of everything.

"Philip, what's a prostitute?"

My brother stares at me as if I'm crazy. "Where did you learn that word? Paul, did you hear what she asked?"

"Mum said it to Dad, last night when they were talking loudly in their bedroom. I heard them."

Sometimes, I wish I could use a dictionary properly, but it's too hard looking up words I can't spell. I can see Philip is not going to tell me. He gets this look whenever he wants to play big brother, and cracks his knuckles. Paul, however, is a different story. Even though Paul's the really good brother who knows when to stop fooling around, he doesn't put on the "you're too young for that" act like Philip sometimes does. I guess that's because Paul's two years older than Philip and really is grown up.

Paul responds, "They're women who make a life from being

with men."

I think about this a moment. "You mean like Mum?"

Philip cracks up laughing and yanks my ponytail. "Sometimes, Ai-Lin, you're just too hilarious."

Paul is smiling, but he replies, "No, not exactly. They're not married women. Many of them don't have much money and so they pretend to be a girlfriend to men who pay them."

"So they're like actresses?"

"Sort of."

This explanation doesn't fully satisfy me, but at least now I know the meaning of the word. I give Paul a kiss and leave him to his school books.

That night, I hear my parents talking very loudly again. Dad has only been home a few days. The last time he went away and came back, I remember my parents talking loudly like this. Sometimes, I wish we lived in a big house, which Mum wants also, then I could have my own room and my brothers could each have their rooms and so could Dad and Mum. But as Dad always says, this is Hong Kong, not Indonesia, and we're lucky to have as big a flat as we do. I'm never quite sure what he means by that, since I've never been to Indonesia.

In my dream, the orange lady has her back to me. Her nails are very long and orange. I go up to her, to ask if she'll be my friend. When she turns around, her face is pale and heavily made up. It's my mother's face, but she stares at me as if I'm a stranger. I scream and run away.

The dream startles me into wakefulness. I can't go back to sleep so I go quietly downstairs and step out on the balcony. It's around four in the morning. Only a few lights dot the hills of Hong Kong island. Everything is calm and peaceful, unlike my dream.

Singing voices rise from the streets below. I can't quite see them, because it's still dark, but I can tell there are two sailors singing and walking along Nathan Road next to the Peninsula Hotel. Their voices ring out clearly. They're drunk. As Mum says, men sing when they're drunk.

I suddenly hate all U.S. sailors. They don't belong here, making so much noise in the middle of the night.

The day my mother fires Ah Yee the cook, two new aircraft carriers dock right in the middle of the harbor. It's a Saturday.

"She dared to raise her voice to me!" Mum repeats several times that afternoon. "She dared!"

I watch Ah Yee pack her things. She lives in a small room with no window next to the kitchen. I don't want her to go. She always makes me lunch when I come home from school, and sneaks special treats or snacks to me while I'm doing homework. She also helps me with my Chinese lessons, which are really difficult. I can't imagine my afternoons without her, when my mother is usually lying down because she's ill or goes out shopping. My brothers both go to full day school now, so there's often only Ah Yee and me at home most afternoons.

Paul says Ah Yee is much too rude to Mum, and should be asked to leave. Philip doesn't care because he doesn't like to eat and never pays attention to her.

Ah Yee leaves quietly, shortly after lunch. I wonder where she'll go. I have no idea where she lives. She told me once that she had a little girl, exactly the same age as me. When I asked if I could meet her and play with her, she replied that her daughter was in China. It seems like Ah Yee has always been with us. Dad says it's fine to have a cook since Mum can't cook, but that looking after us is Mum's job, which is why he won't let Mum hire an *amah* to look after me, according to Philip. Philip says I'm the only baby who still needs looking after.

I feel sad seeing her go. It's not fair. The only reason Mum gets upset at her is because she doesn't understand Mum's funny Cantonese. Ah Yee always understands when I talk to her. But Mum speaks Mandarin - and even then, Dad says she speaks peculiar Mandarin - so she doesn't say her words right in Cantonese. Naturally, Ah Yee doesn't know what she's saying.

Mum spends the afternoon on the phone with friends from church and the Jockey Club telling them about Ah Yee and what a headache she'll have looking for another cook. After that, she lies down for an hour or so because she does have a headache.

I cry in my room, but no one pays attention to me.

That evening, Dad announces we're going out to eat Shantung chicken at Far East Restaurant to celebrate Ah Yee's departure.

I put on my new red dress which Dad hasn't seen me wearing yet, and he says I'm beginning to look more grown up all the time. This makes me happier than I've been all day. Mum is wearing make up and has drawn her eyebrows so they arch. Dad says she looks fierce like an Empress dowager which makes everyone laugh, even Mum.

We all go over the hump to Far East restaurant which is on Kimberly Street, a back street that doesn't join any of the main roads. The walk takes about fifteen minutes. It's not that dark yet because it's only seven o'clock and lots of shops are still open. I love walking the back way. The streets are less crowded than Nathan Road and some of the shopkeepers who recognize us say hello. Paul and I used to roller skate together around these streets. He'd pull me along so that we'd go faster and shout, "hey we're off to Never Never Land!" But Paul doesn't have time to roller skate anymore now that he's getting closer to Form 5 and School Cert, which everyone knows is the most important exam in the world.

"*Hsu sang, Hsu tai, hao jiu bu jian!* Mr. and Mrs. Hsu, long time no see!" Mr. Huang, the owner of Far East restaurant greets my parents. My father chats with Mr. Huang. I don't understand much of what he's saying because it's all in Mandarin.

Philip whispers shu shu sha sha noises in my ear, which is sort of what Mandarin sounds like, making me giggle.

I know the whole menu by heart, because we hardly ever order anything different. Shantung chicken, pieces of cold chicken which is dipped in a soy garlic sauce; crispy pepper leaves and fried bamboo shoots that look like pieces of fish; hot steamed shrimps, without the shells; Hunan ham with long leaves of Chinese cabbage in a white sauce; pan fried pork dumplings. The best part though are the white loaves of steamed bread - silver thread bread - which have the soft, thin shreds of bread inside a spongy crust. Paul takes the end and scoops out the shreds which I eat, and fills his cone with shrimp. I love the bread because it means no rice. Rice is so boring Cantonese.

I love eating at restaurants with my family. I get to stay out late and see the streets of Tsimshatsui at night. My brothers don't fight with each other, and Mum doesn't yell at any of us. Dad talks loudly like he always does, but in noisy Chinese restaurants this seems okay somehow, not like at home. Besides, at restaurants, Mum laughs at what Dad says but at home she doesn't. I especially like Far East, because here, Mr. Huang always comes to our table and chats with my father, and sometimes he even pours Dad a glass of brandy which we don't have to pay for.

Mr. Huang comes by tonight and looks across the table at me. "*Hsu xiao jie,* Miss Hsu," he begins in his funny Cantonese, "what class are you in now?"

"Primary 4."

"*Wa,* clever girl, at Maryknoll, right?" He addresses my mother.

She smiles in acknowledgement. My mother is very proud that I'm at Maryknoll, and the boys at La Salle. This is because of her excellent connections with the Catholic Church. I know this is important, because, as she often reminds me, I failed the Chinese entrance exam into Primary 1, and it was only her connections that got me into a good school like Maryknoll.

Mr. Huang smiles a strange smile at me. "They say Maryknoll is full of ghosts. Japanese ghosts."

Dad laughs. "Yes, Ai-Lin is always coming home with ghost stories."

I feel my face turning red. I wish Dad wouldn't tell people the silly things I say. Philip is snickering - he knows how scared I get. Once, he put a rubber hand covered with red paint on my bed after I told him the story about the nun's hand hidden under the path in our school from the war with the Japanese. I screamed and ran to Paul who showed me it was just a joke. But I dreamt about it for days afterwards.

"Anyway, enjoy your dinner," Mr. Huang says.

Sometimes, I don't like being the baby in the family.

The night air is cool after dinner, and Mum makes me put on a light cardigan. I don't like it because it covers up my pretty dress, but I do what she says. We walk home along Nathan

Road. It's ten o'clock and quite a few people are still about. The moon tonight is as bright as the street lamps.

Sailors mill around the streets, like ants surrounding a dead cockroach on our verandah, looking and leaving and returning again. The sailors don't seem to be going anywhere in particular. But they're there, always there. Like ghosts who must come back to haunt us here on earth.

Outside Chung King Mansion, a flock of women laugh and talk with the sailors. I peer at the women, looking for my orange lady. She's there on the steps, talking and laughing as loudly as the rest. There's something strangely magical about her tonight, like a costumed actress on stage who appears and disappears, declaiming lines to her audience on Nathan Road. She is not a beautiful woman. Her face is chalk white with powder, and her orange hair is a blackish coppery color, like an orange on the market fruit stand that has been scarred and bruised and not fit for sale, as Mum would say. I walk as near to the steps of the building as I dare, to get a closer look at her. And then, I hear Mum's voice, telling me to get away. My mother's face is wrinkled with disgust, and I know she does not like these women.

On Monday, during recess at school, I walk down the path paved with large flat rocks and stop at the black stone halfway between the tower and the covered playground. Under this stone, my friend Helena told me, is the hand of the nun who wouldn't let the Japanese soldier touch her. Helena knows all the ghost stories. I close my eyes and try to imagine Japanese soldiers swarming around the grounds of my school. Instead, I see American sailors in white uniforms surrounding my orange Chung King Mansion lady.

I've been nine for a whole month now, and I think I'd rather be ten. Philip says that until there are two digits in my age, I'm not really grown up yet. This summer during the holidays, Mum says I have to take more private lessons in Chinese, because I've had red marks twice in my report card this year. Miss Yeung, my teacher, told Mum that I would either have to stay back a year to improve my Chinese, or join the English study group next year. Mum was so upset at Miss Yeung that she complained to the principal.

"She dared to say we weren't really Chinese, so it wasn't important for Ai-Lin to learn Chinese! Who does she think she is?" I hear Mum shout at Dad that night. Dad is packing for a business trip to Japan and tells Mum to stop shouting.

"This is all your fault. You should help the children with their homework," she continues. "How do you expect them to learn if you don't help them? You know I can't because my Chinese isn't good enough. I can't help it. My father had to send me to Dutch school because of his connection to the Dutch."

I pull the blankets over my ears. None of this makes sense to me. I've tried hard in Chinese, but it's even harder now that Ah Yee's gone and no one speaks Cantonese to me anymore. My Eurasian friend Helena speaks English. She's lucky. Her mother's Portuguese and doesn't make her study Chinese. Paul used to help me, but Mum made him stop because he had too much homework of his own to do. Philip can't help. He's taking French now in secondary school and says Mum's ridiculous and won't listen to her at all. Philip could help me if he tried. He could have passed Chinese if he wanted to. He understands everything that's said to him because, as Mum says, he has a musical ear. And I know he can read, because I've caught him reading the Chinese paper Dad gets when he thinks no one's watching. But he simply won't study because he's defiant - Mum says Philip's character is bad, and that he will defy everyone to his grave.

Under my blanket, things always feel safer, less scary. It's also easier to think under here when I can block out the noise that doesn't make sense. I know I don't want to study Chinese all summer, but Mum made an agreement with the principal that I wouldn't have to stay back a year if I could pass an extra Chinese exam at the end of the summer.

I've got to do something. Paul says the only way to face the difficult things of life is to persevere. But he's smart, and much more grown up than me. It's easy for him. I try and try but it doesn't do any good just trying.

Tomorrow, when Dad flies off, I'm going to run away from home. I'll pack the B.O.A.C. bag Dad gave me with my latest Supergirl comic, my new red dress and some clean socks and underwear. Oh, and my toothbrush. I don't think I'll need anything else.

The next day Mum has a headache again. She has a headache every weekend and also when Dad goes away. She's so predictable.

I'm going to get her prescription, but I'm not coming back. I don't care if she suffers from her headache. Maybe if I run away she won't make me do all these things I can't do. Maybe then she'll miss me and be sorry and won't shout at me anymore if I ever come back. Of course, maybe I won't come back.

Downstairs in the hallway of our building, I go to the little shop way at the back next to lift number 5 to buy myself a vitasoy drink which I drink right there. Mum doesn't let me drink vitasoy; she makes me drink milk instead which has calcium, but I don't like the taste of milk. The fat man who minds the shop asks me where I'm going this afternoon with my airline bag. I tell him I'm going to visit my friend. When he asks where my friend lives, I say Chung King Mansion.

"So go through this way." He points to a back alley and path I've never seen before.

"Where does that go?"

"*Hei ya,* here you say you're going to Chung King Mansion and you don't even know the way?"

I don't like the fat man. He wears a filthy singlet and shorts, no shirt, and rubber thongs. I don't think he's very clean. His hands are grimy and his long pinky fingernail is yellowish black.

"Of course I know the way. I just want to be sure, that's all."

He chuckles and takes the empty soy drink bottle I hand back to him. "Siu tze is clever, aren't you?"

So because I don't want him to think I didn't know the way, I go through the opening at the back of the shop and through the dark alley. And there I am, in Chung King Mansion.

It's the middle of the afternoon, and a number of people are in the main foyer. It looks like an ordinary building to me, and I wonder now why my mother always makes such a fuss about it. There are some Indian tailors, like the ones in the arcade of the Ambassador Hotel which I pass by often. I see the lifts, which look like the ones in our building.

And then, I see her again, waiting for the lift.

She looks different somehow. Her orange hair isn't quite as orange anymore, and the black roots are prominent. She has no makeup on, and she's wearing ordinary clothes, a pair of cotton slacks and a blouse. But it's definitely my orange lady. I recognize her.

I walk close to her, and realize that she's only a little taller than me. She isn't smiling and laughing. In her hand is a cloth net bag filled with vegetables and meat wrapped in newspaper. She looks just like Ah Yee when she's come home from the market.

The lift arrives and she holds open the door after she goes in.

"Hey little sister, are you coming or not? I'm not holding this door all day."

It dawns on me that she's talking to me. I shake my head and quickly walk away. She makes an impatient noise.

At the entrance of Chung King Mansion, I stop at the top of the stairs and look at the bustle of Nathan Road. There are sailors coming up the steps. I don't know why, but I begin to cry. My orange lady scared me. Her ordinary speaking voice isn't melodious and sweet as I've always imagined, but rather rough and deep, like the hawker woman at the market. But what I didn't expect at all is that she is not really much older than me, like one of the girls in the upper classes at school. She isn't the grown up lady I thought she was. She isn't grown up at all.

I wipe my eyes with the back of my hand and walk down the steps.

That evening, I don't run away after all and return home instead with my mother's prescription.

For months afterwards, I avoid passing Chung King Mansion, especially in the evenings.

I've been nine a whole summer now. Tomorrow, school starts again. I only just managed to pass the extra Chinese exam, because Miss Yeung gave me private lessons all summer and Paul had time to help me. This school year, my mother says I have to improve my arithmetic which also isn't very good.

This summer, there were more battleships on the harbor than I can ever remember seeing. Dad says the Americans have to continue the war in Vietnam, and that Tsimshatsui is turning into a red light district because of it. Mum says Tsimshatsui always was a red light district only slightly better than Wanchai and if my father had any sense he'd buy our family a house in Kowloon Tong. When I ask my brothers to explain what my parents mean, Philip tells me to hang a red light outside Mum's door to really make her mad. And Paul says war is sad and horrible, but confirms that the Japanese really have nothing to do with this one. None of this makes any sense to me.

This afternoon, Mum has a headache because there's been so much to do before my brothers and I start school.

In the evening, I see my orange lady again. She is all orange, her hair dyed to match her orange dress and nails. I hang around in the streets much longer than I'm supposed to and watch her perform. She is smiling, laughing, talking to sailors. After a little while, she takes one sailor by the arm and leads him into the building. Even though I can't see her face, I'm sure she's not smiling anymore.

I walk home slowly, past Chung King Mansion, my mother's prescription in my hand.

2

My Father's Story

On my thirty-first birthday, my father appointed me his official biographer.

"I have begun writing down my life's accomplishments, from my youth in Indonesia and China to my mining days in Java which were part of my profitable and successful enterprises in Hong Kong and Japan," his letter from Hong Kong to me in Cincinnati began. "You will write these memories into a book for me. The next time you come home, we can have some long interviews, and tape record those conversations so that you can have a mnemonic device. After all, Ai-Lin, even the best writers need to gallop their memories."

My father always wrote me long letters, saving him the cost of international long distance while still telling me everything that was on his mind, or so he claimed. I suspected it was because he fancied himself a writer, and was especially eager to prove it to me, the English major. It also gave him ample opportunity to sprinkle his correspondence with malapropisms in English, his third and favorite language, acquired at age fifteen in Jakarta.

On my thirty-first birthday, a cold day in the early April of '85, the last thing on my mind was the story of his life. His letter's arrival on that day was pure coincidence; my father neither remembers nor celebrates birthdays as a matter of principle, although I've never known what principle he meant.

It had been six years since I'd last seen my father, and my home city Hong Kong. When my marriage to Vince da Luca broke up two years ago, I left him in New York and moved my green card life to Cincinnati, where I'd first landed in America as an undergraduate at Xavier some fourteen years prior. I took a job as the Ohio editor of *Tri-State Business and Leisure,* which is what I still do, in between trying to recoup a life.

"Why not come back home?" my father had written at the time of the divorce. "You can get back your job with AsiaMonth, live rent-free with me, and still go back to the States from time to time so that you won't lose your green card. I don't mind about the divorce, no, not at all. I won't disown you for that."

After graduation, I had returned to Hong Kong and lived with my father for four years before getting married. My mother had died shortly after I turned sixteen. Both my elder brothers had not returned from the States after college. Paul remained legally as a computer professional in Austin, Texas, and Philip, illegally as a classical musician in San Francisco's gay community. Paul and Dad don't talk to each other - not even an acknowledgement at my wedding. They quarrelled eighteen years ago before Paul left for the States. As for Philip, whom Dad calls "my amused son," the last time Dad saw him was at my wedding six years ago, and Philip never writes and doesn't call very often, since he's constantly in hiding as an illegal.

Which was why, at thirty one, I was the only Hsu heir left to write my father's story.

So it was April, and cold, which I've already said, when I sat down to compose a reply to Dad.

"I am a business and travel writer," I tapped onto my computer screen, "and am not experienced enough for the kind of writing to do your biography justice." This was a reasonable self-characterization. Besides, it was good, Confucian humility, which might appeal to my father's sense of the order of things.

I re-read the part of his letter that said, "you may not be a good enough writer at this junction, but Dad can editorialize your words and make them better."

"Publishing is very competitive," I tried, "and the chance of selling a biography, especially of someone who isn't famous, is slim."

Forget that, I decided. My father once threw a fortune into an "American real estate investment," about which he was extremely secretive, and which made my mother cry for many days. I was only ten at the time, but Mum's tears are vivid in my memory. The "investment" turned out to be ten acres of the Nevada desert which was artistically rendered in a brochure as a water sport resort. The developer long ago disappeared with my father's funds, although he did send a title deed. As recently as three years ago, my father insisted I go to Nevada and find his land, which I did. It is still a desert, on state property. Dad told me I should file a lawsuit against the state for illegally exercising eminent domain without even notifying him.

"For a biography to be successful," I tried again, "one has to detail both the successes and failures of a life."

My father's words boomed an echo in my brain: "I think my biography will be exceedingly intriguing to Americans because there have been no failures in my life. There is a famous American, I think his name is Horatio Algae, who serves as a parallel existence."

I switched off my computer. I had no words for my father.

It had begun to rain lightly. On a similarly rainy, but warmer day, when I was thirteen, my father took me to meet Lulu.

I had heard her name whispered, along with the derogatory

slur *jaahp jung* meaning "mixed breed" in Cantonese, by my mother to "Auntie" May. The latter was Mum's Portuguese girlfriend from her convent school days in Hong Kong after the war. May was as close as a sister to my mother, whose family was all back in Indonesia.

Lulu, I gathered, was an undesirable friend of my father's according to Mum and May.

Dad brought me to see Lulu without much preamble. That was Dad's way. Although he loved to talk, he never explained anything that was really important. But I was so pleased and flattered that he was taking me somewhere, anywhere, that I didn't bother to question this unusual outing.

We boarded a bus together for the heart of Mongkok, a densely populated commercial and residential district in Kowloon. It was a Saturday afternoon and Nathan Road bustled with people and noise. Dad let me lead him to the upper deck of the bus, where I insisted on sitting by the window.

"Lulu's sick," was all the reason my father gave me for our visit. He carried two bunches of violets. I liked the deep green and purple; the colors were "opulent," I told Dad. He smiled at me for saying a new English word I'd learned at school.

It was a long, half-hour ride. The bus trundled along Nathan Road, passing the cluster of high-rise department stores, hotels, residential buildings and cinemas that prevailed near the harbor area of Tsimshatsui where we lived. I liked going through the tunnel of trees overshadowing the route by the army field, which was across the road from my girlfriend Helena's home, a flat above the Chanticleer bakery. We traveled about fifteen minutes until we had ridden a little over a mile to the junction with Waterloo Road. At this point, the bus continued straight on Nathan Road, instead of turning right, which was the route for the number 7 bus I usually took to school. I didn't know this part of Kowloon too well. The buildings were older and closer together, and there were no trees anywhere.

Throughout the ride, my father was quiet, reflective, not his usual talkative self. The only other times I can recall seeing him this way were when Mum died, and when Philip's letter arrived, announcing he was relinquishing our family name and that he was either bi-sexual or gay. But those two incidents occurred later, and I found myself wary of, and a little perplexed over my father's demeanor.

Lulu's home was in an old, pre-war building, with a dark and narrow stairwell leading up to her third floor flat. It was a far cry from our own modern building with its bank of lifts and wide corridors. The building was on a side street, attached on either side. I saw bamboo poles of washing hanging out of the windows to dry.

As we climbed up the long row of stone steps, I traipsed my hand along the cool walls. I remembered saying to my father, "they don't need air conditioning here in the summer," and he mumbled an incoherent reply. The ceilings were high, unlike those in our building. I wondered if Lulu were very tall.

The woman who opened the door looked tall to me, about five foot eleven in her three inch stiletto heels. She towered over me even more than my tall mother would have. Lulu wore a cheongsam, the high-collared, tight fitting Chinese style dress that was still popular back then in the sixties. Her hair was light blonde, almost white, but her features were Chinese. As I stared at her pink eyes, I realized with a start that she was an albino.

She spoke to me in English. "So you're Ai-Lin, the girl with no English name."

"Say hello to Miss Lulu Watson," my father said. He added

with a laugh, "she calls herself the bloodless Eurasian."

She led us into her living room where she had laid out an English style tea. The high ceiling was complemented by a wide, squarish room with plenty of light. There was a verandah that overlooked the back of the building. On it were several potted plants, a large fern among them that made the verandah look like a tropical jungle. But the most startling thing about her flat was that its perimeter was ringed entirely by rocks of varying shapes, sizes and colors. Around the base of the fern was a semi-circle of crystals. I gazed at these clear, multi-faceted gemstones of nature, fascinated by their sheen.

We sat down at the tea table.

"May I pour for you?" I inquired politely. I had been taught at Girl Guides for my hostess badge that this was the correct etiquette for teatime, if one were a lady.

Lulu guffawed. Her voice was hoarse and masculine. "My, my. Aren't you a princess? Kewey, you old pseudomorph, I can see why you love and adore her."

In my entire life, I had never heard anyone mangle my father's Mandarin Chinese name, Zhung-Qiu, into a nickname, in Cantonese yet from "Qiu" to "Kew", or call him an old pseudomorph. I had no idea what she meant by that, but was too shy to ask. Nor had anyone ever referred to him as "loving and adoring" me, or anyone else for that matter. "Love" was not an English word I heard in our family, except in connection with religion, my mother being Catholic.

My father was laughing, relaxed. He succumbed to her teasing and seemed to expect that I would too. Because I was confused by the whole scenario, I began to pour the tea, not knowing what was expected of me.

She held up a plate of watercress sandwiches, and I took one dubiously, my teacup balanced precariously in my other hand.

Dad seemed to be quite at home. He sat there in an armchair by the window, bathed in afternoon sunlight, happily munching on watercress sandwiches and sipping his tea. Lulu played Paganini's Concerto in D on the phonograph, and cranked up the volume. A neighbor's cat yowled. My father leaned back, closed his eyes, and revelled in the scratchy strains of the violin and orchestra.

While the music played, I found myself wondering if this were where Paul meant my father went to hear what he derisively called "Dad's brain music."

No one spoke until the music was over.

"Lulu and I share a fondness of good music and rocks," Dad said as he opened his eyes. "We have been friends for a long time."

"Rock collecting, child," she rasped. "Began it along the Atlantic coast. Been collecting ever since. Your father contributed pieces from his mines in Indonesia." She went over to a section of black rocks, bent down, picked one up and held it out to me. "Manganese ore, child."

I took the rock out of her hand and turned it round in my palm. Dad never brought any rocks home, and I was only vaguely aware of his mining operation. It was an ordinary looking rock, hard as granite and as ugly as a lump of coal.

"Manganese ore is a ferro-alloy metal," my father spoke up suddenly from his perch. "My Japanese customers buy it for batteries."

I continued looking at the rock, trying to think of something to say. Here was my father, talking to me about his business as if I were a grown up. He barely spoke to Mum about business, treating her with a certain amount of condescension and disdain. His attitude was something Mum had often complained bitterly to me about.

I wanted to ask him if there was a great deal of manganese in his mines, but it seemed like an ignorant question. Wouldn't Miss Watson think me stupid not to know? She seemed to know so much about my father I'd never known.

Lulu straightened up and called, "Ah Ying!" and an amah wearing a flowered samfoo, the shirt and loose pants outfit of servants, came out of the kitchen to collect the tea things. She gave her instructions in rapid, fluent Cantonese about laundry and dinner.

She pulled a cigarette out of a case on the coffee table, and inserted it into a black holder. My father helped himself to one, and lit both their cigarettes.

"Nothing like a good fag," she sighed, settling onto her sofa. "Come here, Ai-Lin, and sit next to me. I want to take a good look at you."

I complied. Her rich, heady perfume wafted round me. It was the kind of musky scent my mother would never have deigned to wear. Close up, her albino face did not seem so strange. I was comforted by this woman my father had brought me to meet, despite a premonition that there was something wrong about her, something bad that had to do with him. But in her flat, where my father did not issue pompous edicts or shout at anyone, where a random order of things prevailed, I somehow understood that he wanted me here to show me that even for him, life was not always to be controlled.

She took my chin in her hand, and her skin felt rough against my face. "You've got Kewey's eyes alright. Mind you don't turn them on the wrong man. All my girls are crazy for him."

"Lulu . . .," my father's voice held a warning threat.

"Mum's the word, Kewey. Mum's the word." She released

my chin. "She'll break a few hearts though."

I desperately wanted to participate, to be grown up, but all I could think of to say was, "I think you must be a very special person, Miss Watson."

She coughed as her voice rasped into a laugh. "Why so, dearie?"

"Because my father respects you."

Dad cocked his head back in the manner he always affected when something puzzled him. Lulu ran her long, white fingers through my hair. "Well, I respect your father too," she said.

"My father says you're not well. Are you ill, Miss Watson?"

"In a manner of speaking."

"I hope you will be well soon."

"Not to worry child. It's nothing a little *sihk fu* won't cure."

She had slipped that in, so deftly, the Cantonese expression "eat bitterness" that I neither could understand nor misunderstand her. I thought about that for a long time afterwards, wondering if I had heard her correctly. But that was the one and only time I ever saw her, so I never found out what she meant.

On the way home, my father said Lulu had a sickness of the heart because she couldn't love. It was the second time that day I had heard the English word love, this word that held so little meaning for me. Dad also said that one day, when his life was almost over, he hoped to cure this same heart sickness he had.

"Dad," I began tentatively, emboldened by his unusual candor and seeming willingness to talk, "what's a pseudomorph? You know, what Miss Watson called you?"

He started to laugh. "Oh, pay no attention to Lulu. She was just joking."

"But is it a real word?" I persisted, knowing he wouldn't

mind my linguistic curiosity.

He hesitated. "Yes. It's a kind of crystal."

"Like the ones around Miss Watson's fern?"

"Maybe, I don't know. Pseudomorph is a geological term. It happens when a mineral changes into another one, but keeps its outer form. Like petrified wood, or certain kinds of quartz. Lulu just likes the sound of the word."

And then, Dad became his old self again, garrulous and overbearing so that I couldn't get a word in edgewise, which Mum always said was the fault of his pride. He did not mention Lulu or our visit again for the rest of the ride home. But I remember how excited and thrilled I was by this unusual event. Most of all, I remember how special my father made me feel that day.

I told Mum about our visit at dinner that evening. She sat silently through my recital. Dad seemed faraway and preoccupied.

Around midnight, I awoke with a start.

"How dare you take her there!"

My mother's voice, raised to that pitch of fury and ire I most feared, reverberated around our flat. My parents' bedroom door slammed shut, and an angry dialogue in Indonesian followed.

Philip crept into my bed. I was trying hard not to cry.

"It's okay sis, it's not your fault. They're just like that."

"But what are they saying?" Our parents always argued in Indonesian, which none of us really understood. But Philip had taught it to himself, and followed much of what went on.

"Mum's saying Lulu's a prostitute, a *mama-san,* and Dad is calling Mum narrow minded and puritanical, and Mum says he must keep his activities confined to Japan and the geishas and if he ever dares to cast a shadow of this into our home again she's leaving him and getting the marriage annulled by the church. You know how Mum gets melodramatic when she's upset. What was Lulu like, Ai-Lin?"

"Oh, kind of glamorous, in a weird sort of way. Real busty."

"I heard Auntie May tell Mum that Lulu's a hermaphrodite."

I gazed at Philip, the only defense I had left against our parents' quarrels now that Paul had left for college in the States, vowing never to return. "Do you really think that's true? She had a voice like a man's."

"Could be. Anything's possible."

I thought about this for awhile, my parents' querulous voices dimmed by my imagination. My brother played with my hand, and his touch calmed me. I always found our kind of talk reassuring. Life, I had discovered by now, simply went on despite my parents' outbursts.

"Philip, do you suppose Dad's really going bust because the new mines are empty like Mum claims? I mean, are we poor now?"

"Paul thinks so, that's why he saves every cent and works all the time. I don't know. You know how Dad is. He doesn't tell us anything."

I didn't want Philip to leave my bed, but knew that even he couldn't make everything right. I hardly slept at all the rest of the night, wondering what it was my father found in Japan that he couldn't find at home, wondering if a geisha was anything like Lulu, wondering who Lulu really was and why she had to sik koo to cure her heart's sickness. I wanted to cry, but couldn't. Tears would have been meaningless, superfluous. I wished my tears could form crystals, like the translucent rocks I'd seen that afternoon. Somehow, I felt that if I gazed long enough at those crystals, those quartz teardrops, all the questions in my head would be answered.

But I hated my mother that night, more than at any other time, for taking away the beauty of this day with my father, for always making him someone I couldn't ever love.

For the rest of the year, my father kept writing me long letters detailing the progress of his biographical notes. My continual silence on the subject of my writing his biography did not deter him. In one letter, he even sent me a neatly drawn workflow chart of his business at its heyday, when manganese poured out of his mines into profitable shipments to Japan. He was so busy in those days, he said, that he had to take long business trips out of Hong Kong, sometimes for as long as four months, but he always traveled first class. I remembered his absences, and how much Mum resented them, especially the ones to Japan which she called his excuse for philandering.

All that year, I read through the pages of airmail paper, filled with his tiny, crammed handwriting. Every week, a new envelope arrived with just "Hsu," our family name, scribbled in English in the upper left hand corner, no return address. Each letter was yet another convoluted story of a deal only he could have closed because of his connections and understanding of the issues involved. Invariably, his letters mentioned numerous people I had never heard of or met. I counted fifteen strangers in one letter.

His letters did shed a little light on the complexities of his business. What struck me most was the unnecessary labyrinth he constructed, both in terms of the organization he managed and the flow of distribution of the manganese ore from his mine. It was confusing. Had I been covering his company for a feature story, I would have described the structure as the product of a neurotic and overly secretive mind.

Yet in all those letters, he never once mentioned my mother or brothers or me. It was as if his trips and business had been his whole life, and we his family had existed only on the periphery. After all, hadn't I come to Cincinnati after my divorce because I simply couldn't stand the thought of living with him again? Four years of life alone with Dad had almost convinced me that Mum had been right, that as much as she admired Dad's perseverance in teaching himself geology to run his business, and his entrepreneurial skills, love could not flourish when pride got in the way.

My father passed away early the next year, a month before my thirty-second birthday. He was seventy nine. I did not see him before he died. A few days later, I burned all his letters to me.

A large and very heavy parcel arrived on my doorstep a week after his death. The box was marked "Lulu's rocks." Where had Dad found the strength to lug this to the post office, so recently before dying, when his health was poor and his body weakened by age? I stared at the box, this neatly packaged gift. On the return address, I saw that he had written his full name, Hsu Zhung-Qiu, in Chinese characters - his official, Mandarin Chinese name which means "middle bridge" Hsu - and not his Indonesian or English names, names he always insisted that didn't count because they were adopted only for the convenience of business.

"Have you been well?" his letter began. It was eerie, but I could hear my father speaking to me. He hardly ever began a letter with a simple pleasantry since writing, he always said, should get right to the point.

"As I do not know when you intend to return for a visit," his letter continued, "I thought I should send you Lulu's rocks so that you would better understand my life. As you know, the business went down for awhile, but picked up again later so that we were both comfortable. This is the secret of my success: to persevere even when everyone thinks I am wrong.

"However, I do have one failure to tell you about, which of course, you will not include in my biography. That failure was Lulu. She was right to call me a pseudomorph, a false form. I had called her that originally, because she became a different person when running her business. But it was I, not she, who deserved that description. Despite what your mother and Auntie May might have thought, Lulu was never my mistress. She represented my only failure: a failure to love and to accept love.

"I am trusting you with this important secret, Ai-Lin, so that you won't make my mistake. A pseudomorph occurs because in nature, some crystals need to adopt disguises. The change in physical properties can yield an exceptional mineral, a true beauty. But it is up to you to recognize, and respect, such a rare perfection if and when you are lucky enough to find it."

So in the end, I did find the words to tell my father's story, though not the story he intended for me to tell. Although I am, these days, a competent writer and editor in the English language, I think I still do not truly understand this English word "love." But each time I look at the rocks arranged around the perimeter of my apartment, I think of my father and feel the strange heart sickness he spoke to me about. And each time the feeling arises in me, a little more of the pain melts away from my heart.

3

Philip and Me

When I was growing up, my two brothers and I shared a bedroom. Dad thought this normal and healthy, saying that most Hong Kong people didn't even have space enough to sleep separately from their children, and that we already had an oversized room, meaning one hundred and thirty square feet. And in our home, Dad's word was law. It was not till I was thirteen and had begun to menstruate that Mum cordoned off half the room for me, since my eldest brother Paul was leaving for college in the States soon.

So Philip and I whispered a lot late into the night during my childhood and early teenage years. He was four years older than me.

"You're an accident. Either that or you're the child of Mum's lover," he whispered to me one night when I was ten. "He was probably a *gwailo* priest."

"Priests don't have children, silly," I whispered back.

This was when Philip came to my bed for the first time. He climbed on top of me and kissed my lips. "Don't you know this is all two people have to do to have a baby, Ai-Lin?" All we did was kiss, me giggling away, while he shushed me. And by five thirty, I fell asleep and he crept back into his own bed.

For days after that, I kept looking at my face in the mirror, trying to see if I might possibly be Eurasian. My girlfriend Helena, who really was Eurasian, said I'd know if I really was, because inside, you know you'll always be different from everyone else. I thought of all the *gwailo* priests Mum knew. There was the old Italian who always looked like he would keel over at the altar. He had startling blue eyes, the kind that made me think of sapphires. He couldn't possibly be my father, I decided, because I didn't have any sign of his white hair, flabby jowls or blue eyes.

And then, there was that young American, the one Dad said flirted with Mum. He looked like Kirk Douglas with the crazy chin. I didn't like him much, because he liked to speak to the kids in his accented Cantonese, as if to show off what he knew. His linguistic attempts made Mum laugh, but I thought he sounded silly. He couldn't possibly be my father.

Which left the accident of my birth.

"Why should I be the accident? Maybe you and Paul were," I whispered to Philip a few nights later. Paul was deep in sleep, grinding his teeth away.

Philip came into my bed and pressed his body close to mine. It made me feel all nice and warm.

"Don't you hear how Mum and Dad quarrel all the time? They never used to do that until you came along. They're probably angry because you're an accident. And don't you see how Dad's always out late at night? He and Mum don't sleep close together anymore, you know, because they're afraid to have another accident. After all, there already were us two boys, so why would they need to try again? Mum says girls don't count among Chinese."

Philip had this intense, serious way about him that frightened me. I began to cry, and blurted out that I didn't want to be a *jaahp jung* Eurasian and would stop speaking English if that's what made me more mixed, like Helena, since it was quite awful enough to be part Chinese and part Indonesian, as well as a girl, and said that maybe it was the priest's fault I made Mum and Dad angry because he hadn't washed away my original sin properly during baptism. At that Philip hugged me tightly, reassuring me he was just teasing and why did I take him so seriously? He started to kiss away my tears, and when I looked at his face, he had this funny look about him, and then he abruptly got up and went back to his bed.

I was so relieved to learn that everything was alright that I didn't think anything more about the night's events, and after that, Philip regularly visited me in my bed where we whispered and kissed and giggled.

It was a Saturday in January when I was eleven and a half, about a week before the Chinese New Year. Philip said Dad had come home around three or four, which was why Mum was banging things round the kitchen and yelling at us. I barely missed being slapped by her this time, but Philip was dealt a sharp blow across his face for playing his music too loudly. As soon as Dad was up and around - it was past noon - Mum stormed out of the house to play tennis. Dad was morose and quiet that day, and then he and Paul got into an argument and Paul slammed the door on his way out to a movie. Philip and I stayed in our room - me with a stack of comics and he hunched over the piano all afternoon.

Paul didn't come home for dinner. Nor did he call. Mum asked Dad why he didn't know where his own son was, and Dad retorted that if she hadn't been gallivanting all over the tennis courts flirting with other women's husbands, she might have better control over the children. Mum began to cry and blubber about what kind of husband goes out drinking all night with loose women and how dare he insinuate that she was up to anything besides playing tennis at the club and Dad kept trying to shush her with not in front of the children but Mum was too far gone by now, wailing and choking, and I remember thinking she was going to die her face looked so contorted.

Philip finally took my hand and we shut ourselves up in the room and listened to our parents shout at each other the rest of the evening. That was the first time I heard anything about Dad giving Mum VD, although Philip couldn't be sure he heard right since they were fighting, as usual, in Indonesian.

Things calmed down round about ten, but at eleven, a new explosion happened when Paul strolled in, recalcitrant and defiant, which was not the way Paul usually was. Paul actually answered Mum back, something he never ever did no matter how bad Mum got, and she slapped him hard across the face and when he came into our room he didn't say a word.

At two in the morning, Paul gave me the worst fright of my life.

Our home was finally quiet, and everyone was in bed when a rhythmic clicking sound by my ear woke me up. There was Paul, kneeling next to my bed, only his eyes were closed, and he had a vicious look on his face. I gasped in fear, loud enough to wake Philip, who sat up in bed and rubbed his eyes.

Philip quickly came over and whispered that I should be very quiet, so as not to wake Paul.

"But what's he doing?" I whispered, because by now, Paul had stood up and was walking right into the piano.

"He's sleepwalking. He does that sometimes, only I've never seen him move around this much."

Philip gently guided Paul, and my eldest brother, the boy I worshipped because he was the smartest, kindest person in the world, climbed obediently back into bed and ground his teeth into a deep slumber.

I began to cry. Philip comforted me.

"He scared me," I whimpered. "Why did he do that?"

"He didn't mean to. He won't even remember he was up."

Philip had climbed into my bed and was kissing my eyes.

"It's okay Ai-Lin. Forget about it."

I cried a little more, even though I was old enough not to be a cry baby, frightened by the strangeness of the day, feeling that our whole family had just been hurled into a colossal pit out from which we would never find our way. And Philip kissed me some more, and hugged me, and the next thing I knew he was doing something new and unfamiliar to me, very gently, so gently that even though I felt a little sore, I didn't say "ouch" or anything because the sensation was comforting in its closeness. Afterwards, he whispered to me, "this is our secret Ai-Lin and we needn't tell anyone. We'll get married someday and we won't ever fight, you'll see. I'm never going to leave you, as long as you promise me you'll always love only me and no one else." And I promised with intense fervor, "I'll always love only you Philip," and saying that made me feel important and complete, a feeling I never wanted to lose.

Philip and I regularly committed incest for several years after that until he left for college.

The day I got my first period, I went to the library and borrowed a book from the adolescent's section, *Questions About Sex,* that explained, with representational line drawings, the whole business of sex, including the meanings of birth control, homosexuality, menopause, impotence and deviant sexual behavior. I liked the book. It was written in straightforward, simple language with just the facts, nothing else. I had made no sense of either Mum's moral admonishings about why I should only let boys kiss me on the cheek and nowhere else now that I was a "woman" or the euphemistic explainings at school passed off as "sex education."

Philip was mortified. "What if Mum sees it? She'll lock your bedroom door every night and not let you out with anyone after dark. You know how she is."

"No she won't. I'll tell her she'll never marry me off if she does, and then she'll be stuck with me, a useless girl. Anyway, I'll mix the book in with my comics. Mum would never look there. You're being a big scaredy cat."

Philip was standing at the door of our bedroom and I was sprawled on my bed devouring the book. My brother came over and sat down. He stroked my arm lightly. "It's still our secret, isn't it Ai-Lin? You haven't told your girlfriends, have you? You haven't told Helena?"

"Oh shut up. I promised, didn't I? Besides, it's not like we're doing anything wrong." I looked up at his handsome face, at those sad and frightened eyes, and felt strong and terribly adult, more grown up than him because I had the knowledge I needed and for me, knowledge was the beginning of power and control.

But reading the book also worried me, especially about pregnancy. So I told Philip that unless he started using condoms, I'd lock my door every night. And I did. Philip pouted and fumed for the next four days, calling me a spoilt brat princess, saying no one would ever want to marry such a difficult girl, laughing at my period, the blood letting he called it, because it was a smelly, filthy thing that only the inferior sex got. I was mad at him at first, but after the first two days, I felt more hurt than mad because as much as I loved my brother, I hated his mean streak, his ungenerous heart that was so unlike Paul, whom I missed dreadfully even though I was happy he had finally escaped to the States.

I refused to give in, however, knowing I was right.

On the fourth night, Philip slid a packet of condoms under my door.

Whenever he made me mad again after that, I would neatly slice all his condoms with a razor, and he'd find out only at night when he tried to put one on and I'd laugh in his face and make him leave my room.

It was not till I was fourteen that I began to feel something wasn't right about the amount of time I spent with Philip.

Philip attended the boy's school La Salle, a five minute walk away from my school, Maryknoll Convent. Every day, he'd fetch me and we'd take the bus home together. Since he had been doing this since I was ten, started at the time because Mum had stopped coming to fetch me, I didn't think anything of it. But in secondary school, where my girlfriends had begun to date boys, I began to feel silly and childish.

Still, I did nothing to stop him for the first three years in secondary school because, to be honest, I liked it. Philip was rather exotic looking, and this made me popular among the girls who wanted to meet him. I felt proud to be seen with him, and to let everyone know how devoted he was to me.

Helena had a dreadful crush on him.

"Helena looks like a bad imitation of Raquel Welch," he used to say. "She isn't slender like you." The fact that the gorgeous Helena wasn't attractive to Philip gratified my ego even more.

Besides, Philip always made up for any bad feelings I might have at night.

One night, shortly before my thirteenth birthday, Philip said. "You don't want to go out with some boy who speaks Chinglish English, do you? Ai-Lin, you are so beautiful can I go out with you?" He mimicked the local sing song English accent.

I giggled.

"That's the way David Wong speaks, isn't it? He has a crush on you."

David was the first boy rumored to have a crush on me. He went to Philip's school and was one class behind him and two years ahead of myself. I wondered how Philip had heard.

"And furthermore," Philip carried on in the same choppy, sing song voice, "you are also very intelligent. Therefore I think you can my girlfriend be."

"Oh stop, Philip," but I couldn't help laughing.

"Shh, you'll wake Paul." He put his hand over my mouth from behind me. Philip always liked to curl up into my back. Much later, when I was married, my husband Vince would complain that I was always turning my back on him in bed.

"He won't mind, he's leaving for the States soon."

"Lucky stiff."

"Oh don't be jealous, you're going in a couple of years. Besides," and I turned around to give him the sweetest smile I could, "we'll have the whole bedroom to ourselves. And I don't even like David. He's a *syuhtauh* potato head."

In the darkness, I could just make out the smile on his face. Philip had Mum's smile, which was warm and kind, but he resembled Dad more closely, right down to our father's handsome features, dark complexion and protruding Adam's apple. Girls liked Philip, because he danced well and was charming and polite. I suppose that was why I thought I was lucky he cared so much about me.

The thing is, Philip was right about the Chinglish English. Even though I could speak Cantonese fluently, I was really more comfortable in English. That was what our parents wanted, for us to be Westernized and English speaking so that we could make a future life abroad in the West. They were, after all, immigrants themselves, outsiders from Indonesia who made few local Cantonese friends. Though they were ethnic Chinese, Mum could barely read her characters, although she could speak both Cantonese and Mandarin pretty well but with a distinctly foreign accent, and Dad only spoke Mandarin, having refused to learn the local dialect, which he considered rough and lower class.

So I abhorred Chinglish English, although I had plenty of Chinese friends and chattered away happily in Cantonese to them. I would have had more Portuguese or Eurasian friends, because they spoke English, but Mum was prejudiced against them, although she didn't admit it and even had Portuguese friends herself. Philip said you could tell by the way Mum joked about them, calling them second class Europeans who thought they could be equal to the colonial British. But Mum made an exception of Helena Choy, even though she was both Portuguese and Eurasian, because her father was a doctor. Besides, Helena had been my friend ever since primary school and I wouldn't have let anyone stop our friendship.

My family was simply not like anyone else's I knew.

Philip and I had our first fight over Ricardo da Silva.

I had been invited to a spring dance at Philip's school. It was a huge affair, and all the girls from Forms 3 through Lower 6, the equivalent of American high school years, were invited. I was in Form 3 and terribly excited because it was the first dance Mum would let me go to since the teachers would be chaperoning.

Philip was peevish. "You don't want to be dancing with every Tom, Dick and Harry. Some of the boys have bad breath. I'll tell Mum not to let you go."

I had a new dress and shoes and even secretly bought some make up which I planned to put on at Helena's place before the dance. Mum didn't approve of make up for me yet. So I was going, regardless.

"Don't you dare," I snapped, "or I'll tell Mum what we do at night." My own viciousness startled me.

Philip recoiled. "I'm sorry Ai-Lin, of course I wouldn't do that."

"And furthermore," I continued in Chinglish, "you should not be jealous. Otherwise, you cannot my lover be."

Philip left me alone for a few days after that, not even coming to my room at night, and although I was a little disturbed by his absence, I was too thrilled at the prospect of my first dance to care.

It was there that I met Ricardo.

He was a dark-skinned, Portuguese, Form 5 arts student, a classmate of Philip's, and incredibly handsome. Helena knew his family and introduced us. He danced well, spoke beautifully unaccented Cantonese and English - unlike many of the other Portuguese kids I knew, he didn't say "already" after every sentence - and made my heart somersault every time he said my name. We sat out three dances in a row and talked.

The band was playing several insipid pop songs. They were a local group, Adam Ho and the Zounds, and most of my girlfriends were crazy for the lead singer, who looked like a Chinese Paul McCartney.

"Pretty bad, aren't they?" I remarked.

He laughed. "I'd rather be listening to 'Purple Haze' or Motown."

His taste in music mirrored Philip's. I was in love.

"In fact," he continued, "some of my classmates brought a sound system into our classroom upstairs, and we have a bunch of terrific albums. Want to come up and listen?"

"Do you have The Doors?"

"Is 'Light My Fire' good enough for you?"

It was one of Philip's favorite songs. I felt myself blushing but nodded happily and followed him upstairs. We hung around with his friends, and listened to albums. Helena was in a corner necking with one of the guys. Most of the kids were older than myself, and I felt cool, grown up and proud to be with Ricardo. He offered me a cigarette, and taught me to inhale, and I even took a couple of sips from the bourbon he had hidden in his jacket pocket. We smiled at each other a lot and kept a watchful eye for passing teachers. All the time, he either held my hand or kept his arm around my waist or shoulder.

It was an hour and a half before we went back to the auditorium.

Philip marched over. I realized, a little guiltily, that I had completely forgotten about him.

"We were in the home room," Ricardo said quickly. He was holding my hand. "You should have come by. It was your kind of music."

Philip ignored him and addressed me. "Don't you think you might have at least told me where you were going."

"Philip, please." I was horribly embarrassed.

"Excuse me," Philip said to Ricardo, "I'd like to dance with my sister."

"Sure." Ricardo held out my hand to Philip, but did not let it go.

And then, Philip suddenly turned away and placed his hand on Ricardo's shoulder. "Go on, you dance with her. I'm sure she'd rather dance with you than her brother." And he walked away, leaving a puzzled Ricardo to lead me to the dance floor.

It was a slow dance, and Ricardo held me with both his arms round my waist. I liked the feel of his body close to mine and leaned close to him. I felt him kiss my neck and ear, and his hand close to my breast excited me. Philip watched from across the hall. I wished he would ask someone to dance.

Halfway through the second song, Ricardo asked, "Does your brother have a girlfriend at your school?"

Of course Philip doesn't have a girlfriend, I wanted to exclaim, I'm his girlfriend, and suddenly, I saw the complete absurdity of my life, the insanity of my "secret" with Philip, which caused this one innocent question to throw me completely.

My silence must have betrayed some of my inner turbulence, although the chaos lasted only a moment, a mere fraction of time, because Ricardo looked at me in a funny way and said, "Are you feeling alright?"

"Oh yes, I'm fine," and we continued dancing as before until Philip came by, and I saw his eyes were furious with jealousy. Although Ricardo couldn't have possibly known, I think he sensed something, because this time he stepped back as my brother almost snatched me out of his arms and took me home, though everything was terribly polite and no one would have known anything was really wrong.

I would not speak to Philip at all during the cab ride home, and locked my bedroom door that night.

Ricardo asked me out to see *The Thomas Crown Affair,* but I had to say no because Philip told Mum that Ricardo was a wild one whose brother was a radio deejay and that the movie was unsuitable, so of course Mum absolutely forbade me. I sulked and pouted for days, and wouldn't even let Philip fetch me after school and took the bus with some of my girlfriends instead. But Ricardo and I did make it to the movie without Mum knowing, because I lied and said I was going out with Helena who promised to cover for me, and it was wonderful because once Steve and Faye gave up on their chess game and whirled into their windmill, Ricardo French-kissed me the rest of the movie in our back row seats and told me he loved me. But Philip suspected and followed us to the cinema where he watched us and later confronted me. I was furious and slapped his face for being jealous and mean and for spying on me, and he went and told Mum. She slapped my face and called me a prostitute, and said she would tell Dad if she ever caught me again.

I cried for days and was desperate to see Ricardo, but Mum had Philip watch me like a hawk. I hated Philip passionately and locked my door every night for two weeks. After awhile, Ricardo started going out with one of my girlfriends whose parents let her date. The day they started going steady, Philip was sweet and gentle, absolutely princely, and that night, he kissed away all my tears, promising he would never be unfaithful like Ricardo and made me his lover again.

I never dated anyone. Helena told me not to be such a bore, but even she couldn't get me to change my mind since I couldn't tell her why. Mum said I spent too much time at the library and in my books, because I turned into a terrible bookworm, and that boys didn't like eggheads. She even told Philip not to be so protective of me, and encouraged me to go to dances and parties with my friends, as long as she approved of them. I went only to the ones Philip was invited to, knowing he couldn't bear for me to be with other guys when he was around to see it, but that he was much more cautious now since the Ricardo incident because he didn't want to let slip about our secret. At those parties, I would torture him by dancing as close as I could with every guy who asked me. I got a reputation for being a cock-teaser, because I would neck at parties, letting guys touch me all over, but wouldn't go out with anyone. But my brother and I always went home together afterwards, and he would be so excited he'd even kiss and fondle me in the taxi which both aroused and infuriated me.

When I was fifteen, Philip and I made love for the last time, the night before he left for college. He stayed with me almost the whole night, just holding me. His eyes were wet when he promised me he would come back for me one day, that he would love me forever. And though a secret part of me was glad he was going away, I cried all the same because I knew I was losing the one person who loved me more than anyone else in the world.

I woke up with a start from the same dream every night for months after Philip's departure.

In the dream, Philip and Paul stand over my bed where I lie, naked. Philip moves towards me, his arms outstretched in a ready embrace. Paul protests, saying don't Philip, but Paul's eyes are closed. Philip advances, Paul's voice fades until it's barely a whisper, and then he turns into a shadow, Philip's shadow, as Philip lightly plays his fingers all over me at which point I wake up, my body agitated and unsatisfied.

Each night, as I stared into the darkness, my insides would feel cold, as if I had been frozen into a block of ice. Although by now I no longer expected to marry my brother, I couldn't imagine never feeling him close to me again. In a strangely childish way, I felt his departure was my fault because I had been unfaithful to him once - even though reason told me otherwise - and clung to the hope that if I remained faithful to his memory, he would appear magically one day and love me again. I refused to go to any more parties, and spent all my time reading books and listening to The Doors, which Philip used to listen to incessantly, hoping, I think, to "break on through" to whatever other side it was he searched for. In fact, until I went to college and met Derek, I never even held another boy's hand.

Philip's letters stopped after his first semester at college. I felt betrayed, and despaired at ever hearing from him again. Paul wrote all the time, and said Philip's phone had been disconnected and that it appeared Philip may have dropped out of school. And then a year later, Philip's letter arrived announcing he was abandoning his family name and that he was gay and proud of it.

"Your brother is so irresponsible," my mother said, after shrieking at Dad that Philip's fall into a living hell was all my father's fault. "You better not turn out like him, Ai-Lin, when you go to the States. Especially since you're a girl."

I wanted to shout at my mother, to tell her she didn't know anything. Instead, I locked myself in my room, only to find that I could shed no tears. I took his last condom, one I had preserved for his return, and sliced it cleanly through. My heart closed up that night and I hated Philip, hated him for this, his ultimate desertion.

Over the next ten years, I only saw my brother twice. Philip had remained illegally in the States after college, living mostly in San Francisco, and I had attended Xavier in Cincinnati and gone home after that. Once was during my junior year, when he and Paul drove into Cincinnati to see me - Paul was living and working in Austin, Texas at the time - and the three of us were all so happy to be back together again that Philip and I didn't spend any time alone. The other time was four years later during my business trip to the West Coast, by which time Philip was determinedly gay, or at the very least bi-sexual, and living with Frederico, his albino male lover. That time, he was happy and charming and playful, and we never once alluded to our "secret."

On my wedding day, Philip danced the fourth dance with me at the reception, he being last in line of all the men in my life. Vince and I had arranged for all sixties music, to take us both back to our adolescence. The deejay was spinning Motown, a Four Tops number, very slow and romantic.

Philip held me very tightly and whispered into my ear. "We were going to marry each other once, remember?" For a second, I felt a familiar agitation, the prelude to his nightly visits. "You were going to love me forever, and I promised never to leave you."

I pulled back and looked into my brother's eyes, wary and a little frightened. He wore a sad smile, and I saw his Adam's apple bulging up and down, up and down, the way it always did when he was excited.

"We aren't supposed to speak about it. It's our secret." For just a moment, I wanted to play along, wanted to hold onto a long hidden past that I neither understood nor dared to fully feel.

"Forgive me for Ricardo?" He looked sad, sadder than I'd ever seen him. "Forgive me for leaving you, for everything?"

I leaned my head on his shoulder. His arms around me felt comfortable, familiar, as if they always belonged there. "There's nothing to forgive," I said.

And then, we were dancing like brother and sister again, not lovers, and I felt a little frightened and sad, because I knew that marrying Vince was the first real break I was making with the strange life of my family and my intimate world with Philip. Because even after all those years, I had never been truly intimate with any man until Vince came along.

Philip kissed me after the dance and whispered, "don't be

afraid, Ai-Lin," and I went back to my new husband, reassured that at least one person in the world could read that chapter of my mind.

The wedding was the last time I saw Philip. He was a little better after that about calling from time to time, although we never spoke for long. And each time I heard his voice, my insides would feel warm and safe and even a little excited.

Philip died of AIDS several years later, in the arms of the lover who gave him the disease. He was thirty seven.

After his death, I began psychoanalysis.

My therapist keeps telling me it's normal to feel anger, because I was the "victim" of incest. She doesn't understand though. Every time I try to feel this anger she tells me about, so that I can "work through it and forgive myself, if not forget," I hear Philip's sing-song Chinglish-English voice saying, "I can your girlfriend be." And then I laugh, because it makes me remember, and the truth is, I don't ever want to forget about Philip and me.

4

About Vince

The September day the call came from Cincinnati offering me the Ohio editor's job at *Tri-State Business and Leisure,* I packed my bags and took the next flight out of New York.

"You're crazy, Ai-Lin" Vince said as he drove me to the airport. "They roll up the sidewalks at sunset. I was there once on a shoot. It was like a morgue downtown after dark."

Vince was my soon-to-be-ex husband. Three months of our trial separation had convinced me our four-year marriage was over. It hadn't convinced him. "Morgues are quiet. And clean."

"If all you want to do is roll over and play dead." He reached over to tickle the back of my neck.

I suppressed a smile. "Cut that out and watch where you're going." Damn Vince. He could make me mad and happy at the same time.

He pulled his hand away. "Look, forget what happened to us. You'll suffocate there, Ai-Lin. And you won't be able to get decent Chinese food."

"I'll cook."

"Hah! That'll be the day."

I looked out the window at the disappearing Manhattan skyline. No more filthy subway rides, polluted air or expensive boxes that passed as apartments. No more frantic deadlines at BusinessWorld. No more feeling like I was constantly on the edge of insane. No more Vince da Luca. I felt an unnerving calm approach.

Vince had cut off a Hassidic driver and was swearing at him. The way he drove set my nerves on edge.

"Will you slow down?" I asked.

"Why should I? You're the one who's running."

"Enough. You promised you . . ."

"Goddammit Ai-Lin," he exploded, "what the hell did I do to deserve this?"

That was it. Whenever Vince yelled, something froze inside of me. I clenched my teeth and stared out the window for the rest of the ride, shutting him out of me completely. Vince drove in silence; he knew when he'd lost.

But at La Guardia, he insisted on walking me to the gate.

"You don't have to," I protested, but he was already on the ramp to the parking lot. I could hear him say to himself - give me ten more minutes with her and I'll change her mind. His tenacity drove me wild, even though it was what had attracted me to him in the first place.

I was agitated and upset inside, despite my outward cool. As we walked together to the gate, he tried to play with my hand, and then my neck, bypassing my "cut that out" with his "I know I promised but it's been three months." Even when I managed to get across "no" to the man, he'd get his way somehow, like today, showing up to drive me to the airport even though I had said I'd take a taxi.

But at the gate, as I heard the last call for my flight, he took me in his arms and kissed me until I was almost ready to turn around and go home with him. I could feel the tears inside, but I wouldn't cry, wouldn't give in to him because to give in meant letting go of everything I'd held onto for so long in my life, and not even Vince could make me into someone else although of all the people who loved me, which in my case amounted to only my two brothers and perhaps my father, Vince came closer than anyone else.

I pulled away from him. "We agreed."

"I know, I know."

"We've been through everything."

"That doesn't make it final."

"It does for me."

He lit a cigarette. I could see he was suppressing the urge to shout another protest, sorry as he already was for the last outburst. I watched as the final passengers trailed through the gate.

"So can I call once in awhile?"

"It won't do any good. Vincent, I have to go."

His eyes were both angry and sad. I began to walk towards the gate. And just as I entered the tunnel to the plane, I heard Vince's shout, loud and resonant, "I'll always love you, babes."

As my Delta flight touched down, I found myself gazing at the Greater Cincinnati Airport with the same trepidation of twelve years ago when I had first arrived as a student at Xavier University.

"Cincinnati," Vince had said in surprise when I first met him, "what a way to encounter America."

We had met on board a boat in Hong Kong, one of those cocktail reception evening-on-the-water media affairs the advertising crew and publisher at *AsiaMonth* loved to throw. I had attended with some misgivings. Vince was a visiting freelance photographer, and I was the command performance editorial staff guest.

I was at the quiet side of the boat avoiding the schmooze when Vince gravitated towards me and introduced himself. "You don't sell space, do you?" he asked. "How come you don't wear glasses like every other person in Hong Kong? And has anyone ever told you you have the most gorgeous hair?"

"Yes, I'm single, twenty-twenty vision and space sells me.

Does that answer all your questions?" I was surprised by the ease of my response.

He laughed. "I know, I know, it was a corny pickup line. So sue me. Is it my fault you're single? What's your name?"

"Hsu Ai-Lin."

He shook my hand. "Pleased to meet you Ai-Lin. So, you ready to split this pop stand yet?"

I laughed in spite of myself. "Does it show that badly?"

"I'm afraid so. I hate these things too but I couldn't pass up the boat ride since this is my first trip here."

Vince was a blast of clean air. I had earlier sidled away from some Swiss hotelier, a major advertiser, who practically had me at dinner and in bed after "proper" introductions and his complimentary dribble about an article I hadn't even written.

I liked writing for *AsiaMonth.* I could lose myself in researching facts until the story came clear to me. Four years with the magazine had given me just enough status to get occasional decent assignments and travel around Asia, and once in a rare while to Europe. What I didn't like was the business end of publishing, entertaining with the advertising crowd, which I studiously avoided whenever I could. Tonight had been a compromise, because it was budget renewal time - "they like to meet our journalists," my publisher pleaded, "makes them think what they do has legitimacy." I had finally agreed, because my editor bribed me with a trip to Rome, an assignment he knew I wanted, especially since it meant showing up my chief rival at the *Far Eastern Economic Review,* a Dow Jones publication with much larger editorial budgets and salaries than we had.

Vince made up for the evening.

"So tell me the story of your life," he said.

"Why don't you tell me yours first?" I responded.

"Okay. Brooklyn, circa 1950. My mother howled because I came out feet first, kicking my way into the world. Your turn."

It was impossible not to like Vince. Not only was he incredibly handsome - dark eyes, jet black hair, olive complexion, and a warm flashing smile - but he made me laugh and want to throw caution to the wind. There was something passionate and open about him that I liked; he had spirit and made me imagine possibilities. In many ways, he reminded me of my brother Philip, right to his being exactly four years older than me.

"I was a quiet baby," I said.

"I got into street fights a lot."

"I tried to be a model child."

He lit a cigarette and offered me one which I took. "If I promise to kiss you very quietly, will you go out with me?"

I could feel him edging into my being. Cynicism did not prevail, although my head was already buzzing with a thousand unspoken protests. "That depends."

"On what?"

"The persuasiveness of your kiss."

Dinner that night was wonderful. He told me all about his family in Brooklyn - four sisters, three brothers, two Dobermans, a thousand relatives and the most wonderful mother in the world - and his life in Manhattan. When he spoke about his city, it was with what amounted almost to reverence. Coney Island, City Island, the Cloisters, Prospect Park, the GW Bridge. He reeled names off like a litany, all the spaces he liked best to photograph. I had never been to New York, and had always been curious to go. He made me see the city in my mind.

That night, Vince kissed my hand. "Tomorrow?" he asked.

The evening had ended too soon for me. I wanted him

never to let go of my hand, and was already regretting my too-persistent request to go home, citing work and a father who still sat up and worried as excuses. Vince had brought me home without protest. I both resented and admired his gallantry.

"Tomorrow?" he repeated, kissing my arm and forearm.

I nodded. An unaccustomed feeling of security enveloped me.

"I guess my kiss must have been persuasive," he said as he walked away.

The plane rolled up to the gate and discharged the passengers in a smooth and steady flow. There was no one to meet me in Cincinnati, as there hadn't been when I arrived before. But this time, the journey was easier, perhaps because this time, I knew I was better off alone.

Walking down the ramp towards the arrival hall, I suddenly recalled my first encounter with the notion of this city.

"So you found Xavier in some reference book at a library in Hong Kong, and that made you go to Cincinnati? No relatives, no friends, nothing else?" At the end of our second date, Vince was still having trouble with the story of my life.

"Not the library, the I.I.E., Institute of International Education, where hopeful Hong Kong students research their collegiate futures in lines of fine print."

"Whatever." He pulled me away from the door of my flat into the stairwell. "Tomorrow night again, okay babes?"

"But Vincent . . ." My protest was silenced by a kiss, a light brush across my lips and over my cheek. I shuddered. It was the identical way Philip had always begun our lovemaking. I was aroused without fearing the passion for the first time in years.

"Not Vincent. Vince. Please see me tomorrow?" He kissed my neck lightly as I leaned against the concrete wall; the cool surface felt strangely sensual through my silk skirt.

"Maybe, I don't know."

"We belong together, don't we?" He was stroking my arms and back lightly, with Philip's gentle, pianist's touch.

There wasn't much I could do except say yes.

At home, my father was up. He looked at me in a peculiar way. "You're working late a lot."

"Out of town visitors."

"Hmmph. They shouldn't make women work so late, or travel so much. Make me some tea."

I headed towards the kitchen, his command grating my nerves.

When Mum first died, I had only been sixteen, and Dad still looked after me as a parent. Although I had overseen the housekeeping, he did not demand unreasonable attention. But ever since my return from college, his demands had grown over the past four years until I often found him impossible to bear. I could not share in his morose, unforgiving grief, in his need to blame my mother for abandoning him. Luckily, my job gave me some independence from and financial power over him that made filial piety, which included living at home, tolerable.

"Who was that with you at the door?" he called out from the living room.

So he had been watching, listening. A scream of protest stuck in my throat. I replied calmly, "Just a colleague who was kind enough to see me home."

"Daughters," Dad muttered just loud enough for me to hear, "all they do is get married and abandon you."

In bed that night, I pretended Vince was making love to me,

and I gave in to him, deliciously, completely, with a liberating abandon I thought I would never feel again.

I saw Vince the remaining five nights of his stay in Hong Kong, and he was incredible and I felt more in love than I'd ever remembered feeling. Each night before the last one, I would feel my body burn against the cool bed sheets. It was as if Philip had returned for his nocturnal visitations, and nothing, not my father, not the memory of my mother, not the cautionary voice in my head could stop this sensual abandon. Every ugly detail of my life vanished into an oblivion of comforting forgetfulness. My father's habitual grumblings and complaints did not trouble me that week.

On the last night, we stood at the Star Ferry pier in Central staring at the black water of the harbor. It was one in the morning. I had been trying to end the night, but the words simply wouldn't come.

He lit a cigarette. "I'm not leaving you like this."

I evaded his gaze, unbearably kind and loving. "You'll never see me again."

"Is that what you really think?"

No, I wanted to shout. I don't think that at all. Instead, I lied. "I've never been with a man before."

He was silent for a long moment, and then he put his arms around me in an embrace and what with his kiss and his body against mine and the metal guard rail pressing my legs and waist from behind, the alternating sensations of warmth and cold intermingled and it was only the public-ness of the place that kept me from pulling him into me then and there I was so desperate with desire, a desire I had kept hidden for so long, too long because until this moment, I had not believed that the power of this passion could last beyond these few days with Vince.

My Avis rental car was ready for me and I picked up my luggage in record time. The weather was warm and a little humid. I drove past miles of Kentucky bluegrass; due to Cincinnati's reluctance to finance an airport within its own boundaries in 1955, the "Greater Cincinnati" Airport, a one time temporary facility, was still located in Boone County, Kentucky. In the distance, the bridges across the Ohio River to downtown Cincinnati emerged. I suddenly recalled Union Terminal, that wonderful art deco building, where Derek Anderson, my one and only boyfriend before Vince, showed me how my voice could carry from one side of the hall clear across to the other.

"No one? Not a single guy? I'm really the first?" He had come to Hong Kong to meet my father after he proposed and before I accepted.

I stuffed Derek, and Philip, into the furthest recesses of my being. After all, Derek and I never consummated, and Philip, well, Philip didn't really count, did he? "Not a one."

"Come on, you can tell. I'm not the jealous type."

"Zip it. Come on, my dad's waiting."

I had wanted to prevent this meeting, even suggesting that we both went to Austin so that he could meet Paul instead. As strange as Paul was, I knew I could count on him. Dad was another story. Vince naturally wouldn't hear of it.

It was the first time Vince had ever been in my home. Our flat, a duplex penthouse which once commanded a spectacular view of the harbor, was now shadowed by the Sheraton Hotel. Dad was quick to tell Vince about the way things used to be.

"Far East Mansion was once the tallest building in all of Kowloon, that's what we lived in. When I bought this flat, you couldn't find a better place. You can't imagine the trouble I went through to turn the two floors into a duplex!"

I cringed. The walls of our flat, once a cleanly light, pale blue, looked grey now after years of neglect. Vince followed Dad out to the verandah. The metal railing, painted a matching blue, peeled and flaked like a bad case of eczema, rust showing through, the result of too many typhoon seasons. I saw Vince's photographer eyes snap every detail, right down to the missing tiles by the drain.

"It's in an excellent location." Vince lit Dad's cigarette, declining the offer of one for himself. "I can see why it's special."

"The best." My father beamed proudly.

"Tell me about the mine in Indonesia," Vince began. "Ai-Lin told me that you used to be in the business. Sounds exciting."

And Dad was off, an ancient mariner with a willing audience. I wandered outside to the verandah. How was it Vince could appease and humor this difficult man? I had not seen my father this happy in years. There was something magical about Vince. It was as if he could elicit all the forgotten joy that existed once, somewhere, in me, in my family. Around Vince, Dad was not morose or tiresome, and did not control me with his customary possessiveness. Since Vince entered my life, I no longer remembered old pains. Even my colleagues at work finally decided I was human, and no longer made cracks about my ability to freeze over the equator.

I suppose that was why I agreed to marry Vince.

Even after we got engaged, Vince could not believe that I wasn't seeing anyone at all when we met.

"She's the only woman I've ever met who doesn't talk about her old boyfriends. That's why I'm marrying her," he declared to his youngest brother Don.

I was visiting him in New York to meet his family, now that my Dad had told me I would be a fool not to marry Vince. Don was supposed to be the easy introduction who had stopped by to drive us all out to Brooklyn. I took an immediate liking to him. He resembled Vince, except that his features were finer and more chiseled, and he had a delicacy that Vince lacked. Don was an architect who restored old buildings. Just like Derek. The coincidence unnerved me.

"Don't let the family overwhelm you." Don winked at me. "Vince has been a nervous wreck for weeks now."

"What're you talking about, nervous? Get outta here. You ready yet babes?"

"Vincent, patience."

"Aha," Don smiled. "Just like mama. She's got you all figured out, Vince."

My fiance tapped his brother on the side of his head playfully. We headed out of Vince's Upper West Side apartment to Don's car, where Vince insisted I sit in the passenger seat so that I could see "the real New York." I glanced at the ring on my left hand. My fiance, my husband. The words rolled through my mind like the ebb and flow of waves at the shoreline, perpetually commanded by the romance of moonlight, the prospect of eternity. Despite the nervousness I felt at meeting his family, I had already decided nothing about them would deter me.

The da Lucas lived in a two-story brick house on a short block off the southwest corner of Prospect Park. It was early Sunday afternoon. We found a parking space right in front of the house on the tree-lined street.

Mr. Da Luca opened the door as Don switched off the engine. He was a tall, handsome, dark-skinned man, about sixty, who wore a happy, excited expression. Vince looked exactly like his father, who, when introduced to me, looked me up and down with his dark, southern Italian eyes and said, "I approve," in a deep, resonant accent, and rounded all three of us into the house.

The rest of the family were already there. The two other married brothers and their families, four sisters in various marital states, surrounded by children and husbands, various uncles, aunts and cousins, some elderly women who wore all black; all of these people's names and faces went past me in a blur. Italian and English flew around the living and dining room. I realized, with a start, that every face there had a distinctly Italian cast.

Vince plunged into a prolonged round of greetings. I heard him babbling in Italian and I thought how wonderful he sounded, so warm and mellifluous, without the hard edge in his voice which I heard when he spoke English. He seemed to have forgotten about me, caught up as he was in family gossip and exchanges. Don guided me through the mass of people. "Downstairs," he whispered, "my sisters can't wait to get you alone for some girl talk." And he led me to the basement where the sisters congregated, all of whom kissed me and welcomed me into the family as if I were already one of them. It was intoxicating, being surrounded by this rush of warmth, the aroma of garlic and sauce wafting through the house, voices raised in shouts of laughter, not anger, this joy of a family celebrating the occasion of my engagement.

Just before we sat down to dinner, Vince took me to meet his mother. First, he put out his cigarette. He had been chain smoking all day.

I had wondered when she would appear, although I had been warned ahead of time that she tended to be sickly. I was unprepared for the stark severity of her room. Downstairs, there was an abundance of flowers and colors amid rich, dark wood furniture - Mr. da Luca was a furniture maker who had immigrated after the war - and the house felt solid, dependable and permanent. Yet upstairs, in Mrs. da Luca's room, the colors were pale, delicate and ethereal, a startling contrast to everything I had seen so far.

She sat in a rocking chair, a thin woman of medium height, dressed in a classically cut cream colored gaberdine suit and Bally pumps. Her hair had begun to gray, but still showed its original rich chestnut color, and the long tresses framed her face exquisitely. Her fair skin evidenced her northern Italian origin. Don had told me his mother had been a dancer before getting married. There was a grace and elegance in her movements as she rose, like some regal bird, to study me.

Vince kissed his mother's hand, wrapping an arm lovingly around her shoulder. "Mama," he said softly, "this is Ai-Lin."

She did not speak for several minutes. I gazed at her. Nothing Vince had told me about his mother - whom he clearly adored and respected - had prepared me for her demeanor, in some respects much like my own mother, except that my future mother-in-law's eyes did not border on the edge of insanity. I was glad I had dressed conservatively but well for the occasion.

"Vincent is my oldest and most precious son," she said slowly, with only a hint of accent. "You must always be proud of him and do your duty to him." And then, as if the strain of speaking had been too great, she leaned on Vince who fussed about, putting a wrap around her despite the warmth of the day, and escorted her carefully down the stairs, as if I did not exist, for the moment, at all.

Cincinnati's skyline began to appear in the distance. I went to light a cigarette and stopped myself. In college, Derek had tried to get me to quit, and I almost had, but when he dumped me, I started up again with a vengeance.

Vince smoked too much, especially when he was nervous.

"But why shouldn't we have at least a small reception in Hong Kong? Wouldn't your father want that?"

It was two in the morning. I was exhausted from all the planning. Vince persisted with his arguments for over three hours. I had emptied the ashtray three times.

"You don't understand," I pleaded for what seemed like the tenth time, "Dad won't invite Paul. If we simply have it in New York, then your family can call the shots and we'll invite whoever we like, including all my family."

"But it's your wedding, Ai-Lin. They'll make up long enough for that."

"You don't know my father."

"What about Philip? Wouldn't he want to see you married at home?"

"He's illegal. He can't leave the U.S."

"I've got a friend who's an immigration lawyer. He can help."

"It's not that easy. Besides, Philip won't take that kind of help."

"Come on, Ai-Lin, doesn't family and home mean anything to you? What about all your relatives in Indonesia? Don't you think your dad would want them at the wedding for his only daughter? And your friends, like Helena? And 'Auntie' May? I thought she was almost like family to you, at least, that's what you told me. Come on, Ai-Lin, surely a little of the Chinese tradition of family, ancestor worship, something must have rubbed off on you?"

"I've told you, I don't want a huge wedding full of strangers.

Mum and Dad never took us to Indonesia, and I hardly know my Indonesian relatives. Every so often, relatives would appear for a week in Hong Kong and ooh and aah over how big the children had grown and then disappear, and I wouldn't know them again if I saw them. And the only people who matter, Helena and Auntie May, will come to New York."

Vince shook his head. To him, family and friends meant everything. I tried to tell him that he was everything to me now, but he never quite understood that.

I had been reticent about my family's history, deflecting Vince's inquisitiveness by talking about my friends instead, like Helena. Helena, who was trying hard to get married, thought Vince wonderfully romantic and envied me my good fortune. My family didn't seem to matter anymore now, not even Philip. I would not make the mistake of telling Vince about Philip and me, the way I had with Derek. I wanted to hide away the past in this new life I'd discovered with Vince. It was difficult when he wouldn't let me.

"Look," I continued, "if I could have my way, we'd elope."

Vince stared at me in horror. "God, you're cold."

I felt something close up inside. The look on his face was unloving and mistrustful. I wanted to lunge at him and scratch his face, to destroy any trace of this momentary absence of love. The violence of my emotions frightened me. How was it that this man held such power over me? I began to cry.

"You just don't understand," I whimpered.

He came over and put his arms around me. "Hey, I'm sorry. I didn't mean to push you. We'll do it just in New York, okay? For my family?"

It was the first time I had cried with Vince, the first time, in fact, that I had cried in years, although Vince couldn't possibly have known it at the time. An unfamiliar sense of relief overtook me as the violent feelings subsided. Vince led me over to his bed where he cradled me in his arms and kissed away my tears. I felt like an incompetent child, being comforted by my brother Philip. But when Vince and I made love that night, I felt closer and safer with him than ever before because up till then, as much as I believed I loved him, I realized I had kept him a little bit distant from me, high up on a pedestal as My Romantic Lover, and not known the man I loved.

So I married Vince, and through the festivities, he met my two brothers, both of whom he found a little strange. My father came to the reception, although neither he nor Philip would go to the church wedding. Paul gave me away. Dad and Paul glared at each other, unforgiving, and never exchanged even one word. I could hear the entire da Luca clan whispering away about my strange family, the weird Chinese in-laws that Vince was not ashamed of no matter what they did. My mother-in-law would not kiss me, protesting that she had a cold although I saw no sign of any such ailment. But on my wedding day, I didn't mind terribly much, because Vince gazed at me with so much love in his eyes that said forget everyone you're my family now that my whole being felt like a dam ready to burst.

As I sped over the suspension bridge into downtown Cincinnati in my Avis rental car, the radio station played country western. Rock and country. That was all I ever heard in Ohio. And a little classical.

Shortly after our second wedding anniversary, Vince started listening to opera. Puccini. He wanted to go to Italy.

"To live?" I demanded.

"To Rome, where I first proposed to you," he replied. "We can even send your dad a ticket so that you can see him again."

"What makes you think he'll go?"

"I don't know. But it's worth a try since he refuses to come to New York, and you won't go see him in Hong Kong."

"And what will we do in Rome?"

"You'll live with me and be my love." He rolled over and lay on top of me. "Come on, Ai-Lin, talk to me. Tell me what's wrong."

We were sitting in bed on a Sunday morning. For the past several months, Vince had been complaining about our conjugal relations - "I'm not getting enough, babes." - was his way of putting it, to which I always evaded reply.

I pushed him away. "There's nothing wrong."

He let out an exasperated sigh. "Goddammit, there is. Why won't you tell me? Don't you love me anymore?"

"Stop swearing," I said, and walked out of the bedroom to the kitchen.

Vince was always trying to relive the romance of our original meeting. When I arrived in Rome on one of the most important assignments of my career, there were flowers in my hotel room and a wire from Vince that said "marry me?" At five thirty the next morning, he knocked on my hotel room door. Thanks to him, I showed up late for my first interview with a run in my stocking, which didn't sit well with my editor. Vince followed me around for the next four days until I gave in and agreed to consider his proposal. And I had known the man for only a little more than two months.

From the kitchen, I could hear Pinkerton's and Butterfly's duet. It irritated me, because it turned Vince on. I knew he was masturbating in our bedroom. My body froze. I tried to concentrate on emptying the dishwasher. The clock in the kitchen ticked with an unbearable loudness. I stood very still, my arms piled with clean, white dishes as the operatic voices reverberated through our apartment. A part of me wanted to go to him, feel him in me, but something held me back, tightening my every fibre so that passion had no outlet. And then, I heard the shower come on, and my body relaxed.

How was it that love had come to this?

Vince appeared fifteen minutes later wearing only a pair of jeans. I averted my eyes from his lean, bronzed body and poured him a cup of coffee.

"You used to shower with me." His eyes accused over the rim of his cup.

I turned my back to him. "I didn't know you were in the shower."

He reached for my arm.

"Don't."

"What the hell is the matter with you?" he exploded. "Why are you being such a goddamned bitch?"

I wanted to tell him, but when he yelled like that I froze inside and couldn't talk to him. I wanted to tell him that something was happening to me, something I didn't understand that had to do with a growing fear that he would leave me. But the words remained buried inside me because that feeling seemed irrational, insane and completely without basis since it was clear to me and everyone else that Vince loved me, and not understanding my fears made me even more afraid.

That afternoon, I went for a long walk by myself down around South Ferry. Vince was working. He worked all the time these days, partly, I think, because it was the only time he could let me be completely alone. Vince seemed to understand a lot about what I needed, even when I wouldn't talk to him.

The sky was overcast. I walked around the park, and lingered at the memorial for the veterans. Staring at the stone slabs of names, these men who had never asked for war, I felt a sudden urge to cry.

"Ai-Lin? What's the matter?"

Vince's brother Don was standing beside me, and I turned and looked at his concerned face that so resembled Vince, except that it was even more handsome and gentler, and before I knew it, he had his arms around me and I was saying something about how much I loved Vince, and I didn't know what could possibly be the matter but something was stopping me from loving Vince completely.

Don took me to his apartment which was in this marvellous old brick building on Front Street, a short walk away, and poured me a glass of wine. We sat by the window which looked out to the East River. In the window was a vase of white and purple orchids, just like the ones my mother used to fill our home with.

"Reminds me a little of home," I said, sipping my wine.

"Then that's good. Everyone's childhood has some memories worth keeping."

He talked about his childhood with Vince, how he had always adored his brother who protected and loved him. They were alike, he and Vince, he said. The wine and the talk and the breeze with its faint salty odor from the fish market were marvellous, and I could feel my entire body opening, relaxing. When he leaned close to me to pour the second glass, I felt his arm against mine and I put my hand on it, whispering, "and are you alike in the women you desire?" He stopped, looked at me, and kissed me firmly on the lips and before I knew it, I had my tongue in his mouth and minutes later we wound up on the couch. I was so aroused by the feel of his body close to mine, his passion that was evident and I hadn't meant to do it but I began caressing him and he groaned "Ai-Lin, please, I won't be able to help myself" and Don and I wound up making love that day into the night and it so relieved me to feel open and happy that I didn't even think about the wrongness of it all until much too late, until much too much passion had overtaken and conquered me.

Vince was watching TV when I returned. The ashtray was filled with butts.

"Do you know what time it is?" His voice was quiet, even.

I looked at the clock. It was past midnight.

"I'm sorry. I went for a walk and forgot the time." I could feel my panties still wet between my legs and blushed hotly. I turned my back to him so that he wouldn't see my face.

He gripped both my arms from behind. "Ai-Lin, I've been so worried, I . . ." he bent to kiss my neck and then stopped. "You've been with someone."

His voice, flat and toneless, frightened me. When Vince yelled, I cringed, but I was never afraid.

"Look at me." He spun me around. "You were, weren't you?" His eyes were sad, and bewildered. I kept waiting for an explosion, even for a slap across my face although in my wildest dreams, I could never imagine Vince hitting me, he was simply too good a man for that. But the explosion never came. He simply sank back into his chair, lit a cigarette and asked, "but why, babes, why?" and then, almost in a whisper so that I could not be sure I heard correctly, "why did you have to prove mama right?"

I fled to the bedroom, afraid to confront the consequence of my desires.

I rented an apartment in the downtown Cincinnati area

after only two days of looking. It was on Fourth and Plum, in a renovated industrial building full of painted pipes. I took what struck me as a huge two-bedroom space, furnished, for a little over seven hundred dollars a month. "Luxury in Cincinnati, slumming in New York and Hong Kong," I told Vince once I settled in. "Swines before a pearl," he retorted.

"Swine before a pearl," he said, when he punched Don in the eye.

"It was my fault, please don't Vince," but my voice faded away in the force of emotions.

Don had come over the next evening to confess.

"We're all weird," Don said, as I nursed his rapidly swelling black eye, "but at least we keep it in the family."

"Bastard." Vince rubbed his hand.

"It's all mama's fault. No girl's ever good enough, not even her own daughters. I can't believe she talks to Ai-Lin. She must really think a lot of you, you know."

"Leave mama out of this." Vince lit a cigarette.

Don pulled out three wine glasses and a bottle of Bardolino from his bag and uncorked it. "Talk to me. Come on Vince, you know it wasn't what you think. You know me better than that."

Vince and Don talked into the night until early the next morning. Words tumbled out, about the da Lucas and their family secrets, most of which I knew as open secrets, about what he and Don called Chinese sex. "You know about Chinese walls?" Vince asked and I nodded, having just researched a story about a recent corporate merger in which the law firm representing more than one interest had established a so-called Chinese wall - the lawyers involved were separated as much as possible and could not exchange documents or discussions until the deal was consummated. "Well in our family, we have Chinese sex - in-laws screw each other, a bunch of illicit stuff goes on, and everyone guesses but everyone pretends nothing's going on because we're one big, happy family that forgives, forgives and forgets."

"And you and Don?"

"We stayed out of it, till now." Don gingerly touched his black eye. "We said we'd be above it, because mama always said this tendency came from our father's side of the family."

I didn't say much, because this was about Vince, not Vince and me. Don had always been a catalyst for Vince's emotions, like a sort of second self that drew out his inner life, the way Vince was for me. This was a necessary exclusion, I thought, like the world of Vince and his mama that I was privileged to enter only in discreet, unassuming ways. How everything had happened with Don didn't seem to matter anymore. But as I listened to the brothers talking, I felt as if I would always be on the outside looking in, trying to say to Vince all the things about myself that really mattered, above and beyond the passion I felt for him, which for reasons I couldn't fully explain, seemed to have contracted within myself these days. I didn't know how to say that each time the passion ended, I couldn't bear its departure. Vince was stronger than me. He believed that love and passion would thrive and expand beyond the present. I did not have such faith. I was afraid love would leave me, the way it had when Philip left me and later when Derek dumped me. And so I ran away to escape the possibility of pain.

But these were not words I knew how to say, unlike the words that flowed so freely now between the brothers.

By the early hours, Vince and Don were pretty drunk. Vince forgave me, completely, saying he knew this was just a one time thing, a momentary lapse of judgment under the influence and not some horrible adulterous desire on either of our parts, and everything was fine because whatever problems he and I had had nothing to do with this and he and Don were fine afterwards and nothing ever happened again between me and Don because Don made sure of it but I always felt funny and never quite got over the feeling that I simply lacked the insight required to appreciate that love invariably leads to forgiveness.

Sometime over the course of the next two years, Vince entered therapy. He also planted several pots of basil.

"You like that in your food, don't you?" He countered, when I complained that our tiny balcony didn't have room for all those pots.

"A little, yes. But we'll never eat all these plants."

"You take life in such tiny doses, Ai-Lin. Don't you ever get hungry?"

The phone rang. "It's Don," Vince said, his hand covering the receiver. "He wants to know whether we want to go get pizza at Patsy's. We could do it after my session."

I shook my head, and continued to read on the couch.

"Come on, you love Patsy's. We can watch the sun set from under the Brooklyn Bridge." He was grabbing my foot playfully. I shook his hand away.

"Some other night," he told Don. He climbed on top of me and tried to kiss my neck. "You know, it's okay if we see Don."

"I know."

"And it's okay if you want to come for a joint therapy session, too."

"I don't want to."

Vince eventually gave up trying to persuade me and left. Alone at last, I stepped onto our balcony and stared at the sky.

Didn't he understand anything? I didn't want to see Don, because every time he touched or kissed me in even the most brotherly way, I felt an awful rush of desire, one over which I had no control. And this was something I couldn't tell Vince, like about Philip or Derek, because then he would leave me. To Vince, everything was okay. I could be as cold as ice to him and that was okay. We could not make love for weeks at a time and he would accept it. Everything was okay since he started his weekly therapy and was locating the key to his psyche.

The phone rang again. Don's voice, like some horrible temptation, asked an ordinary question about some family event next week. I replied, but as I hung up, I felt the weight of a thousand secrets choking me, burying me alive, and the leaves of basil loomed over me like a giant jungle trying to swallow me into its heart of darkness. And Pinkerton's and Butterfly's duet soared in my brain, piercing my eardrums with a decibel level loud enough to waken all the crypts through the centuries and my body chilled and turned to ice.

When Vince returned, he found me curled up on the floor in a corner of the bedroom behind a locked door. I had smashed every basil pot except one. Vince never said a word. He put me to bed, cleaned up the mess and continued to live with me and love me as before, more sadly perhaps, but patiently nonetheless.

During the six months prior to my leaving Vince, I had visions of physically wrecking our home. I cannot name a specific cause or emotional state accompanying these visions. When I told Vince of these visions, he would hug me very tightly and say "it's okay, babes, it's okay. Let it out." It was Vince's idea that I needed to talk through all my feelings and cry, which felt good when I did, but made me uncomfortable afterwards. I began to sense the loss of that delicious, sweeping feeling that used to engulf me when I felt Vince's body close to mine. And I felt sad and alone, what had been a normal condition of existence before Vince came into my life. Vince tried to get me to talk to his family, even to Don, as well as to his therapist, but I told him to get rid of all of them because I wasn't insane, I had never been insane and would never be.

Three months before I left Vince, I ran away from home.

It was a Sunday afternoon, and I had refused to join Vince at one of his sister's birthday party.

"Tell her I'm not well."

"Okay, babes, whatever you say."

Before, Vince would have protested, first shouting, later calming down and cajoling me into going.

"Aren't you going to try to convince me otherwise?" The edge in my voice seemed to have always been there, hard and cynical, justified by some unknown persecution.

"You know I'm not like that. Not anymore. My therapist says . . ."

"You and your goddamned therapist! What about me? Don't I count? Or does some overpaid quack matter more than your wife?"

"Ai-Lin, please don't pick anymore fights with me. I haven't the energy."

I was about to counter with yet another high pitched insult - my voice was often frenzied these days - when I looked up into his eyes and the overwhelming sadness and compassion I saw shocked me into silence.

"I'll see you when I get back." He picked up his coat and left.

That afternoon, I packed an overnight bag and checked into

a midtown hotel. I kept saying to myself, over and over again, I'm not insane, I'm not insane. It was the frantic nature of New York, the frantic nature of being loved by Vince that was to blame. "Why aren't you afraid of me? Why d'you still love me? Don't you see I don't know how to love?" I had screamed at Vince only two days ago in what had been the prelude to a typical weekend. We not longer saw any friends, only visiting family when we had to, and I often begged off. But I wasn't insane, and I wasn't going to let Vince's psychobabble get to me. I wanted to be alone with myself, the self that had been slipping away from me for too long now.

Sex with Don. That's what did it. Chinese sex.

In that anonymous, gray hotel room, I began a communion with myself that lasted for hours, days, years.

If I hadn't left Vince he surely would have left me.

I made it to Cincinnati to get away from Vince after four years of marriage. It's been six months since I left, and I'm still waiting for him to sign the divorce papers. Vince won't let me go, because he says we're still in love. He keeps asking me to try to remember, when all I want to do is forget. Vince tells me the basil is flourishing despite its tiny pot, and that it's grown into an enormous, leafy plant. Somewhere deep inside I believe he may be right about this love he says we have. But I've only just begun to find the words that make remembering easier to bear. And until I can remember and laugh as well as cry, I don't know if there'll ever be anything more to say about Vince.

5

Paul Is My Mother's Son

Yesterday, I said goodbye to my brother Paul. He took off to travel throughout China as a celibate Shaolin monk, who will modem his impressions from a laptop computer to a publisher in San Francisco. Paul tells me I might never see him again, because he does not know where his search will lead.

I have spent a week with my brother in Austin, Texas, his home for the past nineteen years, helping him terminate his material life. Yesterday was our last night together.

I feel hollow. The shock of his phone call, over three months ago, telling me of his decision to abandon life as a computer programmer for a spiritual existence, has still not worn off. I watch him making tea for us in his kitchen, his face serene and contented. Now there is only Philip left. All the men in my life do not remain. I want to cry in protest, but the tears die in my throat.

"Mum would be proud of you," I say.

Paul pours boiling water over the leaves, and sets the pot of tea next to the sink to steep. "Doubt it. She wouldn't be happy unless I became a Franciscan priest."

Paul's thirty eight. He has my mother's Chinese features and her height. But he is not particularly handsome, unlike Philip. Paul always worried too much, which creases a permanent frown on an otherwise youthful brow. He worried over my education after Mum died, and later, over my career and marriage, giving me support and understanding when I left Vince two years ago. He worried over Philip's illegal immigrant life, bailing him out on several occasions by providing money and the means for Philip to move around quickly and often. Paul's a classic number one Chinese son. Yet he never passed judgment on either Philip's or my actions, being ever the stoic big brother who never complained, never scolded, never needed help, never married.

"Tea's ready."

He puts a tray down on the cardboard packing box in front of me. Paul always sat on the floor and had hardly any furniture even before he decided against material life. The steam rises out of the chipped teapot spout. I pour us each a cup of the strongly flavored iron Buddha tea,

"Cheers." I raise my cup.

"To the pursuit of happiness," he replies.

"Say your dynasties," my mother commands, and we three children begin our recitation, first in Mandarin, then in Cantonese, while Mum listens for mistakes or mispronunciations in Mandarin, as if she could tell the difference. We drone our litany, a litany we know almost as well as the Our Father, Hail Mary and the I Believe.

I am six, Philip ten and Paul twelve. It is 1960. Paul recites the loudest, to cover up Philip's mistakes and my giggling.

"Again," Mum commands. "You must always remember you are Chinese no matter where you might live. In Indonesia, when I was small, I could always recite the dynasties from the time I was five. And it had been eight generations, eight, mind you, since my ancestors left Fukien for Java. But as my father always said, our family is pure Chinese blood through and through."

We recite again, and Philip tickles me to make me giggle. Mum's face is turned away so she can't see me squirm. Paul stands up the straightest, reciting the loudest so that at the end of this ordeal, Mum will say, "Paul is my good boy, while you two monkeys are just too naughty for words." Then Paul will beam with pleasure, his funny face and little eyes glowing at the sound of our mother's praise.

"I think Mum would be proud," I say in between sips. "Shaolin is still a religious pursuit."

Paul pauses. "I've made peace with my choice."

"Paul, it's not like she's going to object."

He grimaces, and right away, I know I've said the wrong thing. Although it's been thirteen years since our mother died, Paul still feels her absence.

"She'll always speak to me."

I stare at the reddish gold liquid in my teacup in silence. I love my brother Paul, but will never understand him completely. Of course, he wasn't around Mum, and I was, during her last year alive, as she went progressively insane, smashing things in the house, invoking her Catholic God to oversee her salvation and redemption from a loveless marriage.

When I look at him again, his face is serene. "I think Mum approves of my choice."

"I know she does," I reply, although privately, we both know our mother accepts no other religion except Catholicism since her conversion during her convent school days at St. Mary's in Hong Kong. Any conflict this may have caused with her Chinese identity never seemed an issue.

Paul stands up suddenly and gets a bulky package in a manila envelope which he hands to me. "My legacy."

I open it. A current bank statement summarizes some $150,000 in liquid assets - mutual funds, CD's, cash. Even I am surprised, despite my awareness of my brother's frugality. Behind the statement are the titles to his mortgage-free condo and fully-paid-up six year old Honda Accord, and a power of attorney giving me sole authority over all his worldly possessions.

"Do whatever you think best," he says. "I don't have enough time to find Philip, but I expect you'll take care of him. After all, you always have."

I want to say, Paul this is crazy don't do it, but I bite my tongue. There is after all a part of me too that would abandon all for something far more tenuous than his spiritual odyssey.

He places his hand on my shoulder. "It's okay Ai-Lin," he tells me. "I'm not crazy, really I'm not."

Paul is fifteen. It is two in the morning. The three of us are awakened by our father banging on his bedroom door. Mum is crying loudly, chanting over and over again in English, a mantra of defense. "You have committed adultery again. You are not worthy of entry to our chambers." And Dad hisses in a mixture of Indonesian and English, "Be quiet. Stop being such a child. Think of the children."

Paul gets out of his bed and walks over to the adjoining wall to our parents' bedroom. When we were younger, the wall could swing open into the next room. Mum had designed this wall-door for easy access to us in case we were sick. But Dad sealed it shut two years ago saying we were old enough by then to separate from our mother.

Paul leans against this forbidden partition, and his face seems to glow in the dark. He is angrier than I've ever seen him. He turns to Philip and me and declares, "One day, I will kill him. That man is not my father."

I pull the covers over my head, and wait for the silence that invariably returns.

"But when," I ask, "did you first leave the Church?"

"Mum's voice came to me in a dream," he begins.

I hear Mum's voice in Paul's monotone, her slightly shrill, excitable tone that can rise to a shriek. I stare at this man, this almost stranger who can invoke the woman I am inextricably connected to yet also despise.

"She was telling me the story of her conversion, you know, when she was sixteen. How she was swinging in the garden reciting her Chinese homework when suddenly, she couldn't remember a single word of Chinese. How she heard that voice, telling her she could now find herself. 'When I met your father,' she said in this dream, 'he knew I was very devout, that I went to Church every day. And so he agreed to raise all our children as Catholics. He even was baptized. But then he spent our entire life fighting me over the essence of my soul.' And then, her face appeared to me," Paul continues, "and it was soft and warm and beautiful. I remember all the times he hurt her, all the other women he ran after. And I ask myself, why did he marry our mother? Why?

"You know, Ai-Lin, and I've always felt this deeply in me. He is not my father."

I feel my childhood fear return, the fear that surfaced whenever Paul sleepwalked, whenever Mum stared at me with her vacant, beautiful eyes as if I did not exist, whenever I needed to run away from Mum before she slapped me, whenever the scream would stick in my throat until I felt I would choke to death under my covers.

Paul kisses me goodnight, and I know he is saying goodbye. An earthly goodbye, he tells me, has no meaning in eternity. I hug him, trying not to cry. He whispers to me, "*ngoh haih siu fei lihp, neih haih bihn go aah?* - I am Peter Pan, who are you?" And I whisper back in the excited voice of a six year old child, "Wendy! Tinker Bell!" "Klook, klook, klook!" He mimics the sound of the roller skate wheels over the concrete pavements of our memories.

Paul tucks me in bed, the way he sometimes did when I was a child. He is ever ready with his distant love, but I know his heart and mind have already begun on his life's journey, a journey I can never share.

My brother took off early this morning, a private departure before dawn while I slept. Although forewarned, I still wake up to his presence, unable to accept that he has truly left my life. How much longer before Philip too will depart, succumbing to the AIDS virus that already inhabits his body? I lie on Paul's bed, praying for a metamorphosis that will remove me to an easier existence. Even now, the tears will not flow.

I stay around Austin for a couple more days to take care of business. The condo I list with an agent for sale. What little furniture and personal possessions he had I move to a storage company in Cincinnati. I decide to keep the car, thinking Philip might use it, and arrange to move it to Cincinnati. The only equipment I keep behind is his computer, because he told me to read the relevant files after he's gone.

The one other thing I keep is a small, black metal box safe which I find under his bed. It is locked, and I've looked everywhere but can't find either a key or a combination. The box is heavy. It looks vaguely familiar, but I can't quite place it. I will take it back with me to Cincinnati and have a locksmith open it. This is odd, because it is so unlike Paul to leave a loose end.

As for the money, I dump the bulk of it into an account in Philip's name, keep a nominal amount for expenses, and donate five hundred dollars to the American Shaolin Movement, an organization I never even knew existed.

It is my last evening in Paul's home. How eerie this silent chapel. Paul was a quiet boy and man, and is only talkative to me on the phone, when wires and distance separate us. These last days with him have been like a series of meditations, or the silence of a chapel retreat, broken only after the course of reflection and penance have been run. To break the silence, I try to reach Philip. I call every telephone number I have for him, careful to use the right code words for each number, to no avail. The best I can do is to leave a message with Frederico, the albino lover he always eventually contacts again.

Finally, I switch on Paul's computer. There is only one file on his drive, named "Ai-Lin." I open it.

"He is not my father," Paul's letter begins. "I am my mother's son."

Paul is nineteen. It is the eve of his departure for college in Austin. Dad is out. Over dinner, Mum is telling us, again, the story of her wasted mathematical genius.

"I was the best math pupil in Upper 6," she boasts. "All the other girls used to come to me for coaching. May wanted me to let her copy my answers on tests, but I wouldn't let her. Then she used to get angry at me, and say nasty things about me. Portuguese. They're all like that. Pretend to be friends to your face, but behind your back, they make fun of you because you're Chinese, and because the nuns favor them.

"My brothers in Indonesia were going to send me to university. In fact, I took the entrance exam, and Hong Kong University would have accepted me to read Mathematics. My second best subject was Physics. I could have become a professor!"

Paul is the only one listening, enthralled, as if he has never heard this boring tale before. Philip has an earphone stuck in one ear and is listening to the BBC music broadcast. There was a time, once, when I would listen enthralled, and pray fervently afterwards to be as good as my mother in Math. But I am thirteen now, and have endured her scolding for too many years, first over my poor Chinese and now my mathematical ineptness. I want to demand - so why didn't you become a professor, why didn't you go to university, why did you marry Dad and then drive him away, why did you condemn Dad because he couldn't always be rich enough or smart enough for you?

But these are not words I dare to say because I don't want to feel the sting of her slap across my face.

"You know," Mum says suddenly, "you'd think your father could be home the evening before his son will leave for abroad."

"Where is he?" Paul asks.

I hear the scorn in her reply. "Sullying himself as usual."

I whisper under my breath, "It's not true."

Mum shoots an angry glance at me. "What was that?"

I feel Philip's hand on one arm, and Paul's on the other. "Nothing."

"I should hope not. You know, I think your sister fancies herself my equal!" Her voice begins to rise in pitch. "In old China, boys, daughters were discarded, considered useless. If a girl couldn't marry well, or be the first wife of a rich man, her best hope was to be a concubine."

My face turns red with shame and anger. I cannot listen to Mum when she talks like this.

Philip pipes up. "She didn't say anything, Mum. Really she didn't."

"Liar!" She rises to her feet and towers over the dining table.

I put down my chopsticks. The rice feels stuck in my throat. This is as bad as the time I couldn't convert decimals and fractions into percentages, and Mum kept shouting, "0.375 is the same as 3/8 is the same as 37.5%, can't you see the pattern you stupid girl!" until Paul intervened and taught me instead.

"Let me talk to her, Mum." Paul's voice soothes, as he stands up to face our mother. "After all, she's still a child. But I can show her the right way, because you've taught me so well."

My mother's face softens into its gentle beauty, and her eyes sparkle with an inner fire. She sits down and gazes at Paul, who has his hand on my shoulder. "What will I do without you Paul?" she says.

The front door opens. Dad enters holding a duty free shopping bag. He hands the bag to Paul. "Here. For your trip."

I watch as the lines on Mum's face harden with contempt. She glares at Paul, willing him to reject our father's gift. I see the torment on my brother's face, an anguish that seems to have always been there.

"Wow!" Philip rummages through the bag. "Look Paul. It's XO." He holds up the bottle. "And a carton of Benson & Hedges. Lucky stiff."

But I know it is too late for Philip's sweetness to prevail. The energy of my mother's wrath reverberates around our home. Paul is still sitting, frozen, unable to move. I want to run and hide in Philip's arms.

"How dare you corrupt my son with your vices!" Our mother's voice, on the edge of shrill, assails Dad. She stands, pulling herself up to her full height. A tall woman, she can look Dad in the eye, even without her heels.

Dad's voice remains even. "There was a time you used to enjoy my vices."

"You've never been able to distinguish between the sacred

and profane."

I hear the fatigue in Dad's tone. "To some, they are the same."

She begins to scream her words, slowly at first, and as the volume rises, her words slur into a shriek. "You are sending my son away, and now you want him to mirror your vices. You want him to become as dirty as you are. Because of you, I am filthy, unclean, unfit for holiness. I hate you! I hate you!"

"Stop it! Stop it!" Dad comes towards her, his hands raised to cover her mouth.

"Don't touch me, don't you ever touch me again!"

And then, our father lunges at her. His hand shoots for her mouth, and she bites him hard until he shouts out. In the rush of madness around us, I become aware that Dad is tripping, falling, and his weight against Mum sends her sliding across the dining room floor into the living room where she bangs her head against the pillar.

"Leave her alone!" Paul charges into action. He punches Dad in the face and runs to Mum, who is sitting against the pillar rubbing her head. "You could have killed her." He stares accusingly at Dad.

I take Philip's hand and we run to hide in our bedroom. "It'll be alright," he whispers, trying to soothe me. "Mum's not really hurt. Paul will take care of things."

"But Paul's going away. What's going to happen when he's gone?"

"I don't know, Ai-Lin. I don't know."

Outside, the front door slams loudly and quiet returns.

Paul shows up in the bedroom several hours later. Philip is fast asleep, but I wake up as soon as he enters.

He sits on my bed next to me.

"Have you been out?" I ask him. His breath smells of alcohol. I am frightened. This is not like him at all.

"Yes I have. Dad would have killed me otherwise."

"Oh Paul, he wouldn't. You know that was just an accident tonight."

"I know." He begins to cry quietly. I've never seen my brother shed a tear. "Ai-Lin, how am I going to take care of her? I'm not fit for her."

"What do you mean?"

He dries his eyes. "Go back to sleep Ai-Lin."

"No, you're not okay. Where've you been, Paul?"

"Chung King Mansion." Paul's eyes are shining, strangely vacant, not unlike the unreachable distance I've seen in my mother's eyes. His voice takes on a frenetic quality, and he speaks faster and faster. "I know she doesn't like it, but what else can I do? I've asked her to leave him. I've told her I can take care of her. But she won't. She hates him and curses him, but she won't leave him. And then, she hurts you, and Philip. It isn't right."

Paul strokes my hair, twirling the long strands between his fingers. I hug my brother, wishing I were still a little girl being pulled along on my roller skates while he pretended to be Peter Pan, wishing he weren't going away, wishing that Chung King Mansion would vanish up in smoke because I know it's a place that makes Paul unhappy.

And then, he lets go of my hair and stares through me, vacantly, as if I am not there. "I denounce him," he declares. "I have no father. From now on, he will never exist for me again."

Paul's letter continues, "I confess to almighty God and to you my sister, because there is no one left to hear me. I am my mother's son, but I wanted to be my mother's lover. Why didn't she live instead of him?"

The letter is rambling, at times incoherent. I skip-read, unable to accept what might be the beginning of madness. As I read, the words do not connect. I hold onto the image of my sane and rational brother, with his letters of brotherly advice, with his long phone calls where we laughed and chatted about philosophy, computer programming, the best investments, the car I should buy. The letter goes on for twenty single spaced pages in nine point type.

There is an abrupt shift in tone at the end of his letter.

"Delete this file, Ai-Lin. You are smart enough to know why. I have a lot of faith in you because you are a survivor.

"There is one more thing I must ask you to do for me. I'm sorry to bother you with this, but I didn't have time to tie up this one loose end. You've found the box, no doubt? In your usual sensible way, you've decided to take it to someone back home to open it. This box represents the only kind thing Dad ever did for me. He sent it after Mum died. You'll find the key taped to the pipe under the sink in the bathroom. The combination is right-30, left-14 and right-35. The decision is yours with regard to the contents. Thanks, sis."

I find the key and open the box, and a faint fragrance seems to emanate, a remembered fragrance, the scent of Chanel no. 5, the only perfume Mum ever wore. And then I remember - this is my mother's jewellery box, the one she guarded with such pride. Inside, I find Mum's jewellery, or rather, her imitation jewels, the substitutes she had made when she sold all her jewellery to feed us. They lie there, a glittering heap of rhinestones, winking and smiling at me in Paul's empty apartment. A diamond brooch, pearl and diamond earrings, a deep red ruby pendant, necklaces and bracelets of all descriptions and more, lots more replicas of what once represented a fraction of my father's fortune. A vision of my mother, wearing one of her Dior evening gowns, conjures up before me. Her long hair is pinned up, netted in a fifties beehive. She is wearing make up and jewellery, and the aroma of her perfume envelops my senses. My father is wearing his shantung silk suit, tying his tie. And my mother is smiling, laughing, happy to be going out with important business acquaintances of my dad's. I am very young, sitting on my parents' bed, bouncing up and down. For once, Mum doesn't stop me. Philip is polishing my father's shoes, brushing hard, holding up the gleaming leather for Dad's inspection. Paul stands before my mother, like a valet, her silk stockings lying across his arms, prepared to serve his queen.

And slowly, I began to cry, for the fragile, tenuous moment when our family was whole, when my mother laughed and smiled, when my father kissed my mother and made her happy, when my brothers and I could be children forever, a part of that whole, and all that has been strange and frightening in our lives had not yet begun to be.

On board my flight back to Cincinnati, I look out over the clouds and wish Paul all the best in his solitary search. Perhaps he will combat the madness, if that is what it is. Or perhaps, he will die alone, in a faraway Chinese village, to be buried by strangers who know him only as the local idiot who arrived many years ago from some unknown place. It will take time for me to come to terms with my brother's distant love. What I hope is that my growing isolation is, as my father asserts, the natural state of being. As the plane begins its descent, I recall the time I couldn't convert decimals and fractions into percentages, and finally, after Mum had given up scolding me, Paul put his arm around me while I fought back my tears. He then patiently wrote out the numbers on a large sheet of paper, going over and over each section, drawing me a picture of interlocking parts, until suddenly the whole dark and terrible mystery lightened in my brain and I saw, and understood, the true meaning of the number 1, and then all the decimals and percentages fell into place with no difficulty, no difficulty at all.

6

Loving Jade

The hospital room is glaringly white. I am thirty three. It is April of '87 in Cincinnati, six months after Paul's departure for China and solitude, and a little over a year after my father's death.

Dr. Felicia Cheung, my psychiatrist, says she prefers not to prescribe me any drugs. I look at her blankly and agree, mostly because I hate pills. She advises me to begin intense psychoanalysis with her, as an outpatient, as soon as possible. I nod, because I seem to be short of words these days, but remember to ask if my Blue Cross will cover this. Dr. Cheung is clinical and Freudian. I wonder if her couch is comfortable.

My name, I tell Dr. Cheung who speaks no Chinese, means "Loving Jade." I was never given a Christian name, neither when I was baptized nor when I was confirmed into the Catholic Church.

"But everyone has at least an English name," Mum objects. "She's entered secondary school and most of her classmates have English names or will be given one." Both Paul and Philip succumbed to my mother's religious naming process.

"Call her 'Loving Jade' then," my father says, translating literally my Chinese name Ai-Lin.

My mother rolls her eyes in despair, but Dad remains adamant on the subject. He has had enough, he claims, of Western nonsense.

So on my first day in secondary school, I tell my teacher my name is Hsu Ai-Lin - I make a point of saying it in Mandarin, the way my father says it, as I hate the Cantonese pronunciation Hui Oi-Lem - and that I will not be taking an English name.

"Are you sure?" my form mistress asks me, surprised. "Your family must be *wah kiu,* because you speak English so well. Don't they want you to have an English name?"

Her reference to my being "overseas Chinese" catches me unawares. My parents never refer to themselves that way, although they are obviously *wah kiu.* Several generations of both their families are rooted in Indonesia, and ancestors in my father's family even intermarried Indonesians, yet they consider themselves ethnically and culturally Chinese, which is a very *wah kiu* attitude. Secretly, I would have liked an English name, and even went through a book of the lives of the saints to pick out names I like. There is no way I dare disobey my father however.

"I'm sure," I tell her. "After all, an English name is merely a convenience for a British colony. My father says it should be possible to inconvenience the British from time to time. Wouldn't you agree, Mrs. Gupta?"

My form mistress, an English language and literature teacher from India, smiles. "Very well, if that is your family's decision."

That's the end of it, I think, but a few days later, Sister Rose Marie, the headmistress, summons me to her office. She is an American who speaks halting Cantonese. I've already discovered that the girls all call her Sister *Louhsyu,* which is a close enough transliteration of her name, but sounds like "rat" in Cantonese. She is small and wiry and rather rat-like, her thin lips pursing to a point when she's annoyed. The peaked habit Maryknoll nuns wear doesn't help her appearance.

"I understand you won't be taking a religious name in English," she begins. Her long, wooden rosary clicks against the chair as she rearranges her skirts.

I stand in front of her desk. "No, sister."

"Your family's Catholic."

"Not my father."

"What religion is he?"

"He doesn't have one, sister." I hesitate before continuing. "It's not that he's atheist, but he doesn't like religion."

"And do you?"

"I'm baptized, sister."

"I see. Very well."

She dismisses me after that, and no further mention is made of my taking an English name. I feel I've achieved something of a victory, because several of the other girls hear about my interview with Sister Rose Marie, and congratulate me on the fact that I emerged unscathed. When I find out my classmate Wong Siu-Lan, who isn't even Catholic, has taken on the English name Agnes, I begin to feel pleased that I refused.

I tell my family all about it at dinner.

"Interfering nuns," is all Dad says.

"I told you," my mother moans. "Your father is the most stubborn man in the world. As proud as I am to be Chinese, I would never be so impractical, so stupid. Stubborn he is. Stubborn."

Philip chuckles. "Pretty cool, sis."

Paul's the only one who doesn't say anything, although later, he takes me aside and says, "I hope it's what you want," and for a moment, I want to tell Paul that in fact, I really did want an English name, but now that everything's settled, with the headmistress no less, I feel foolish and I simply didn't know how to change it.

They feed me bland food and refer to this ward only as the

fourth floor. But everyone in the hospital knows it's the floor for the insane, which is what I must be. A few minutes ago, this middle aged woman carrying two bags full of unfinished knitting wanders into my room. "Want a scarf, hon? Or a pair of socks?" she asks. "I'm taking orders." I turn away from her and refuse to answer. "Huh," she mutters as she walks away. "Another high and mighty snob. We'll see how long she lasts."

I don't belong here. The number four in Chinese is unlucky, because it sounds like death, both in Mandarin and Cantonese. I can make peace with death, but not insanity.

So you want me to talk about my adolescence. I haven't talked about that in years. Aren't you just supposed to grow up and leave all that behind? Not in my case, huh?

Well, Dr. Cheung, I am an anomaly in secondary school. Only two of my classmates have Chinese names, and they're both Buddhist. That's just the way things were. Hong Kong's still a colony after all. I also discover that at eleven and a half, I'm the second or third youngest girl in school, being underage for Form 1. And then, I speak and write unusually good English which gives me a linguistic edge in our Anglo-Chinese school where all subjects save Chinese are taught in English.

"It's my native tongue," I tell Agnes Wong, as I breeze through grammar and precis exercises, and score 100's on my compositions. "We speak it at home."

"Sister Rose Marie likes you, because you write for the school paper," she says. The paper is only in English, since Sister Rose Marie can't read Chinese, the native language of ninety five percent of the students.

"No she doesn't," I reply, "because I won't write what she wants."

It's true I argue with the *Louhsyu* over editorial matters, but

Agnes still calls me the favorite of the *gwaipo,* the foreign devil woman. "And she also likes you because you're not a real Chinese," she says.

"Don't listen to Agnes," my best friend Helena says. "She's jealous." Helena says she doesn't care about being only half Chinese anymore and that when she grows up and gets married, she'll only marry a *gwailo.* "After all," she says, "they all call me *jaahp jung,* so I might as well be more one *jung* than trying to be both."

At home, I tell Paul that I want to be a real Chinese.

"You are," he says. "Don't you let anyone tell you different."

Paul tries to make me feel better, but he's a whiz at everything that matters - Chinese, math, science. I finally flunked out of Chinese in Primary 6. Both Philip and I did, and take French instead, which is easier and a beautiful language for our love games.

"How can you expect your children to learn Chinese if you won't help them?" My mother's refrain echoes from my younger years. Dad's only reply is always that he doesn't speak Cantonese. "But the written language is much the same," she protests. "Your father is the most difficult and unreasonable man I've ever known," she always concludes. "He has no idea what children need."

But I muddle on through school somehow. In Form 4, when academic "streaming" takes place, I flow right into the Arts class, with only math and biology to get through for the School Certificate public exams.

This creates a small uproar with Mum. "You're just like Philip. Stupid! What do you expect to do without Science? Stay back a year and try again. You can get into the Science stream if you try."

"I don't want to stay back," I protest.

"As if it's not enough that your father goes bankrupt, now you're going to waste your life. You're too influenced by that tsap tsung friend of yours. Can't you see Helena isn't as smart as you, and that's why she's taking Arts? Oh, why are none of my prayers answered?" And she slaps me hard across my face, although by now, at fourteen, I am more or less immune to her rantings and tirades. I go to Helena's home where I spend the night whenever things get out of hand. Mum calls Helena vulgar because her breasts are quite large and boys chase after her. It's not her fault she's attractive.

But I make up my mind that I am quite happy as an Arts student, despite the stigma, and this time when Paul writes from America to say he hopes this was really what I wanted, I can honestly tell him that yes, this is indeed what I have chosen for my life.

Must I remember? There's so much pain in memory. The day my mother dies, I'm sitting for my mock exams.

It's right before Easter holidays, and I've just turned sixteen. Philip left for the States the year before. Dad's home most of the time these days, morose and cranky, waiting for the next big "deal" to pull him out of his slump. Mum goes to church every morning, cooks dinner for the priests every Friday, arranges flowers for mass every week and has sold the last of her jewellery to feed us and keep up our middle class appearances. Paul stopped taking money ages ago, being smart enough to win academic scholarships, and diligent enough to work two jobs every summer as well as a part time campus job during the school year. And Philip, I learn much later, prostituted himself to both men and women so that he wouldn't have to ask for money from home.

I'm in Form 5, the School Certificate public exam year, and

the mock exams are two and a half weeks' worth of preparatory exams taken at our own school to simulate the real thing. Nine subjects tested by multiple choice as well as essays for most subjects, each one with a standard syllabus covered over the past three academic years. Each subject exam lasts between three to five hours.

In the middle of the history essay portion, I hear my name called. I look up from the desk, my head still buzzing from the vagaries of the Ottoman Empire, which I am trying not to confuse with the reign of Louis Phillippe, the Boxer Rebellion or Woodrow Wilson, all of which are part of the syllabus.

"I'm very sorry," Sister Rose Marie says. She points to the box of Kleenex which I refuse. I don't know how to explain that crying is simply not something I do terribly well or at all these days.

I miss the rest of the week's exams - "lucky thing" I overhear some of the girls say, since I don't seem broken up over Mum's death. Helena is the only one who cries for me. Dad is hopeless about everything, and I finally call Auntie May who helps me make the funeral arrangements.

The church is dim despite the summer afternoon's glare. May arranges for an open coffin. The only matter Dad has paid any attention to is this, insisting that Mum be dressed in her last, remaining Dior gown.

I walk towards the coffin in the empty church, empty except for a few strangers in the back pew who have wandered in. Where are all her friends, from church or the Jockey Club? Are they, as she used to say, only friends when you have money? I look around for Linda Yue, her jeweller, but she isn't there.

My mother looks beautiful, surreal, many years younger, her wrinkles smoothed away by the expertly applied make up. I cannot connect this person with the living dragon who tormented me in her last years of life. Gone are the worn, haggard features, marred by an incessant anger. Silenced forever are the shrill tones of hatred for everything and everyone. Life has victimized her, torn away the beauty and intelligence she prized. Death is kinder, giving her a smiling mask of tenderness.

I cannot cry.

"Her hell is over," May whispers to me. May, the only friend who stuck by Mum through the end.

I was one of the top students in Indonesia, and the beauty queen in my native village - Mum's voice echoes. And I was cursed with a girl as stupid as the devil I married. I shut this voice out of my thoughts. She is gone now. I need never be afraid again. She will be buried soon.

"She was a beautiful girl, and so smart," May says, her eyes wet. "Such a waste."

I look at my father who is staring, stony faced, at the priest throughout the mass. What does he think? Why does he cling to this woman who hated him? For he does hang on, cutting me and the other children out, refusing to let us into his grief.

Where is Paul? I didn't find out till later that my father never told him till after the funeral.

"The last mass," my father whispers fiercely to me as the requiem draws to a close. "The last mass. And those so called friends of hers didn't even have the decency to attend!" I am surprised at his vehemence, surprised he attends, since he never sets foot inside a church.

So there's Dad, angry and sullen and feeling abandoned although how he can blame Mum for dying is beyond me. All he cares about is his own depression, his losing a housekeeper. I barely exist for him during the first few months after Mum's death. He sits in his armchair, night after night, and finishes off half a bottle of Dewars White Label. No Paul to turn to, no Philip to comfort me in our bedroom at night. And I am alone, with this strange and difficult man, arranging our domestic life, trying hard to keep my head above water, praying I'll make it through the real exams.

I don't have time to cry for Mum.

The day the real exam results appear in the papers three months later, I hold my breath as I search for my identification number. I skip over all my other subject scores and look for Mathematics. I've passed, just barely with a 5, but I've passed. It's only then I miss Mum, the once sweet woman of my early childhood, for the first time.

The walls of the room are colorful and remind me of a kindergarten classroom. There are watercolors and macrame and all kinds of other "creative expression" toys. A man with a twitch is building a cockeyed Lego building. Some skinny old woman sits next to me and gossips about everyone else. "He was going to be an architect," she says of the man with the twitch. "Imagine. And see fatso? She just checks in here when she wants to get away from her husband and children. Hates housework with a passion, she does. And . . . "

"What about you?" I cannot listen to her blithering nonsense and think this will shut her up.

"I'm Schizo Jane, at least They think I am. Either that or I'm the Queen of Sheba." She cracks up at her own joke and wanders away to bend someone else's ear.

The fat lady quickly takes her place. "What's she been saying about me? Don't you believe her, not about anything. She gets her facts wrong all the time."

I think I will go insane if I must stay here another day.

Of course I couldn't wait to go abroad. What was there to stay for? I was a kind of a freak, neither Chinese nor Western. Besides, my brothers were both gone and Helena was going to England.

The year after Mum dies, Dad's business takes a definite upswing. His former Japanese customers of manganese begin taking an interest in Indonesian artifacts, and my father becomes a sort of middleman who arranges the movement of goods and money through Hong Kong. This leads to German customers looking for batteries and toys from Japan, and Filipino customers exporting a plethora of crafts to the Netherlands and Germany. By the time I'm ready to go abroad, his financial condition has improved sufficiently so that I don't really have to worry about affording college the way my brothers did.

Freshman year is the happiest year of my life. Away from home at last, I actually begin to feel as normal as the next person, or at least, I can pretend to be like everyone else. I get letters from Helena in England where she seems also, like me, to be having the time of her life. I major in English and Journalism, and hang out with the foreign student crowd. My friend Rajiv's (the "Raj") favorite line is "man is by nature polygamous," to which I add, "and uses woman more than woman uses man." Raj is a future nuclear physicist; he also has skin the color of chocolate creams and a propensity for parodying Iron Butterfly's "In a Gadda da Vida" which always cracks me up. I know he has the hots for me.

By the end of sophomore year, I have a 3.7 GPA and am the most likely candidate for editor of our college paper. My best girlfriend is Sylvie, a Lebanese-French mixture who's a theater major and the belly dancer in our annual foreign students show. I smoke pot with her and Raj a lot. I like pot. It makes me relax and forget about things. I don't hang out with the foreign Chinese student crowd exclusively, the way most of them do, which makes me a sort of "banana" in their eyes, and more so because of my indulgence in drugs. I continue to stay away from guys, with the excuse that I'm too busy to date. But I'm furious when Raj coins my nickname, "Bamboo Ice."

Yes, I'll call you Felicia. All the college guys want is sex, and don't even care if they have nothing else to say to you. Raj is at least good natured about it because he isn't pushy, which is why I remain his friend. Besides, he and Sylvie are getting it off together.

No I don't think Raj and Sylvie are "bad" for me. Around them, sex doesn't seem bad or dirty. They are just enlightened, I guess, or something. Sylvie wants a *ménage à trois.* But they don't try to force me when I say no.

But I hate the way the American guys try to pick me up all the time, especially when they come out and bluntly say so. They make me feel dirty. Philip used to make me feel dirty too, sometimes.

But in October of my junior year, I meet Derek Anderson at an off campus party.

Derek's an architect at the largest firm in the city, and a graduate from the University of Cincinnati. He is twenty three, four years older than me.

"So you're Catholic, but not a regular church goer, right? What did you say your name was again?" he asks me for the third time the night we meet.

"Ai-Lin Hsu," I shout over the music, because by now, I've learned to flip my surname to the end, American style. "Americans call me Alan," I finally add.

He leads me away from the path of the speakers. "You don't

look like an Alan. Does your Chinese name mean anything?"

I am pleased by his question. Up till now, only my foreign friends ever ask or manage to pronounce my name correctly. "Loving Jade."

"Loving Jade," he repeats, smiling. "I like that. May I call you Jade?"

He has deep blue eyes, the color of lapis, and soft wavy brown hair that curls past his neck. I like his smile and the musicality in his voice. Although I hear Raj and Sylvie hooting with derisive laughter in my mind at his "China doll drivel", I reply, "Sure."

I'm not sure what makes me trust Derek. He holds my hand when he walks me to my dorm and I like the feel of his palm against mine. When he kisses me goodnight, I find myself thrusting my tongue into his mouth, which he accepts willingly. "Wow," he says, when he lets me go, and his face is hot and flushed. He is smiling, the way Philip used to smile when I pleased him.

Derek asks me out the next week and I agree, too readily, to see him. He gazes at me a lot and makes me feel silly and fluttery and foolishly happy. The week after, when he invites me to see his place I simply follow without question.

He lives in an industrial building downtown. "Camp," he says, when we arrive.

Only a quarter of the floor he occupies has been turned into a livable area, cordoned off by a single wall. There is an elegant simplicity and openness about it. The remaining three thousand seven hundred and fifty feet is raw space. There are two set ups for rock bands, including large sets of outdoor speakers and all the musical equipment. I've never seen anything like it.

"So what do you think?" he asks tentatively.

I am completely impressed, but not about to let on that easily. "Did you fix this all up yourself?"

"I designed it myself, and a couple of my buddies and I did the work." He walks me to the row of windows which overlooks the river and Kentucky. "So what do you think?"

"Not bad."

He looks so crestfallen at my response that I want to throw my arms around him and say I'm just kidding silly it's wonderful, but I check myself because the feeling is so foreign. He looks at me strangely, and suddenly, I begin to feel frightened, wishing I hadn't agreed to come to his place.

"You're a virgin, aren't you?" he asks abruptly.

I nod, feeling guilty about the lie.

"He brushes his finger gently across the side of my face. "That's nice."

And then he kisses me, and my insides go all warm and his arms around me feel just like Philip's and it's wonderful to feel that way again, that delicious, secret way that used to make my body erupt with pleasure in the silence of the night.

I think, this is it, I'm in love and this time Philip can't stop me. I'm ready, completely ready to make love to him right away, because he's touching my breasts under my blouse, under my bra and I can feel him getting hard against me, and I haven't felt this good since Philip left me.

We move over to the couch where we continue making out for awhile and I tremble with an impatience I didn't know I had as he unbuttons my jeans, his hand sliding between my legs but he suddenly pulls away from me, an anguished look on his face, "I'm sorry," he says. "I got carried away."

He might as well have put an ice cube in my vagina.

"It won't happen again, Jade."

I am bewildered, sitting on his sofa, rearranging my clothes, my underwear damp with lost anticipation.

He gazes at me. "I shouldn't have brought you here. Too much temptation."

I want to say, no, please you didn't have to stop, but it seems wrong somehow to want something so badly you would lose yourself this much, so I say nothing and let him bring me back to my dorm where I sleep, badly.

These watercolors look like a box I had when I was a kid. I never could draw, and I put all the wrong colors together. But I suppose I must do something to shut them up. If I participate, if I do something, maybe Dr. Cheung will let me out.

So I fool around with brushes and paint.

"What's that?"

"My Chinese name. My family name."

"How do you say it?"

"Hsu."

"Hey, that's pretty cool."

I smile for the first time in weeks. Joe, the man with the twitch, is a sweet guy after all.

Derek and I go out for about six months. Sylvie takes an intense dislike to him.

"Sylvie's a pain," Derek complains. "She's always going on about how stupid Americans are. Why the hell doesn't she go back where she belongs?"

"You don't understand her. She doesn't mean it. She's really a great friend."

"She's a bitch."

It hurts me that they don't get along, but Sylvie doesn't pull any punches.

"He's too possessive, Ai-Lin. And he'll probably want to get married. All that rock musician thing and artist lifestyle is just a front. He's really a closet white picket fence suburbanite, " Sylvie says. "Look at him. He's too straight to even smoke pot. And he lectures you, treats you like a child, tries to stop you from having fun. Is that what you want Ai-Lin? Or is it 'Jade' these days?"

Sylvie's words make me cringe. They hold a disturbing ring of truth.

Raj is more non-committal. "Man, meaning humankind, is by nature polygamous, unless he forces his true nature into the strait jacket of social conformity. We'll wait and see Ai-Lin."

It confuses me that my two closest friends don't approve of him. Derek can be possessive, and jealous, and he tends to whine, but most of the time I don't mind since I like being with him. He doesn't like me hanging out with my friends, or spending too much time away from him. I study at his place while he rehearses with his rock bands. I just wish he wouldn't nag about the things I work hard at, like getting good grades and writing for the college paper. He calls me "superwoman," which hurts.

But Derek makes me feel safe and protected, so I stay with him. We neck a lot at his place, especially after his rehearsals. He stops though, before we can go too far.

"Tell me more about yourself," he says, one night after he's gotten so excited he's actually almost completely undressed me. "It'll take my mind off this." He pulls my blouse around me, hiding my nakedness.

I let the blouse slip off. "I don't want you to take your mind of it." I try to kiss him just under his earlobe, which he finds unbearably sexy.

"Stop it." He pushes me away. "It's not decent."

I am horrified by his words. "What do you mean?"

"I mean, it's not right."

I want to ask why not, but something stops me. The expression on his face, the serious intensity in his eyes remind me of my mother in her worst moments. I suddenly feel my nakedness.

"I'm taking you home," he says.

In our group therapy session, I tell them I know suicide attempts are a cry for help. I am lonely, I say. I am scared to be so alone. Our leader, nods quietly and everyone listens; she has a master's in psychology and is not as young as she looks.

I nod, and schizo Jane nudges the knitting lady and points at me, "See, I told you she'd last."

But Dr. Cheung, I mean Felicia, sex always gets in the way. I know you think Derek was merely crazy, and I his victim. But surely I had something to do with it too?

"It's my problem, not yours."

"It isn't a problem if I love you." It's the first time I say the word "love." I feel a strange, prickly sensation, at once pleasurable and awful. The only person I've ever said "I love you" to in a romantic way is Philip, but I can't tell Derek that, at least I don't think I can.

We are sitting on his bed after yet another drawn out necking session. His jeans are wet, and he is embarrassed. This is the first time it's happened.

"You don't understand," he says, when he returns after changing in the bathroom. "I want to be sure of us before, well, you know. It's sacred. Like marriage."

I gaze at his eyes, those lapis jewels, and want to take him, all of him, until there's nothing left. The brutality of my emotions startle me.

"I don't think it's a problem if I love you," I repeat.

"You don't even know if you do."

"I do, I know I do."

His eyes turn cold, like a crystal fire. "If that were true, you wouldn't tempt me so much." He takes me in his arms, and his hold is powerful, crushing. "Don't you know I dream terrible dreams about you? That I ache at night because of you? How can you be so cruel?"

"Derek, you're going to hurt me." I am frightened. He is intense, but I've never seen him like this.

He lets go of me like a petrified animal. "I'm sorry. I'm sorry."

That night he takes me home and before I go back into my dorm, he takes me to the field behind the building where his hands slide under my skirt and rip my panties and he presses his desire against me with such force that what sexual cravings and longings I harbored all night disappear, in an instant, in the face of this new and unknown frenzy.

"He said what?" Sylvie is incredulous. Raj passes me a stick of Thai weed.

"He wants to get married."

"You'd be mad to do it. Wow, some nuclear holocaust, this, eh?" Raj inhales and holds the smoke, sputtering out words between his teeth.

I look down at my wine glass on the floor where I sit. "He has this thing about virginity."

Raj and Sylvie roll their eyes at each other.

"You, my dear, are nuts." Sylvie places a hand on my arm, a look of genuine concern on her face. "Come on, Ai-Lin, I thought we were friends. Surely you wouldn't do this?"

"Man is by nature polygamous," Raj declares. "And marriage the institution made in hell."

This is the last time I visit my friends, whom Derek forbids me to see.

We are in Derek's loft after another rehearsal. I look at this man, whose vacant eyes and serious smile are like family to me. Raj and Sylvie do not understand, I think, as I play with the diamond on my left hand. Derek will give me a new life here in Cincinnati, which is a little bit like home. What does it matter if his ideas about women are a little old fashioned, or that he can be crude and vulgar? I love him, and he wants me. A high G.P.A. guarantees at most a job, not love.

In my head, my mother snarls, "Girls are useless, born to be a burden to the family until they marry."

Derek looks hungry tonight. I can tell when he will desire me so much it hurts. By now, I almost enjoy and anticipate our passionate necking, my unfulfilled desire, his need for contrition afterwards.

Tonight, a night in early spring, I am wearing a tight leather skirt and sweater. He buys me these clothes which I wear only at his place. Already, he is feeling me, under my skirt, under my sweater, breathing in my ear, over and over again, "cock teaser, cock teaser, that's what you are," and I shut up the voice in the back of my mind that tells me he's crazy, crazy, because I want the passion, I want to be teased, I want this if this is what love is.

We are on his bed and he is sprawled on top of me. He is like granite against my body. I feel his fingers inside me, long and spidery, as he brings me close to a climax and just before I reach it, he withdraws, whispering, "not until we're married," and I beg him, "please, more," and he says, "you're a wicked girl Jade and I won't love you anymore if you don't behave" and I pull down my skirt and sit up and straighten my hair because I know that is what he wants.

I cannot tell you how many times I enacted this or a similar scenario. I am ashamed of the passion that controlled me, ashamed of my desperation in his promise of love. But I thought if I pleased him enough, he would love me a little, like Philip did.

That semester, I do not make editor of the college paper or the Dean's list.

"Ricardo," he muses. "Did you get him hard?"

"Yes," I reply. I am seated on a chair as he walks around me, conducting the inquisition.

"Who else?"

"Other boys, at parties."

"And did you ever sneak away with one of them, to a motel, or a bedroom somewhere when parents were out for the night?"

"Never."

"I don't believe you."

"I let them touch me, under my bra, even between my legs when we necked. And other guys watched."

"Tell me again."

And he would make me repeat this litany, over and over, while he masturbated. Through all this, I sit still, watching him, my face made up like a whore's, wearing a get up that would put Frederic's of Hollywood to shame, a manifestation of all his fantasies. It is what proves, he says, that I love him.

It is the eve of our planned elopement. No family, he says; he long ago disowned his. He has picked out the church and priest. My wedding dress, which is snowy white, lace, is an old fashioned one with a long train, a dress he designed.

"At least let me tell Philip, since you won't let me invite my friends."

He finishes installing a new and stronger bolt on the front door of his loft - "this will keep out people we don't want to see" - and begins to put away his tools. Derek is obsessively neat. He smashed a glass in anger once because I'd put it on the wrong shelf, but was remorseful for days afterwards.

"He's my brother."

"That doesn't mean anything to me. I have no siblings."

"I'd like to tell Paul too, but Philip is special and I really want to tell him."

"Is he the fag?"

I bristle. I hate it when he calls Philip that.

"Philip is homosexual, yes."

"So, he's a faggot. Right? You're the English major."

"Derek, please . . ."

"What's the matter? You a faggot lover?"

Something wells up inside me. I can't take this anymore. I don't have to take him anymore. Controlling my voice as much as possible, I say, "Yes, in more ways than you think."

He stops what he's doing and looks at me strangely. "What do you mean?"

"I was Philip's lover, since the time I was ten. I'm not a virgin." My voice is rising to a pitch as frenetic as my mother's. "I haven't been a virgin for years. I didn't break it riding a bicycle. My brother Philip broke it." I am screaming now, screaming at this lunatic, at the insanity in myself that would brook such a lover as he. "And he was ten times the man you are. I'll never love anyone as much as I loved him."

He is silent, white with anger, and then he yanks the diamond off my finger and slaps me hard, across one cheek, and then the other. "You are unfit for me," he shouts, and raises his hand to slap me again but I run away, pull open the heavy metal door and run down the stairs, as I hear "whore, slut, bitch" over and over and over as I continue to run away, through the streets of Cincinnati, until I am back at the dorm.

Sylvie finds me later that night in my dorm room, my wrists slashed, and that spring Paul and Philip drive out to see me while I recuperate, glibly cheerful in the infirmary, laughing off the whole thing as my Dorothy Parker imitation. When Derek tries to see me the next week, upset and contrite, I scream at him to get out off my life and that my name is not Jade, my name has never been Jade and will never be.

So that's the end of Derek, and after that, life is less emotional but exciting enough in its own way. I graduate *magna cum laude* in '75, go home to Hong Kong and live with Dad. He's a misery to live with, but at least, he's relatively harmless. I wind up at *AsiaMonth,* as you already know, which is a good job because I get to travel and write. I'm happy in those years, not the way I was happy in college in Cincinnati before Derek when everything was new and exciting and wonderful, but I am reasonably content, which is, I suppose, a state of being that has some merit. In '79, I meet and marry Vince and move to the States. And the rest I've said before.

*

The Western Union telegram, crumpled on the floor, was from Frederico telling me Philip had finally died of AIDS. I am thirty three, and have virtually survived my entire family, except for my ex-husband Vince. He doesn't count though. His blood doesn't flow in my veins.

My secretary found me last evening, semi-conscious in my apartment, when she got worried because I hadn't shown up to work and hadn't called in or answered her telephone messages on my machine. I had apparently consumed a bottle of scotch followed by not quite enough sleeping pills. She called Vince who, from New York, managed to locate the one, female, Chinese-American psychiatrist in all of Cincinnati and told Dr. Felicia Cheung, no, ordered her to put me in the hospital for a few days. I was diagnosed as clinically depressed. My colleagues at *Tri-State Business & Leisure* are shocked. "She's the most together person I know," the publisher says. "She's always efficient and organized," my secretary says, "which is why I knew something had to be wrong. She doesn't ever not call in."

After Dr. Cheung leaves, I go back to sleep. I dream about Philip, whom I haven't seen in three years. He and I are dancing at a party and we're both teenagers. And then I see Paul standing at my mother's grave. He is talking to the earth. My mother rises up out of the ground like a Chinese ghost - long black hair streaming down her back, her face chalk white, eyes hollow and red. Paul waves a hairbrush at her and begins to brush her hair and suddenly, my mother turns into a beautiful young woman covered in jewels, holding an abacus in her right hand, saying, "find the square root, calculate the cosine." I find myself walking along the Great Wall and my father stands below, leading the way. I seem to walk forever when out of nowhere, a map of Indonesia spreads out before me like a carpet and Dad and Mum begin jabbering in Indonesian. Paul is standing where Irian Jaya is and reports on the progress of his computer program design. He speaks one sentence in English, and then translates it into Cantonese, and continues monotonously in this vein. Philip dances up to me, then steps back onto Bali and bows, saying, "I can your boyfriend be," in Chinglish English but instead of laughing I begin to cry and cry and cry.

I wake up and find my pillow soaked with tears.

My name, I tell Felicia, means Loving Jade. My father named me that because he thought jade was the perfect gem, the only truly Chinese gem. Mother despised jade. She found it commonplace and boring, and preferred the exotic emerald.

I have yet to discover the true meaning of my name, if indeed there is one. Until then, I don't and won't wear jewels.

7

Repeated Practice

"Cincinnati," Don says, "is a far cry from Hong Kong."

"I know."

"But don't you ever want to go back?"

"Yes."

"Then why not do it?"

My ex-brother in law, like my ex-husband, is a man who does what he wants. But unlike Vince, Don goes about things a little more slowly, with greater patience and care because, as he says, time is the only test of what will endure.

It's May. We are at Vince's wedding reception. Dr. Felicia Cheung feels like a lifetime ago, although it was only four years earlier that my life finally exploded around me. Vince has remained my friend through it all. When he told me he was getting married again, I felt an enormous joy because I knew his life had changed and moved on. I also felt absolved, relieved of the guilt I harbored, despite the psychoanalysis, that I had been responsible for so much unhappiness in a man who had only wanted to love me.

So I went to his wedding where Don took it upon himself to be my "date."

"After all," he says, leading me to the dance floor, "you're still a part of this family no matter what, and we da Luca men like to look after the women in our lives."

I am comfortable in Don's arms. Perhaps this is what Felicia meant when she said that if I could forgive myself, my life could go on. I stopped going for sessions last October, because as necessary therapy may be for the walking wounded, it had become too much of my life, replacing life itself. Also, I couldn't accept a reality dictated by continual connection to this woman who remained perpetually a stranger. A therapist is after all not a friend. She shares memories only for analysis and revelations of inner neuroses; life, however, goes on without her.

Don feels like a friend, even though it has been years since I've actually seen him. We've talked on the phone from time to time, although it was always he who called. It is easy being with him now. He dances well, better than Vince, who grips you a bit too tightly and doesn't let the rhythm flow. With Don, you feel the music. I've forgotten how much I like dancing.

"So I should just pack up my life in Cincinnati and move back to Hong Kong?"

"Why not?"

"Well, I haven't any friends there really."

"And you have hordes in Cincinnati, right?"

He has a point. It's not as if I've rooted myself there. I still rent, although I could easily have bought a place by now if I wanted to, and I've not exactly plunged into the social world, and certainly haven't made any close friends. In fact, I probably know a wider circle of acquaintances in Hong Kong.

"Unless," he says, "there's someone special there you haven't told either Vince or me about?"

"A lover? I haven't dared."

I hadn't meant to put it quite like that. But the da Lucas have an unnervingly likeable way of eliciting the heart of the matter.

"So about Hong Kong, will I do, as a friend I mean, until you re-connect?"

I pull back and stare at him quizzically. He smiles.

"I'm serious," he continues. "In fact, *wo xianzai xue*

Putonghua. How does that grab you?"

I laugh. "Pretty good. Better accent than mine."

It turns out Don really is going to Hong Kong. His firm was contracted for a project in Guilin of all places, and Don agreed to a posting in Hong Kong for at least two years.

"In fact, I went out there last month to take a look. It's a terrific city. So I really have an ulterior motive to all this, because I'd love to have a friend there who knows her way around."

The thought is tempting. The tenant in our family flat is moving out this summer, and the agent wants to know what to do. That is still the only place I think of as home, which is why I didn't sell it when my father died.

We whirl past Vince on the dance floor. Vince is still the most sexually attractive man I've ever known. But he only has eyes for his bride, which for him, is the way love is. There are some happy endings after all.

You are afraid of intimacy - Felicia's observation, clinically delivered, echoes like an unfinished accusation.

In my apartment in Cincinnati, the first night back in my own bed is a sleepless one. I still often suffer from insomnia. My trip to New York has reawakened voices I thought were long mute. Felicia's words, first spoken to me shortly after I began outpatient sessions with her, flit around my wakefulness, as does Don's voice. I had been wary of being around him, our one indiscretion weighing on me even after all these years. But he was fun to be with, relaxed and natural. He is my age, and doesn't condescend to me. I think he can be a good friend if I let him.

I did not always like listening to Felicia, because she spoke truths in terms that wouldn't connect for me. It was easier submitting to slings and arrows. I told her this once, but she didn't know what I meant.

You don't let people into your life, especially men, even when you are physically intimate with them.

One thing I have learned is that listening and talking to Felicia doesn't necessarily bring solutions. Even now, my body still sometimes aches for Philip. Incest is a terrible word, a terrible thing in her books. How do I explain to her that Philip was the awakening of passion, which Derek continued and Vince tried to satisfy?

Life in Cincinnati hasn't been about people, just existence. I chose this city because it once contained the happy memory of two celibate years in college, before I met Derek. The years since my return have been celibate. But what Felicia doesn't understand, because of the constraints of her profession, is that passion, sexual or otherwise, never dies. It just goes to sleep for awhile.

I sit up and smooth my pillow. Paul's voice speaks to me often lately. He is trying to tell me something about who I am. These are the kinds of things I've learned not to tell Felicia, not if I don't want to risk another stay on the fourth floor. How do I tell her, in her stubbornly comfortable second generation banana skin, that for a perpetual non-belonger like myself, the only questions worth finding answers to are to know who I am, to know what love must be for me, to know why passions, mad or otherwise, control me? Madness is merely a metaphor for life lived to its fullest.

My connection to my family is the most important connection in my life. Their seemingly bizarre world is my path to sanity, and not all our "talking cure" sessions about how I deal with the men in my life.

Can't she see that letting people into my life, especially men, in a white bread city like this one, will only bring more of the

Derek Andersons?

No, I guess she can't.

It is getting closer to summer, closer to sinus season. I don't know whether to open or close windows when the air hangs like a dusty theatre curtain. The weather in the Ohio Valley sometimes reminds me of Hong Kong. But the oppressive atmosphere here is the result of nature, of climactic forces. The real oppression back home stems from the overpopulation, the shadows of too many buildings, the frenetic heart of its people, like me. Frenzy doesn't immigrate well.

I get out of bed and stand by my window. The river is black, and there are no lights in Kentucky. I can hear my brother's voice calling me in Cantonese. I still count in Chinese, even after all these years in the West, even though English is supposedly my native tongue.

Paul liked Texas because the weather was dry. I haven't seen or heard from him since he departed on his pilgrimage, only from his "ghost." The publisher in San Francisco stopped receiving modem messages three years ago. Can he ever have loved me if his only link with me are my imaginings, my memory?

I must try one last time to find him, I think, whatever that means.

Besides, Cincinnati is getting too quiet and clean. Too morgue like.

I think it's time I blew this pop stand.

"Ai Lin! Great to hear from you."

There is affection in Don's voice.

"I'm going home, Don, and it's all your fault."

It's July. Yesterday, I called the agent in Hong Kong and told him not to rent out the flat anymore. There isn't anyone left to look after me, now that Vince is remarried. It's time I started looking after myself.

I tell Don my plans. I'm going to try and make a home for myself for the first time in my life. He offers to help me remodel the old flat.

"After all, I specialize in restoration," he says.

I ask about his girlfriend, the one he didn't bring to his brother's wedding.

"She wants to split up. She says if I go away I won't come back, to her that is. It was really over in her mind the day I was offered the opportunity, even before I said I'd take it."

I hear the sadness in his voice and my heart feels his pain. Don wants to marry her, but she doesn't want to leave New York. She's a singer. He understands why she feels she has to stay.

There are many unanswered questions in my head when I hang up.

Felicia never said much about Don's calls in the past, or my continued connection to the da Lucas. Once, after Vince called, I confessed to her in a session that I sometimes entertained fantasies of being made love to by both brothers at once. She tried to disguise her reaction, but the horror was clear to me. Her thoughts about my "healing" involved a "healthy" relationship with a nice man in Cincinnati, to show me that intimacy did not have to be perverse.

I refuse to pretend that Don is not attractive to me. I also refuse to pretend that the "adultery" with Don was not the result of my passion. Perversion is an attitude, not a fact.

The men in my life just happen to evolve from the same strange (okay Felicia, neurotic) roots from whence I came.

By the fall of this year, I will be back in Hong Kong. My decision to return is only just now beginning to feel real.

Calling Don is a way to make it more real. It suddenly seems like a huge weight has fallen away from me. I don't understand this sensation, just as I don't understand what I expect to find at "home."

Don meets me at Kai Tak International. He is bronze. I'm startled by his tan, by how much more he resembles Vince like this. When he kisses me though, his lips firmly planted on my cheek, he is Don again, the man about whom I'm not entirely sure how to feel. All I know is I do feel.

"So does it look the same?" he asks as our taxi makes its way towards Tsimshatsui.

I stare at the highways that weren't there when I left twelve years ago. It still frightens me that I've been away so long, and am back now with no real idea of what I will do. The late afternoon sun adds to the surreal environment.

"It's not exactly what I expected."

"Hey, I know my way around a bit now. I'll be your tour guide if you want."

We laugh. Don's been here since August, and it's taken me till late November to get back. There was a lot more to ending my life in the U.S. than I thought.

"You know, I was beginning to think I'd never get back."

Don puts his arm around me and gives me a hug. "It really is good to see you. I'm glad you made it back." His arm rests on my shoulder. I've never liked being touched by people, especially men. The American habit of affectionate greeting hugs is distasteful to me, and I indulge in it only out of respect for local custom. With Don it seems alright somehow.

As we approach Tsimshatsui, I gaze at the Hunghom railway station complex. Nothing looks the same. The long flight and jet lag insinuate their way into my consciousness, scrambling my senses into a weird state. But then I see Rosary Church, which looks almost exactly the way I remember it. It was my mother's church, where she dragged me and my brothers each Sunday, about a twenty minute walk from our home. I begin to recognize buildings on our right along Chatham Road.

"My brother Paul used to pull me along on roller skates down this road."

"You were close to your brothers, weren't you?"

"Very."

"Then you must miss them a lot."

"Yes, very much." I don't talk to people about things like this except Felicia. She says I should. Don is my closest confidant now that Vince no longer is.

He is silent awhile, as if he senses my discomfort. Vince would have pushed me to the edge, wanting me to talk some more. I must stop comparing Vince and Don. It isn't fair to Don; it overly affects how I deal with him.

"Hey, I hope you like what I did, with your apartment, I mean,"

"I'm sure I will." True to his word, Don did redo my family's home. Give me a sense of space - that had been the extent of my brief to him - and I let him do the rest. I had not seen the place since my father died, and I put the responsibility of upkeep into the hands of a property agent friend of Auntie May's. But I knew there had been no major structural changes. My last instruction to the agent was simply to clean out everything and get rid of any old appliances that no longer worked.

When we walk into the lobby of Far East Mansion, I am struck by how much like home it feels. The tallest building in all Kowloon, right in front of the harbor - how proud my father had been of this building, of its grandeur, its facade swelling out on the lower floors like a pregnant woman. I am glad he is not alive to see the extent of the waterfront's encroachment of the harbor at Tsimshatsui East, and the usurping of his building's place of importance. It was hard enough for him when the Sheraton Hotel went up in front, obliterating the view forever.

"It was a surprise, this building," Don says as we wait for the lift. "Ugly architecturally, and the kind of location you'd expect some developer to snap up and turn into a more profitable enterprise. Hard to believe it was once residential."

"Never really was. My dad would be the last to admit it, but there were home factories and offices and even a brothel on the fourteenth floor when I was a kid."

"No kidding?"

"This is Hong Kong, land of free enterprise."

We go up, and an even tension arrests me. Can I go home again, really? I hear echoes of Thomas Wolfe, that the "simple joy" of being among familiar things does contain "an element of strangeness and unreality."

Don unlocks the door, which he has repainted black from its original blue. "Close your eyes," he tells me. "I want you to see it the way I imagined it when I first came here." He covers my eyes and walks me into the center of the living room. "Okay." He stops me. "Take a look."

I blink. It is home, but without the clutter.

Don has stayed with its rectangular box shape and extended it, having opened up the kitchen, American style, giving the room an even longer tunnel effect. He has replaced the three doors to the verandah with matching floor to ceiling glass doors, so that the entire downstairs is one continuous room and verandah with a wonderful sense of openness. The bar my father had put under the staircase is gone, and that space is empty.

But the best thing he's done is around the pillar. My brothers and I always laughed at that pillar, a round tree trunk in the middle, chopping up the entire room. And my mother disdained it as an eyesore in a poorly designed flat. I suppose it is there out of structural necessity. Don has built a wooden bar table that extends out of the pillar towards the dining room and kitchen. There are three barstools under it. It is basically the only piece of furnishing in the room.

I look at Don who seems slightly anxious. "Well, what do you think?"

I fling my arms around him and give him a great hug. His body feels exceedingly good next to mine. "Thanks," I say, "it's exactly right."

He breathes a sigh of relief. "Thank God for that."

And then Don becomes animated, telling me he sees an L-shaped sofa and a rectangular glass top dining table to complete the downstairs. I follow his train of vision, substituting pieces of my own where I see something else. We go upstairs which he hasn't touched, except to paint all the walls white. There is a futon on the floor of my old bedroom which Don threw in there for me. Otherwise all the other furniture is gone.

Now, I feel a prickly sensation mixed with contentment and relief. This is home, and it feels right. For the moment, this is all that matters.

It's January 2nd. Don's girlfriend visited for the holidays as a concession to try to keep things going between them, and is leaving today. My flat is still empty, although I did buy a sofa, L-shaped, which Don and I shopped for together.

The phone rings.

"Can I come over, Ai-Lin?" His voice is very sad and I think

I know what he will tell me.

"Sure."

Don is at my place half an hour later, carrying a bottle of wine.

"She said no," he says as soon as I close the door. "And I don't know what I'm doing here in Hong Kong anymore. Why the fuck do I want to be married so much?"

I let him talk. We finish his bottle and open another. I am just as confused as he is.

The initial excitement of coming home has worn off. In trying to re-connect in this city, I find the pace exhausting, people unable to keep up with themselves and inflation horrendous. Also, voices now babble at me in too many languages and accents after my monolingual life in America, and I mix up the meaning of words. Felicia's voice meanders in and out of it all, sometimes drowning out Paul, whom I try hard not to shut out.

And of course there is Don, whom I feel destined to fall in love with. Destiny disturbs me however. Funny currents pass between us, perhaps sexual, perhaps not, about which we won't say anything. He is my best friend here.

He sleeps that night on my sofa, having finally begun to accept the end of his relationship with his girlfriend.

I walk through my home city in the aftermath of festivities. Were Januarys always so overcast and wet? I seem to remember dry winters of sunshine. I had a royal blue woolen dress when I was about seven which had a pleated skirt. When the sun shone, my mother said the blue of my dress matched the blue of the skies. I remember always feeling too warm in that dress in January.

Tsimshatsui is clean and crowded these days. It is still exciting. But there are no more orange ladies. My girlfriend Helena Gilbert, née Choy, says you can't tell the whores apart from the ordinary women anymore. Helena runs her own very successful public relations agency, and is married to some executive at the Hong Kong Shanghai Bank. Her hair is streaked with reddish brown highlights and her accent and manner are very upper class British. From her appearance and style now, it's sometimes hard to see the Chinese in her. She lives in a flat on the Peak, and can't understand why anyone would live in "Tsimsy" anymore.

It's true that ordinary girls wear overtly sexy clothes now. Maybe I'm just getting too conservative. Or maybe Cincinnati has sanitized me too much to ever make Hong Kong seem right again.

Canton Road has turned into a highway and a glitzy new waterfront. I could be in America.

I find I don't like walking around Tsimshatsui like I used to.

Paul's voice is more insistent. Sometimes, I wake up in the middle of the night and think I see him sleepwalking. Perhaps he is dead, and his ghost must walk our Far East Mansion home until he and I connect. I don't like to think of him gone, and will him to be alive. I see him wandering in a village in the outer reaches of Mongolia, or somewhere in Tibet, holding spiritual conversations with the Dalai Lama. But where he is on earth doesn't matter as long as he still speaks to me.

I spend my days re-connecting, looking up people, thinking about the kind of work I want to do.

I sleep, badly most nights, on my futon on the floor of my childhood bedroom. Sounds I have long forgotten come back to me. Like the voices of drunken sailors singing the night into the dawn; my father's smoker's cough from the room next door, especially after my mother's death; my mother's shrill screams out of nowhere, frightening me into Philip's bed, or activating Paul's frustrated, angry outbursts. And always, always, I feel Philip's touch, when I least expect it, his long piano playing fingers exciting my body, drawing out the passion that hibernated through the years in Cincinnati after my divorce.

I think I am almost ready to learn the meaning of love.

"Maybe I should give all this up and go home."

Don has some of Vince's persistence. Even though his girlfriend has turned down his offer of marriage three times now, and has begun dating his best friend back in New York, he hasn't entirely given up.

"These phone calls get drawn out, Don," I say. "Can't we just meet halfway in the middle of the harbor and talk?"

He laughs. "Vince said you had a sense of humor when you wanted to."

I squash the paperback I was reading just before he called more firmly on the ground so that I won't lose my place. The beauty of these long, idle, non-working days has meant that I can indulge in my second favorite pastime, reading. My favorite one is still on hold, until I can bring Don around.

"My brother Paul taught me a lot of things, one of which was the uselessness of too much talk."

"Okay, okay. I know I sound like a broken record. Tell me what else Paul taught you."

"Math. How to save and invest money. How to work to live and not live to work." I like these long drawn out conversations. They're like the ones I used to have with Paul, when he lived in Austin and I in New York, which sent his phone bills through the roof. He used to call me his one extravagance.

"He really treated you well, didn't he?"

"I think," I say uncertainly, "that he probably loved me better than any other member of my family."

Talking to Don is good for revelations and is becoming a serious hobby for me. I tell him this.

"I'm flattered," he replies. "You've even been known to call me these days."

"I get lonely sometimes."

"For me or my voice?"

"Whichever I can get."

"Is that a proposition?"

"Maybe." The safety of the phone makes me more daring than I intend. Besides, Don and I like to play these verbal games. Even Bamboo Ice can melt, as Raj said when I turned him down for Derek. My mistake. Raj would have been less complicated, more irresponsible and less demanding. But by Felicia's standards, uncompromisingly perverse.

"So that's why you followed me here."

"You sure it wasn't the other way around? I was here long before you even if you did beat me back."

There is a pause on the other end. I wonder if it's love and marriage or love and sex. Either way, love keeps getting in the way.

"Sometimes," he says slowly, "I wish I hadn't been such a sucker for guilt."

Now it's my turn to be silent. I've never known what Don really thought about all that, whether or not our one afternoon fling was all me or also him.

I break the silence. "How's Vince?"

"Very married. Are we always going to bring him up?"

"You did first, sort of."

"Yeah, I know."

We both speak at once. "There's only one way . . .," I begin.

"You know it's not like . . ." he begins.

"You first," he says.

"Okay. How about you make your mind up about her first?"

"And then?"

"And then it's just a matter of repeated practice, isn't it?"

Tonight, the voices are quieter. Philip's fingers recede as I try to recall other hands, a firmer touch and a completely different sensation one afternoon less long ago in an old brick building on Front Street in lower Manhattan.

I sleep well.

Don is taking me out to dinner tonight, to celebrate his final breakup.

The doorbell rings.

It's Paul.

I stare at my brother for several minutes. He has very long hair, tied in a ponytail. He's wearing blue jeans and a soft cotton white shirt, and carries a beat up leather bag on his shoulder. Otherwise, he looks much the way I remember him.

And then I let out a shout that startles me. I hug him and drag him into the living room where his first words are, "I love what you did with that pillar," and then asks for a glass of water.

"But how, but where . . ."

"I was passing through," he says as he wanders towards the verandah. "Thought I'd look up the old homestead. I had no idea you were here."

"So you'll stay?"

"I suppose I will now, for a little while. Hey you're all dressed up. Going somewhere?"

"Got a date," I reply, conscious that until this moment, I

had not articulated this as a "date," not even to Don.

"Anyone I know?"

It is Paul again, a little older, his hair streaked with white and gray, but still Paul. Nothing could seem more normal than his sitting here, talking to me as if we'd never been apart. Don arrives, and looks quizzically at Paul, but does recognize him. So we give up the idea of going out and order food in, and the three of us sit around and talk. At first we are all a little awkward because after all, Don and Paul don't really know each other except that Don probably knows more about Paul than vice versa. But we loosen up - Paul is different in that he speaks more quickly than I remember, with greater lucidity and loquaciousness. He talks about his wanderings, in China and elsewhere. And then he talks about love, about the meaning of love which, he says, is not an alien concept to himself as he feared when he first set out on his pilgrimage. I ask if Shaolin has helped him understand this and he replies that only a complete rejection of all principles and tenets and religions have allowed him to come even a millimeter closer to understanding the power and necessity of love.

"I came back to Hong Kong, Ai-Lin, because I wanted to try to get in touch with you again, and figured it would be easier doing it from here."

I can feel a strange joy in my heart. The pain of all our separation dissolves in an instant. Paul has always been with me. I just didn't know it.

Then, Don begins to talk about his lost love but that soon takes an unexpected turn when he stares at me and says, Ai Lin, I thought that by going to Vince I was saving your marriage but I was wrong because that meant accepting a right and wrong about what we did, which should never have been confined to such narrow terms. Paul looks at him and then at me and acknowledges he didn't know about this but guessed that there was something else besides the so-called nervous breakdown that everyone, including me, assumed was happening to me, because a breakdown implies that the machine once ran smoothly and had an inherently correct movement that simply got disrupted somehow.

Don leans towards me and kisses me, saying that if he hadn't loved Vince as he did it would have been much easier to try to take me away, because he wanted to, but that love gets mixed up with loyalty. I can feel tears beginning to brim because this moment makes up for all the years of feeling that what happened with Don was only about lust, deceit and my inability to love Vince or anyone. That he felt something more than a moment's passion is what I've needed to know.

"Force of circumstance," Don says, "is no one's fault."

Paul dabs his handkerchief to my eyes. "You blame yourself for everything and always have, even when it wasn't your fault."

Finally, I tell them about the years in Cincinnati and Felicia, filling in the blanks I never talk about, when suddenly, shortly before dawn and after many bottles of wine, everything starts to become clear and I stand up, face these two men in my life and say - let me tell you about Philip and me. When I finish, I am crying and Paul takes me in his arms and says - I should have known, poor Ai-Lin, poor Philip, you were only trying to protect each other - and Don says - you should have told Vince, he would have understood, even he would have understood - and for the first time in my life, I understand, if only for just a second, the meaning of love.

Paul stays for two weeks. He has been all over Asia. He meditates on mountain tops and communes with the gods. He goes to Bali and hallucinates on mushrooms. It is not a bad life. When he needs money, he "assists the third world with their computer requirements."

This will be his home base for as long as I'm here, I promise him. I think he must continue wandering, in his quest to discover the reason for remaining alive.

These two weeks have been the truly happiest days I've known in a long time.

On his last night at home, I offer to read to my brother.

"I used to read to you when you were little, remember?"

I nod. "How could I forget? *Siu Fei Lihp,* the Chinese comic book Peter Pan."

He stretches out on the sofa, his long body curled to fit the length of one side of the L. "Peter Pan has no nationality. Just like your Supergirl."

"Nothing that matters does."

Paul's face is serene. He never was one to smile. At least now he doesn't frown.

"So what will it be?" he asks, as he rearranges himself more comfortably.

"Going home." I open the book to the page I've marked and read, "'Discovery in itself is not enough. It's not enough to find out what things are. You've also got to find out where they come from, where each brick fits in the wall.' He always came back to the wall. 'I think it's like this,' he said. 'You see a wall, you look at it so much and so hard that one day you see clear through it. Then, of course, it's not just one wall any longer. It's every wall that ever was.'"

"Who said that?" Paul asks.

"George Webber."

"Don't know him."

"No one does. He isn't real."

"That's why he makes sense. Unlike the Great Wall or the Berlin Wall."

Paul will leave tomorrow for somewhere, but will come home again now that he has a home to come to. On that we are agreed because he has promised to stay in touch with me from now on, and modem messages when he can. He is a part of me, wandering around wherever he does, and that is as good a reason to be alive as anything. It's also a good reason to make a home here for the time being.

My big brother kisses me and turns in for the night. Just before I go upstairs, he says, "I hope I'll see Don again the next time I see you."

In the morning, I will make him breakfast before he leaves.

"Now how about that date?" Don says when he turns up on my doorstep several nights later. He has given Paul and I a lot of space, knowing how much we would need it. There is an unselfish sensitivity about Don that I like. It is very different from Philip or Vince.

"Is that what this is?"

"Maybe." He comes in and hands me a bunch of orchids, giving me a kiss on the cheek. *"Song gei ni."*

I love orchids. The good thing about Hong Kong is that increased imports has un-inflated the price of orchids. I tell Don this.

"There were orchids in my apartment that afternoon," he says, as I put the flowers in a vase.

"That was a long time ago," I say cautiously.

"Yes, but it doesn't mean we can't remember, right?"

My eyes take in his face, the finer version of Vince. "I remember," I say. There is no fear, I realize, in memory.

"But it doesn't mean . . ." we both say at once, and then I

laugh because I understand that what is happening with Don right now is only the beginning of an evolution which will take its own course for both of us, and our wounds.

We go to the French Restaurant in Stanley and are seated overlooking the beach. The waters lap against the sand, washing up the remains of Hong Kong.

I don't know how to feel about this new chic. I don't feel so different here anymore now. Chinese faces speak to me in English and Mandarin as well as in Cantonese, and I routinely hear Singaporean or Malay accents which sound a lot like Indonesian. I see faces that make me think of a whole nation of Chinese, not just Cantonese Chinese. American expatriates, unlike their English counterparts of yore, do try to babble in fluent Mandarin and even surprisingly fluent Cantonese without being police officers. And everyone has been everywhere, or so they would have you believe, and return to Hong Kong because, well because this is where they belong.

I didn't come home to belong.

"So will you stay?" I ask Don over our appetizers.

"For now. What about you?"

"Same. Or forever."

It's easy being with Don. We shoot the breeze and laugh about the same things. He is an acute observer of people. Paul, he says, appears calmer than he really is. I know he's right. Paul still grinds his teeth when he sleeps.

Somewhere around the salmon, I stop eating for a moment and look at him. I share something with this man, because of our accidental connection, something palpable and significant. It isn't as simple as sex or even love. I just need time to find out what it actually is.

"What?" he asks, half smiling.

"Nothing," I reply, glancing back at my food.

"Come on. I'm not letting you off that easily."

I lay down my fork and look straight into his eyes. There's no Vince there, only Don. "Lets just say that fish can be good for revelations."

He laughs. "Here," he says, handing me the bread basket, "have a loaf."

DAUGHTERS OF HUI

FICTION COLLECTION
a novella & three stories

For Tamas Aczel, in remembrance,
of guns and complications . . .

Moreover, acknowledgements, in lines of fine type . . .
thanks to ***Kingsley Bolton,*** *and his powers of persuasion at*
the University of Hong Kong's Library, a fine establishment;
and to ***Kirpal Singh****, for the truth in lies on a Singapore summer's night.*

Your name or your person,
Which is dearer?

Book Two: Chapter XLIV *Tao Te Ching*
Lao Tzu
(translated by D.C. Lau)

DANNY'S SNAKE

Novella

1

The Monday afternoon Rosemary picked up Danny hitchhiking, his van had a flat tire. A snake coiled around his neck.

"Is it poisonous?" she asked.

"No, but it'll squeeze you to death if you let him."

She had recognized her former student, a tall pale figure, standing along Route 9 midway between Amherst and Northampton. Leyland, she remembered, as she slowed down for him. Halfway down last semester's roll call computer printout - a Hampshire College student.

But a thirteen foot boa! In her eight-year old Toyota Celica. What would Manky say?

As she drove, the reports of the recent Tiananmen Square massacre dominated the news. She could feel him watching her as they listened to the radio.

"Rosemary Hui." He let her name rest on his tongue, as if luxuriating in its shape and sound. "You're Chinese, aren't you?" His voice was deep, almost a bass.

"Yes," she replied.

"I hope you have no relatives in China."

"No. Only in Hong Kong," she said.

He did not raise the subject again, much to her relief. Since the start of the Tiananmen episode, she had found the China events painful to discuss. Everyone she knew, all her friends, colleagues and even her students, seemed to expect her to have a lot to say about it. It was not a subject about which she trusted herself to speak.

They stopped at a light. Rosemary felt the summer sun warm her elbow, propped on the window edge. From the corner of her eye, she peered at the snake, which hung in a double loop around her passenger. Why wasn't she afraid of it, she wondered. Was it because its handler appeared calm, making the danger safe?

The news reported that a still unknown number of students were dead or seriously injured. She switched off the radio, and tried to quickly brush away a starting tear, hoping Danny wouldn't notice.

"I was going to go to China," he said. "To Tibet." He gazed out the window as he spoke.

That surprisingly deep voice again. Too rich and sensual for such a boy. Rosemary recalled his apologetic face the day he sat in her office last semester and said he was dropping her course. And how she had tried to tell him it was okay. She heard the same apology in his tone now. "You still can," she responded.

"Perhaps." He was silent a moment. And then, "I think my snake likes you."

She kept her eyes on the road. "Why so?"

"It's trying to say hi."

She glanced at her passenger. The snake had unwound itself from around him and was slithering towards her. Its head was almost at her shoulder. She drew back, startled by the proximity of this sleek reptile, imagining, for just a second, that she could feel its breath on her cheek. Danny yanked its head away, and placed it against his shoulder.

"I'm sorry," he said. "I didn't mean to scare you."

"That's okay. I wasn't really scared." But she felt a knot tighten in her stomach as she said this.

Danny had shifted and was leaning against the car door. The snake had circled its way around him, and its tail was an inch away from the gear stick. She glanced at him. *Lengjai,* a beautiful boy, although she hadn't thought so before. There was an angular precision to his New England features. These were softened by the grace of his movements. He could be a dancer, the way his body seemed to flow into the too small passenger seat. She saw him dart out his right leg, winding his ankle in a swift, neat movement around the snake's tail to draw it away from the stick shift. He gazed steadily at her as he did this. Rosemary found herself blushing under his scrutiny.

They did not speak again the rest of the way.

She dropped him at the Sunoco off Route 9 near Haydenville.

"Thanks," he said as he closed the door. "Hope I see you again."

She watched the snake slither down his body as he walked away. Her skin reacted, not with goose bumps, but of something much lighter, less prickly, smoothly dry. She wondered if he knew the effect he had had on her, and thought that he probably did. Only the tiniest pang of guilt recalled Man-Kit, her Manky, who inspired such absolute fidelity.

Driving home to Springfield, she switched PBS back on and listened to the jazz program. Charlie Parker playing *How Deep is the Ocean* in his surprisingly languid yet sharply curving tones made her think of the snake. It took a little more than half an hour to arrive at her apartment complex.

Man-Kit was hunched over his computer terminal when she entered. Even when deeply absorbed in his work, he always managed to look neat. His broad and rather flat face was smooth and unlined; the only wrinkles that creased his features appeared around the edges of his eyes when he smiled. Rosemary still marveled at how tidily his straight hair fell into place just above his neck. From time to time he would toss his head back, brushing away a lock of hair that fell across his forehead with the back of his hand.

The same jazz program she had been listening to blared through their sound system. She went over to kiss him, and saw that he was in the middle of one of his top speed computer chess games.

"Hey, Rosa-M. So are you ready to kill the kids yet?" he asked, his eyes still glued to the screen. They spoke to each other mostly in English, with occasional Cantonese phrases mixed in. It was something they had done since they first met in Hong Kong. While his left hand manipulated the keyboard, his right hand hovered over a timer, which he struck with a rhythmic regularity.

"Almost," she said. The swiftness of his moves made her dizzy.

"No mail."

"Good. I'm sick of bills anyway. Any calls?"

He never took his eyes off the screen. "Nothing important."

"By the way, did you hear 'Bird' just now?"

"Huh? Oh why, was he on? I guess I didn't ."

"Okay. I'll go cook."

She smiled as she walked away. Funny, but once he would have been the one to ask if she'd heard 'Bird' and been beside himself if she hadn't noticed. A warm, slightly maternal feeling overtook her. Manky, her Manky may have lost some of his youthful figure - ever since his thirtieth birthday he seemed to have become a little softer, rounder - but he was still the only man who commanded her entire being, the only one who counted on her completely.

Rosemary put away her papers and books, and clipped up her long hair into a ponytail. From the kitchen she heard a slap on a table, and an exclamation of delight. Man-Kit had won yet another game. He appeared in the kitchen, jogged past her, circled back, spun her around away from the sink, and lifted all five feet of her off the ground. She pulled off his glasses, kissed him, and hopped out off his arms, giggling. He left her, then, to finish making dinner, grabbing a Coors Light from the fridge as he went out.

Later at dinner, she told him about Danny's snake.

"Was it edible?" he asked, at the end of her story.

Man-Kit loved snake soup, a delicacy of their cultural cuisine Rosemary could have sooner done without, along with dog meat and monkey brains. She had spent her childhood up till age ten in Malaysia, on the island of Penang, her mother's birthplace, and felt that the infusion of Malay culture made her somehow less Chinese than him. But, as he often teasingly reminded her, she was one hundred percent pure blood Chinese, even if she was part Hokkienese from the lazy tropics.

"Well, I wouldn't cook it for you," she retorted, as she

placed a plateful of fried noodles on the table.

"Look," he said, picking up several strands of noodles off the serving platter with his chopsticks and waving them in the air, "snake, snake!"

She gave him her school teacher look. Handing him the bottle of chili sauce, she sat down to dinner.

Man-Kit ate hungrily, quickly, the way he always did. He ate Cantonese style, the bowl close to his lips, shovelling food into his mouth with his chopsticks. Rosemary picked at the noodles. Cooking always made her feel full. Unlike her husband, she did not like to eat as soon as the food was ready. He insisted that dinner had to start when the food was piping hot straight from the wok, the steam still rising from it. She preferred to wait, allowing the aroma to build up her appetite.

But one thing they both agreed on was chili sauce. Rosemary had converted him to her love for spicy foods, and now, he used chili sauce the way Americans used ketchup - on everything.

They ate in silence.

After about his third mouthful, he said, "So tell me more about the snake man. Was he a charmer as well?"

He laughed at his own joke, and she made a face.

"Nothing to tell."

"Was he a good student? What grade did he get?"

"I."

"I?"

"Incomplete. He wanted it, even though I told him not to bother. My only one to date."

She could feel Man-Kit gnawing away inside her. The terrible thing about their closeness, their incessant togetherness, was that he controlled every square inch of privacy within her. She had liked the closeness at first, even insisted on it, while he had tried to distance himself. Now, after seven years, after he had given in to her insistence, she was beginning to feel slightly claustrophobic.

"You know," she said, "I think maybe I should consider a new dissertation thesis."

"Why, what's changing your mind?"

"Oh, I'm not really sure. Maybe I don't really want a PhD after all."

Man-Kit did not respond.

She let a reasonable interval lapse before saying, "So what do you think?"

"It's a crisis. What do you want me to say?"

"Well surely you have something to say about this. It's not everyday that I might consider making such a big change."

"Is that why you picked up a hitchhiker? So you wouldn't have to think about what you really want to do, like you're supposed to do while driving?"

It was an old joke. Their moving to Springfield meant a commute to the university at Amherst for her. She had insisted on moving, so that his commute to work would be easier since he hated to drive. Her promise had been that the drive would be crisis solving time.

"Eat," she said, pretending not to smile. But she felt the familiar rush of pleasure that assailed her each time she was reminded how truly well he knew her.

Later, in bed, while he fiddled with the alarm clock, she stretched herself across his back and nibbled his ear.

"Make love to me, Manky," she whispered.

He removed her gently, and rolled over on his back. He was silent for a moment. "Listen," he said, "I have to go home."

His declaration made her sit up. It took a minute to sink in.

"Your father?"

He nodded. "He's really bad."

"But when did you find out?"

"Mom called this morning, just after you left for class."

She heard the pain and fear in his voice. Over the last year, they had heard from his mother as often as once a month about his father's worsening condition. And each time, he had dismissed the reality by their distance. Neither of them had been back to Hong Kong nor seen their families in the six years since their arrival in the States. That was mostly her choice, she knew.

And now, she knew he did not expect her to go.

Despite herself, she sensed the usual jealousy creeping in. She fought the feeling, forcing herself to empathize. "You have to go, don't you?"

"I spoke to Ah Chun in New York. There's a flight on Thursday, but on such short notice, it's nine hundred. . . ."

She interrupted him. "It doesn't matter," she said, cradling his head in her arms, "the money doesn't matter."

She had to say it because she knew he couldn't. Most of her life, unlike for Manky, money had simply been there. But, even as she said it, she knew that this meant yet another extension of their already over-extended credit cards. For the first time, the thought frightened her.

Rosemary switched off the light. They curled into each other.

"I don't know if I can face it alone," he whispered again.

She felt his body shaking, ever so slightly, as he drifted off to sleep in her arms.

Her poor, wounded hero - how could he have held that back all day long? Three years ago, she would have reacted with much more annoyance and surprise, questioning him insistently, wanting to know why he hadn't said something sooner, why he didn't trust her enough to ask her help and how he could keep this from her. And he would have retreated further into himself until finally, when he couldn't hold back his temper anymore, he would shout at her to leave him alone and she would retort that he didn't need to yell and they would both eventually fall back, she in tears and he in a funk that would last at least another forty eight hours, if not longer.

Well, at least they were past most of that, and now she could let him sleep, although she knew he would wrestle all night with his dreams. Man-Kit never slept peacefully. He always held everything deep inside himself and let his sleep bear the brunt. In their four years of marriage, she had been awakened many nights by his grinding teeth, flailing arms and kicking legs. Yet when she complained, he laughed and said he was just practising *kung fu*.

Rosemary heard his even breathing. Lying on her back, she closed her eyes and tried, unsuccessfully, to fall asleep. She lay awake for almost an hour. She wished they could have made love. Why did the refuge of their love have to be so fragile and uncertain? Why didn't Man-Kit trust her enough to ask for help? Yet a nagging voice inside told her she shouldn't be blaming Manky. What she hadn't said to him, had trouble saying to herself, was that she did not want him to go away from her. And she knew he knew this.

2

She drove back alone to Springfield from Kennedy Airport. The flight for Hong Kong had actually been on time at noon, much to her dismay. She had hoped for more time with Man-

Kit. Before she knew it, he was kissing her, kissing her so much that her whole being ached. Then he was running towards customs. "I'll call you," he cried.

They hadn't even had time to stop for a meal in Chinatown.

Her only consolation was that they had made love early that morning, and Man-Kit had been as crazily passionate as she knew he could be.

To distract herself, she turned on the radio. More reports of events in China. At the Chinese students' demonstration in Amherst the other day, she had donated, almost without thinking, some fifty dollars to their cause. She had simply looked silently at Man-Kit as she took the money out of her purse. For once, he had not teased her about what he called her lovingly lavish bleeding heart.

On the night they had watched the television reports of the lone student in his futile joust with the tanks, Man-Kit had comforted her while she wept and whispered, "why now, why us?"

How completely he understood.

Suddenly the thought struck her: was it possible that Man-Kit, her Manky, might be gone for a long time?

Their last three days had been a race of frenzied phone calls, organizing and planning. There hadn't been time for her to stop and really consider that in the seven years since they first met they had never been apart for more than even a couple of days.

Despite the anxiety she felt, the realization made her smile.

Seven years ago, she and a group of friends had walked into Rick's Cafe in Tsimshatsui after a dance at the University. Her Shakespeare professor had directed their group there for the must-hear experience of live jazz. Her Shakespeare professor was a horny young South African who would do anything to get close to her in a dark place now that she had graduated and could no longer compromise his position.

But her mind was not on him at all. For the first time ever, she was going to see and hear live jazz in Hong Kong!

It had been quite a novelty. She had listened, not fully comprehending the sounds she heard, trying to piece them into her memory of a late night radio program she sometimes listened to on the English language station hosted by a Portuguese deejay, Tony da Costa, who had already initiated her to the strange jazz albums he brought back from the U.S.

Manky was on the bandstand, drumming away. He was lean and energetic, his lips set in a determined line as he handled the rhythm for the all Caucasian band. Man-Kit, during the break, strolled casually by her group to say hello to someone he knew. And the next thing she knew, Shakespeare was edged aside while Ho Man-Kit glided into position next to her, his arm neatly barring the South African's progress.

"Didn't anyone tell you Hong Kong girls don't like jazz?" he asked, and somehow he kept her laughing and talking for the rest of the night. And before she knew it she was agreeing to see him the very next night. Why had he ever let go of that jazz life?

A siren wail recalled her rudely to the present.

Rosemary pulled over.

"You know you were doing at least seventy?" The officer said, as he wrote up her ticket.

"Sorry about that."

"Hey, didn't I give you a ticket a couple of weeks ago?"

No, she wanted to say, we all look alike. If Manky had been home, she would have done so. But she held her tongue and smiled politely, knowing that the officer was right about the previous ticket.

Stupid laws, she thought, when he finally returned her license. Guiltily, she thought of Man-Kit, who no longer chided her about her many tickets, and who never himself speeded, except at his computer. But the waste of money, she knew, bothered him, although he was used to her extravagances. Perhaps she would never be as worried about money as he was, but a tug of conscience had recently begun to assail her, which she found stifling and irritating. He never said so, but sometimes she thought he had stopped playing drums because jazz simply didn't pay, and computers did. She drove at fifty-five the rest of the way, and stopped daydreaming.

She arrived home to find a van parked in front of her house, and Danny at her door with a bouquet of orchids. He stared at her as she approached. "I guess dreams come true." He spoke softly, almost in an undertone.

Rosemary looked at the tan uniform he was wearing with "Springfield Florists" stitched on the pocket, trying not to react to the timbre of his voice.

Danny cradled the flowers in his left arm. "These are for Mrs. Ho. Do you know her?"

"That's me."

"But . . . I thought you were Rosemary Hui?"

His obvious disappointment pleased her. "Hui's my maiden name. I use it at school."

He continued to gaze as if overwhelmed by her presence. And then, recovering his composure, "Here, I guess someone had these delivered to you."

She fumbled for her keys, and dropped them. When she stooped to pick them up, she almost lost her balance and was steadied by Danny's hand. It disturbed her to be so clumsy.

"Why don't you come in for a moment?" she offered.

He entered.

The card read *I already miss you Rosa-M, Manky.* It made her want to cry.

"I hope they're happy flowers."

"Sort of."

She cried a little anyway, in between smiles and frowns, thinking that despite their modest means, his extravagances were always far more worthwhile than hers. She kept her face turned away as she arranged the orchids in a vase. Gorgeous white, mauve and tiger striped orchids, just like the ones that grew wild in the Malaysian countryside. All the time, Danny stood by the door.

Sentimental fool, she scolded herself. Drying her eyes, she turned back to him, smiling.

"Beautiful flowers, don't you think?" she asked.

"Yes," he paused, "but not so happy."

"No."

It had slipped out, that no, to this virtual stranger. Yet he seemed gentle, she thought, and kind.

"Please," she said, "I don't mean to keep you from your job."

"That's okay. You're my last delivery today. Besides, I've still got that 'incomplete' on my transcript."

She smiled. "Since I hadn't heard from you, I assumed you were going to let it turn into a W."

"W?"

"Withdrawal."

Danny was gazing at her again. His large, rather beautiful green eyes had a disarmingly innocent quality that made Rosemary blush, and she averted her face so that he wouldn't notice. She was embarrassed by the effect he had on her.

"You look like someone I know," he said, abruptly.

"Who?"

"An-Mei, my Mandarin tutor."

"We all look alike," she said, finally dispelling the traffic cop.

But he was undaunted, and continued to talk about An-Mei, "peace and beauty'. He stayed until just before dinner time, talking, telling her all about himself. Boy's stuff, Manky would have called it. He was from Malden, near Boston. Delivering flowers and photographing reptiles for nature magazines earned him a living. College just wasn't his thing, not even at Hampshire's open curriculum, not even as an "older" student, which he was, being twenty-three. He studied Chinese up at UMASS, and wanted to go to China, to Tibet, he said. That would be his education, a life study, not just words in books. The unrest in China only made it all the more important for him to go. When he spoke, his words unwound with a sinuous intensity, as if he had waited forever for this moment of utterance.

Rosemary listened, surprised. He spun Buddhist Tibet and Han China into the same mental tapestry. But students, she knew, suffered from knowledge gaps, pieces in the jigsaw that might take them years to find. It was just their enthusiasm and hurry to embrace all before they were ready. What surprised her more was how much he talked. He had not previously impressed her as the garrulous kind. In class, he had been the quiet American kid among mostly foreign students who fought to get into her section. She vaguely remembered the one paper he submitted. It had been short, little more than a page, and had been about Taoism. He used language well, but didn't really have much to say.

"Tibet must be incredible," he was saying.

"The Chinese don't like the Tibetans, you know." Rosemary interrupted his ecstasy.

"Don't they?" He seemed surprised. "Is Hong Kong much like China? You're from Hong Kong, right?"

She felt just a little sorry for him as he continued to talk. Perhaps he would have a wonderful experience in China. Somehow, she didn't think so. China might be a paper tiger, as Manky and their Hong Kong friends sometimes liked to say, but Rosemary believed the country devoured its young mercilessly. And Danny was young, was full of desire to conquer a world, any world, one which only he would define. He seemed like some of her ESL English-as-a- second-language students. They came to America on the strength of a dream, only to be disappointed, and who, until forced into a private conference away from the classroom, would not open up and speak freely.

It made sense when he told her he was a jazz musician. She had been around enough of them to know. It fitted with his musical voice, his overall fluidity, his odd alienation as an American who wasn't like the rest of his peers, but was still undeniably American.

On Sunday nights, he said, he jammed at a club in Springfield.

"During the last set, with Joel's band?" she asked.

His face perked up at her question. "Yes, how did you know?"

"My husband used to play drums many moons ago. I know the club you mean."

The memory of an earlier life nudged its way into her consciousness.

Danny invited her, then, to see him on Sunday.

"What's your axe?" she asked.

"Bari sax."

She imagined him on stage, his hands wrapped around the

large, unwieldy instrument, which had such a rich, rarely heard sound. At least he was tall enough. "Will your snake be there?"

He smiled. "In his cage."

After Danny left, she wandered around the apartment, trying to decide what to do next. It was almost seven. She should eat. Since a hurried breakfast in the morning, she hadn't eaten all day. Surely there was something she could tempt herself with?

But there was no Manky to cook for. Hungry, lovable Manky.

What a little housewife she had become! When Manky had still been in graduate school, he had done his share of the cooking. Since his graduation a year ago, however, she had taken over the preparation of all their meals, even though he protested, saying that as long as he had the time, why shouldn't he do his share? She had been adamant, insisting that since their future residence in America depended entirely on his ability to establish himself in the work world, she wanted him to be freed of daily chores.

If their friends back home could see her now, how they would laugh. She had always been the one who complained that Hong Kong life was too restrictive for a woman, and that she wouldn't have to behave in such an old fashioned way in America. Even when she and Manky had first arrived in the States, all she had willingly done was cook, which she found creative and fun, and had only done housework grudgingly. And Manky, dear Manky, had not minded in the least. He had taken over the maintenance of their household, his instinctive neatness abhorring the mess she left.

Her dissertation beckoned. Stubbornly, she ignored it.

Funny, she thought, how seven years in a new country could change her.

Now, she would happily be a housewife, Manky's wife, and give up everything she had worked for as long as he would always be there. Of course, they had both changed. It didn't seem so long ago that Manky was telling her the reason he wanted to go to UMASS had more to do with Max Roach's ongoing tenure there and programs like Jazz in July, than with the graduate school in computer science.

She made a small pot of coffee, ignoring all her Chinese teas sitting untouched over the years in their larder, and prepared a ham and cheese sandwich.

She did not touch her dissertation that night.

3

There was something about Danny, she told Man-Kit when he called to say that he did not know how long he would have to stay in Hong Kong.

"Oh, oh," he said, "he'll fall in love with you while you fall in love with his snake."

Rosemary laughed. "He's much too young for me."

"Right. Like Americans don't still card you?"

Both in their early thirties, they could almost pass as college kids, although she teased Man-Kit that his expanding beer belly was the giveaway. They often joked about their youthful appearances, a joke they played on all Americans. It was a joke of which she was growing tired the longer she lived in the States. But she detected some antagonism in his tone - not jealousy, Man-Kit rarely expressed any jealousy - just the tiniest flicker of resentment that he could not be there to share the joke.

She knew that now was the moment to reassure him, to arouse him by telling him she needed him sexually. She could use what they called their ESL sex words. Then, any tension between them would subside, and he would whisper to her the few Malay words she had taught him, and she would reply in Cantonese or sometimes, Mandarin, their love words. *Lingua franca.*

But instead, she said. "He's playing Sunday at The Midnite Lite. He asked me to come."

There was a short, but deafening pause.

"Boys' games," he said, at last. "If you're really American."

"Which we'll never be." She could at least offer him that little bit of reassurance.

"Games are necessary."

She heard the spark in his voice, any antagonism gone. It was something he said often, something that always cheered her. She was glad he hadn't gotten really angry - Manky always got so unreasonably furious, followed by depression when he let his temper get the better of him. Why had she egged him on? To make him jealous? It wasn't something she generally did. But then, being this much apart wasn't something they ever did, and no reason was reason enough for this separation as far as she was concerned.

And then, he told her about the miles of demonstrators, how beautiful and terrible this outpouring was, previously so repressed. People from all walks of life marched into the streets to confront the inevitable change to the status quo, whatever the change would bring. Was it fear, she asked, and perhaps humiliation at their helplessness, their loss of control? No, he replied, people were angry and outraged, not afraid, more indignant than humiliated. It was a protest, a demand to be heard. It was unlike anything he had ever seen in Hong Kong.

"In the end, I'm glad we decided to stay in America," he said.

"Games and all?"

"And all." His tone was certain, without its usual ambivalence.

Before he hung up, he told her that he had run into Sonny Lee, an old friend from his rock DJ days, who was now a popular local singer. He said Sonny's latest single was playing on all the Chinese language radio stations. She thought she detected a note of wistfulness in his voice as he said this. He had drummed for Sonny for a brief time, but complained that the music was a poor sellout to commercial Western rock. Was he thinking now that he had sold out too?

Before she hung up, she told him in Cantonese that she was lying naked in bed, her long hair spread over the pillow, waiting for him. A ripple of pleasure prickled her as she spoke.

When Rosemary walked into The Midnite Lite on Sunday, she was pleased to find nothing had changed. The same iron door marked the entrance to the club, which was located on a back alley in downtown Springfield. A former speakeasy of prohibition days, it legally held no more than forty people; only newcomers were asked to pay the cover charge. Man Kit had played there for at least two years, and it was almost as long since he had played at all. His drum set, he was fond of saying, was his contribution to their as yet non-existent art collection.

The band was on break before the last set. Joel, the house sax player and club owner greeted her with a hug. His arm looped into hers as they chatted.

"And Manky? What's he up to these days?"

"Programming relational databases. Creating confluence for many meandering tributaries of bits and bytes. He's been working hard since he finished his Masters."

"Always the hustler. Tell him we miss him around here. And you, gorgeous as ever, what are you doing these days? What brings you out tonight besides my musical talent and never ending desire to seduce you?"

"Oh, nothing different. Still teaching American and foreign students how to write. Still waiting to have children."

She hadn't meant to say that about children. She and Man-Kit had agreed to wait until their life in America was more settled. The trouble was, she was beginning to feel slightly old, slightly tired of always having to wait for everything as if she didn't deserve what she wanted. Also, she knew that a grandchild, especially if it were a boy, was someone that her dad would embrace happily, even willingly, despite Man-Kit, the "undesirable" father. Age seemed to soften her feelings towards her father, making her want the same things he wanted.

Seeing Danny, she disengaged her arm and indicated the cage he was carrying, glad for the opportunity to change the subject.

"The snake. I came to see the snake."

She saw Joel's eyebrows rise. "Oh, him eh? Didn't know you guys knew him. I should have known Man-Kit wouldn't leave you unattended while he disappeared to the other side of the world."

She heard the chuckle in his voice, but saw him eye Danny suspiciously. Same old Joel. Fat, fifty and twice divorced, he ran The Midnite Lite as a jazz club with a passion. Although he lambasted rock bands, and bemoaned the lack of serious, young jazz musician, a new musician, no matter how talented, never won quick acceptance on his bandstand. And though he flirted outrageously and often, he observed, and protected, the sanctity of other people's relationships with an almost pious reverence. Man-Kit called him the one-man jazz and morality D.O.D.

Danny approached them. Rosemary thought he looked uneasy, and guessed that he had not yet won Joel over.

"Sit in on the second tune, kid," said Joel. "Talk to you later, Rosa-M."

Joel left them.

"May I buy you a drink?" she offered.

They went to the bar together and he accepted a beer. He carried the cage and his saxophone case with him. The snake lay unmoving, entwined in a pile of brown and black scales, its tail sloped over its neck.

She gazed at the snake.

"It's one big muscle, you know," he said. "All muscle."

The house band straggled onto the stage.

"Does he always call you Rosa-M?"

She had not expected the question, had not thought, in fact, that he would have observed this small familiarity.

"Yes, he does. Everyone does."

They were standing at the bar facing each other. Out of the corner of her eye, she caught Joel watching them. Danny seemed oblivious to this surveillance.

"Rosemary. Remembrance. A much prettier name. I hoped you'd come."

His words sprang out suddenly after a measured pause. This was the man, not the boy, romancing her. She was flattered by his attention. He remained so still whenever he spoke, as if speaking were a painful act. Even at her house, when he had talked quite incessantly, he had done so with a minimum of gestures or movement. Yet there was a soothing, fluid quality in his voice which she found sensual. Almost unbearably so.

She glanced down at the snake, avoiding his eyes.

"I'm not making that up, you know. Rosemary really does stand for remembrance."

There was a confidence in the way he said it, in his whole manner tonight, without the boyish enthusiasm that prevailed when he tried to talk about China. He removed his instrument from his case, never taking his eyes off her. As he adjusted the strap round his neck, securing the mouth of the bari sax at the right level for his lips, he suddenly winked at her. It was unnerving. But the way he handled his axe, his whole demeanor, suggested a musician who knew the scene and had no qualms about his own ability to perform well.

The band had launched into *'Round Midnight,* signalling the start of the last set during which outsiders were welcome to sit in. When Joel bought the club ten years ago, he had kept this signature tune which had been adopted by the previous owner. Only the house band played it, never the musicians who came to jam.

The music gave her an excuse not to respond. She turned towards the stage and listened, her back half turned to Danny. From the corner of her eye, she saw him lick the reed mouthpiece in preparation, his eyes still on her. She imagined his eyes on her hair, on her back, and his tongue sliding over her neck. His attention was unbearably exciting.

As the tune ended, he leaned close to her ear and said, "You're very beautiful."

"Thank you," she replied, and immediately regretted her response. It had been too automatic, cutting him off. She had not meant to do that.

He set the cage next to her. "Watch my snake, please?"

She nodded, wondering why she felt no fear. Danny stepped

towards the bandstand where Joel relinquished the stage to him.

Danny called *How Deep is the Ocean.* His tone was rich and layered. Again, she was struck by his seeming wispiness as he coaxed sounds from his bari sax. Except for his surprisingly deep voice, she would have expected him to play alto. He looked too thin and insubstantial to evoke such sensuality.

He played the way he spoke, with a minimum of bodily movement. His notes were varied and plentiful. And then, Rosemary recognized what he was doing. He had taken Bird's version, the same Parker tune she had heard just the other day with Al Haig on piano and Max Roach on drums, and transcribed and transposed it for his axe.

Joel joined her at the bar.

"The kid's got talent I hate to admit," he said at the end of the tune, "even if he is a little too uptight."

"He's just young," she said. "You know, he hasn't had time to shape his sound."

"Aah, he's all over the place. Kids. Never know when it's time to come back to earth."

There was a pause. "You don't like him, do you?" It was less of a question than a statement on her part.

"Do you?"

He spared her a reply by walking away as Danny returned.

She called Man-Kit when she got home that night. He was depressed, and she cheered him by sending greetings from Joel and the rest of the band. He was glad to hear that she had gone to the Midnite Lite. Somehow, the sensuality Danny evoked, which had occupied all her thoughts on the way home, waned the minute she heard Man-Kit's voice.

"And your father?" She wanted to know.

"Bad."

Man-Kit continued. "But not so bad that he couldn't ask if I was still making loud Western noises on the drums."

"And what did he say when you told him about your computer work?"

"*Dihn louh* - electronic brain - is just a Western abacus, and that I was selling out. As if his colonial idolatry weren't worse!"

Man-Kit had only been gone five days. His absence bothered her terribly, and already seemed much longer. Yet her unease at their separation felt natural and inevitable. They had often been told that they spent an unusual amount of time together for a married couple. But then, people didn't understand.

"So how long, Manky?"

"I just don't know. It could be as much as a month, maybe more."

She was glad she could not see his expression, an expression, she was sure, of resignation and complacency. When it came to family, Man-Kit accepted way too much. It irritated her.

"But what is it? What do the doctors say?"

"It's not that. Dad's just old and he wants me to be here to talk to me. You know, like what I'm supposed to do for Mom and all that. He keeps saying that a Chinese son shouldn't be too far away from his father."

"What about your job, and me? Don't your family have anything to say about that? Don't they know you could jeopardize your visa status?"

"They don't understand, Rosa-M. Be fair. They've not been to America. How would they know how things are for us?"

But she knew he would not say to them how much he depended on her, nor that money was tight. It was so important for him to appear successful to them.

She pictured him at "home," in his family's apartment on the nineteenth floor of a building on a hillside of Hong Kong island. His father was a retired Hong Kong government official who had wanted him to study in England and return to Hong Kong. His mother and two sisters lived what he termed a petty bourgeois existence. Man-Kit was the eldest child and only son.

"You can't stay that long. Surely they don't expect you to."

She heard the sigh of exasperation in his voice.

Shortly after they first met, he had told her, "You wouldn't like it at my home. My sisters go to the hairdresser's every week. My mother plays mahjeuk and talks about how little money she has, especially in relation to her friends. And Dad bad mouths America, even though he's never even been there."

"My father's ill, Rosa-M. He might die." He paused. "They're my family. Please don't be unreasonable."

She had soon discovered that, despite his complaints, he was really fond of his family. And she knew she was being unreasonable. She tried to soften her tone. "Don't be impatient. I just miss you, that's all. You're my family now."

When he did not respond, she knew what he was thinking. "Did you speak to my father?" she asked.

"I went to see him. He was kind about my father. You know, he really does care about you. He offered us plane tickets for you to come and visit."

Her own eagerness startled her. "Did he really?"

"Yes he did."

There was a moment's silence during which Rosemary imagined going home to her dad, and apologizing in person for the rift that had separated them.

Manky continued, "You know, he's thinking of remarrying."

She did not know, of course, and the hesitation in Manky's voice made her brace. "She's young, isn't she?"

Manky didn't reply.

"How old?"

"Twenty-five."

So much for the eagerness. "Just young enough to be my little sister. Is she a hooker?"

"Come on, Rosa-M, give your father some credit."

And then, all the contempt she had ever felt for her father returned, and all she wanted was for Manky, her Manky, to be back in her arms, to be the only family she would ever want or need.

"I miss you," she whispered, crying softly. "It's too lonely without you."

"Please don't cry. This won't go on forever."

"I feel so foolish," she said, drying her eyes. "I shouldn't need you so much."

"It's the same for me too," he said.

He told her then that he would come home as soon as possible. She could tell he was unhappy with her.

It was almost one a.m. when she finally let him off. The Man-Kit she pictured putting down the phone half a world away was quite different from the image he had presented seven years ago. Her flashy, independent, temperamental jazz musician was really a family man. She remembered, only too clearly, how bitterly he had complained that his family didn't understand him. *Chi sin*, they called him. One of his sisters had laughingly told her that Man-Kit was even crazy as a baby; he had howled whenever anyone tried to rock him. His retort was that none of his family had enough rhythm to rock him.

But this was their family's way of loving and accepting each other, and she resented it.

Rosemary switched off the lights in the living room, shut all the blinds and headed towards the bedroom. How desolate their apartment felt. The news about her father angered her. It was typical. Years of screwing prostitutes after her mother died - Rosemary had been twelve at the time but had quickly, too quickly comprehended - and now, he was finally going to marry someone who was virtually one.

She remembered, seven years ago, when she first came home with the news that she was applying for an assistantship to study in America. How unsettled her father had been! Her university education, he said, was just the modern way for girls to pass the time before marriage. His idea was that she should marry the son of his business partner, and become a Hong Kong society lady who sat around sipping afternoon tea at the Mandarin. She thought he secretly blamed Man-Kit, who encouraged her endeavors. But if her father were angry at her, he failed to show it, choosing instead a perpetual silence about the subject once she had made her decision and left home. And she responded to his reticence by a stubborn refusal to take any money from him once she went to live with Manky, and none since she arrived in the States. For a long time, their communication had been almost non-existent. Certainly, she had never bothered to go home to visit.

"Apologize?" she had almost shouted at Manky when he first suggested her doing so three years ago. "Why should I apologize to him?"

Manky had remained unusually level headed. "Because he's your father, and because one day he'll be gone before you've reconciled with him."

It had been the year of her father's sixtieth birthday, the age Confucius prescribed for "attuning one's ear to the decrees of the heavens". It would be a sad year for him, Manky said, if father and child still remained at odds, especially at a time when he was surely feeling his mortality.

"But why should I be the one? Why can't he come to me and say he was wrong, as he must know now. He can't always be right."

"This is not about right and wrong. It's a simple, filial matter - you're the daughter, he's the father. End of story. Come on, I don't have to tell you that."

All year long Manky had patiently, persistently tried to persuade her. In the end, she had given in, on the eve of her father's birthday. And she had called to apologize, an apology he accepted readily, saying they need never speak of their rift again. She remembered the warmth in her father's voice, a warmth she had seldom felt. Now, she and her father were at least on tentative speaking terms.

"I'll always be there to take care of you," Manky had said tonight on the phone, just before he hung up. "Don't cry, don't worry anymore. I'll be back and everything will be like it was, better even."

She went into the bathroom and began brushing her teeth. If only she could be angry! She knew she was stretching Manky; her unreasonableness and jealousy signalled to him that she blamed his family for taking him away from her. Anger would be easier to bear than this hollowness, this loneliness in the face of death. Yet what else could he do? This was family. He might be their only male relative soon. She understood his duty. Despite her Malaysian heritage, she was Chinese too. But not that Chinese. She wouldn't know where to stand in the funeral procession if she were there, or be able to mourn.

If only she could really understand this feeling of family for someone other than Manky. But she had never properly accepted her husband's family, and now, could not go back to her own. Yet this Chinese way, Confucius' legacy, was rooted so deeply in them both. It felt all wrong and desperately unfair.

She continued brushing her teeth for almost seven minutes, until the foam covered her mouth. When she gargled, she saw she had made her gums bleed.

4

A week later, she saw Danny again.

He appeared at her office, just at the end of her hours. Neither of her two office mates were there. It was almost five, and the early evening sun streamed through the window, casting the entire room in a dusky, surreal glare.

"Hello Rosemary." He lingered over her name. "I came to do something about that 'incomplete'."

He leaned against the door, his right hip bracing his person. His arm was raised above his head, the fingers resting above the door frame.

"Come in and sit." She watched his movements, flowing and graceful, as he slid into the chair by her desk. He was in cutoffs and a T shirt. His long bare legs stretched out, his sandaled feet almost touched hers.

Rosemary was suddenly conscious of her thin summer dress, and her bare arms and legs. Danny's eyes smiled at her.

"You don't have to do anything about it, you know," she said.

"I want to."

"But why? You know you don't need a writing course."

"I think I can learn something from you."

She felt her age as she looked at him. Her eyes took in his physique, and it both excited and disturbed her. She tried to focus on what he was saying.

"Danny, what is it you think you want?"

"Truthfully?"

Rosemary hesitated. She knew where this was going, but gave in. "Of course, truthfully. And I'll take it with as many grains of salt as I choose."

"I just want to be around you."

She smiled, sure of herself now. "You don't need to write me papers to do that."

He reddened, and she caught herself thinking how sweet and vulnerable he looked. Rosemary leaned forward slightly, and crossed her legs. She watched his eyes follow her every motion.

Danny stared at her, saying nothing for nearly a minute. And then, he said, "I'm sorry. I'm being rude. I don't mean to stare."

The deep, sensual quality in his voice had returned.

"Rosemary, please come photograph my snake with me. It's only a slightly illegal endeavor, keeping a thirteen foot snake, I mean. You know, a cop once stopped me and said I couldn't keep a snake over nine feet long, so I offered it to him to take away. He refused."

"It's not the illegality that's the problem," she said, smiling.

"I just want some company, that's all."

She had no more papers to grade. There was no Manky to bug her into working on her dissertation. Why shouldn't she?

"Yes, perhaps I will," she replied.

She followed his van for about three miles along 116 until they reached a clearing. Games, that was all this was. Just games. Just like the time Manky had been pursued by the

Vietnamese girl who wanted "to be a jazz singer more than anything else in life" until she discovered he was married. And Manky had led her on, knowing full well she was more enamored of him than of jazz, promising to help her with her singing. How jealous Rosemary remembered she had been! And how Manky loved to tease her about it.

Danny parked, took out the cage, knelt down and set it on the roadside. His tall, lanky body curved gracefully as he worked. How unlike Manky he was, she thought as she watched him. Manky, despite his nimble mind, was a klutz except when seated at his drums or computer.

He unlatched the cage and released the snake.

The creature stretched out its entire length on the sandy roadside. Danny had placed it a foot away from her.

"One long muscle," he said. "Digesting, breathing, sensing danger. Did you know snakes won't attack unless you frighten them, and then they retaliate? I've had it since it was a baby, yet to it, I'm no different than the next guy. It could turn on me if I accidentally frightened it."

He held up his camera and began to shoot.

The early evening June sun was warm. Rosemary's gaze never left the snake as it inched forward, going nowhere in particular. It looked remarkably harmless lying there on the ground.

"Snakes like the sun," he continued. "They're timid creatures, kind of repressed, you know. All they really want to do is lie around basking in the sun all day. It's not a bad life being a snake."

Rosemary leaned against his car, her memory stirred by the sight of Danny's snake. In the Penang snake temple, when she'd been a girl, she had seen big snakes like boas and pythons in cages. But the little green vipers roamed around freely, dazed by the incense. Once, she had gone to the temple with her mother and some cousins. Her mother leaned too hard against a gate, dislodging a viper that was curled around the top, and screamed as the snake fell on her shoulder.

"Is all your family in Hong Kong?"

"Just my father. My mother's dead."

"Were you close to her?"

"She always made me feel safe." Rosemary paused, the memories taking over. It was strange, talking about her mother to him. She seldom spoke about her, even to Manky; the loss was still too difficult to bear.

"You know," she continued, almost to herself, "she told me once that I would always be safe if I took my fears and made up silly reasons for them to go away. I was pretty timid as a child, scared of the dark, of the 'oily man' - he was a kind of Malaysian bogey man - even of having to grow up. When I told her I wanted to be her little girl forever, she laughed and said my daddy wouldn't let me. I asked her why not and she said because then, he couldn't grow old and everyone has to grow old, but if she promised not to grow old would I stop being afraid? I didn't know what she meant, but somehow, that made me feel better, and I promised her. Silly reasons are better than no reasons, I guess, even if they make sense only in their own crazy way."

Danny was watching her closely.

"I'm rambling," she said, embarrassed.

"No," he said, "just remembering." He aimed his camera at her. "Smile."

She complied, grateful to break the strange mood brought on by remembrances.

"When did you start playing jazz?" she asked, as he snapped her.

"I don't know. Since I was about thirteen I think. My sister taught me, on the piano, and I spent a year listening to everything I could. Later, when I was about sixteen, I started hanging out in Boston with the students from Berklee. You know, the jazz school? This guy turned me onto Pepper Adams and bari sax, and I've been playing ever since. Yeah I know, I'm pretty good."

It was less of a boast than a statement of fact.

"But why this whole China thing? Why not music?"

He shrugged. "Who knows? I love the music, but it doesn't own me."

He spoke with such certainty, such finality, it seemed. Rosemary felt there was no leeway to probe further.

After he finished shooting and had put the snake back in its cage, he asked her, "So where's your husband?"

She explained.

"Then," he said, "I'll bring you flowers every day. Dozens of orchids to throw at your feet, like the royalty of Thailand."

"And what would you want in return?" She said this playfully, trying to be lighthearted. But she felt him encircling her with his persistence. It stimulated her in a new and unknown way.

"Nothing. Just to look at you. You're . . . special."

"Last time it was beautiful."

"Special and beautiful."

She needed the beautiful, even though she had declined his offer to spend the rest of the evening with him.

Danny and his goddamned snake!

She heard Man-Kit chuckling, somewhere in the distance, as she entwined the sheets around her legs in bed that night. Her only consolation was that she knew he was doing the same thing in his bed in Hong Kong.

It was five in the morning. Rosemary had slept badly, waking up every hour, tossing and turning all night. She got out of bed and took a drink of water.

She wanted to call Man-Kit, but knew that he'd be out with Sonny this afternoon. Besides, the telephone bill had arrived today, and the first of their long distance calls had shown up, much to her horror. There was no Manky now to soothe over the expenses, to juggle their finances in his usual, expert way.

And then, there was something about Danny.

Admit it, she told herself, you're hornier than hell.

An angry flash overtook her as she thought of Manky missing her, but not craving her the way she did him. Sex was a funny thing with him - it seemed he could take it or leave it.

She finished her glass of water and went to the bathroom to get another. The air was stiflingly humid; her sinuses reacted to the oppressive climate, clogging her nasal passages to an unbearable level. For the last three hours, she had fought a mounting desire to take a Sudafed. She gave in at last, and waited for the relief to set in as she sat up in bed.

The phone rang.

She grabbed it eagerly. "Manky?"

An unfamiliar woman's voice spoke in Cantonese. "*Hui siu je?*"

Hearing herself addressed formally by her family name, in Cantonese, took her aback. "Who's calling?"

"I'm your father's fiancée, *siu sing Chan,* 'humbly surnamed' Chan."

Rosemary felt the tension mount in her. She loathed what she considered pretentious Cantonese humility, even as she recognized this woman's words as simply the polite language of Hong Kong.

"Do you have any idea what time it is here?"

There was a short pause, and then she heard an exclamation, "Oh, I'm sorry, I miscalculated the time."

It figured, she thought, that her father would pick some bird brain to ease his post midlife crisis. Her mother, an energetic, intelligent and educated woman, emerged in her memory. What an insult. She would be absolutely rude to this woman, Hong Kong rude.

"Please forgive me," she continued. "Maybe I should call back."

"Well, you've woken me now. What can I do for you?"

"I wanted to introduce myself. Your husband said he told you about me, and that makes me think you can't be too happy."

Despite herself, Rosemary began to soften a little. But she couldn't let her guard down that easily.

"Well, you're right. I'm not happy."

"Please understand, it's not money I'm after. Your father said you will get a green card soon, and that you could get him one too. He said that if I married him, I could get one and that way I could also help my family leave Hong Kong."

So that was it. She listened on, unwilling to bestow an easy sympathy.

"You won't believe me now, I know. Your father doesn't know I'm calling you. He would probably be angry if he knew. But you must understand that I sincerely respect your father. He's a good man, very kind but so lonely. He likes me and just wants a little happiness for his old age. That's not so bad, is it? A man likes to feel young by having a young woman. I'm not very clever or wealthy, but I'm young and quite pretty."

The woman had spoken hurriedly. Rosemary heard the fear and apprehension in her voice. It was a strange desperation, something she had seen in some of her ESL foreign students here in the States.

Taking advantage of the silence, the woman continued. "Your father tells me you haven't been back to Hong Kong in six years. Things are very different now. You wouldn't recognize half the buildings along the waterfront on both sides of the harbor."

"Miss Chan, are you and my father formally engaged?"

"We have an understanding."

Rosemary sighed. Things seemed so ridiculously out of control, so far away from anything she knew.

"I believe your father needs me."

"You've made him need you."

"Please, you're angry. I apologize. I woke you up. You can't be expected to know how things are here. In the last week, especially, since Tiananmen.

"My mother left China almost forty years ago. Her family were landowners. You know what that meant in China. My mother is seventy, but she still hasn't forgotten what it was like then. My father died in China; he couldn't get out."

Rosemary's head began to spin. Her sinuses had cleared, but this woman's words nagged at her, forcing her into an uneasy acceptance of her plight. It wasn't that she had anything to fear, but she did have a duty to her mother. Rosemary forced herself to speak politely.

"Miss Chan, my father is free to do as he pleases. Of course, if he wishes to marry you, I will give you the proper respect. And if my father wants me to get him a green card when I have mine, I will do so. You understand, of course, that my father has to ask me."

"Then, Miss Hui, although I should really call you Mrs. Ho, we understand each other. I'm sorry to disturb you. I will not bother you again. Thank you."

She hung up.

The entire exchange, carried on in Cantonese, had an efficacy that collapsed time. Six years was a long time to be away from home, to adapt to and adopt the milieu of the university and surrounding New England towns. She found herself picturing this Chan woman - an artificial Hong Kong beauty with too much make up. But at least she had acknowledged Man-Kit's place in the family, and called her Mrs. Ho. Rosemary knew it had to be her father who had somehow conveyed that acceptance to Miss Chan.

A little glimmer of light peeped through her bedroom window. She would be exhausted in class this morning.

5

Rosemary barely made it through class. Then, her best writing student from Cape Verde failed to turn in his assignment on time, and the only excuse she could get out of him was that he hadn't finished his research. He was writing about a national hero in his country, and could not let go off his draft until it was perfect because, he said, too few people knew about his hero. She gave him an extension.

Around noon, Celia, who shared her office, said, "Rough morning?"

Celia Wong was an ethnic Chinese ESL Education grad student from Jamaica. She and Rosemary had commiserated over many a coffee break.

"I'm too soft on these kids," Rosemary moaned.

"So why don't you be the mean teacher who accepts no excuses?"

"You mean, force Chinese discipline on them."

"Discipline isn't just a Chinese trait."

Celia, she knew, made the kids toe the line much more than she did. Their other office mate, an Irish-American woman who had grown up in Japan, was even stricter than either she or Celia. Rosemary decided she was simply not cut out for teaching. Her students' personal miseries had a habit of emerging during conferences, sometimes to the detriment of their lessons.

ESL simply did not strike her as a sufficiently serious subject to discuss compared to the problems of adjustment that plagued her students!

"Come on," Celia chided, "what's really bothering you, darling, or are you just missing Manky?"

Celia always called him Manky, never Man-Kit, and there was almost always sympathy in Celia's voice, colored by her musical Jamaican accent Rosemary had come to like.

"I guess that's part of it."

Celia gathered up her books and papers into a tote bag, imprinted on the side with the logo of the local public radio station. "Well, whenever you want to talk, you know where to find Auntie Celia, if she doesn't find you first." She gave Rosemary a hug. "Got to go. Jamie'll be wanting his lunch," she said, referring to her four-year-old son.

Rosemary smiled at her. "Thanks."

It was late afternoon. Rosemary uncorked the bottle of wine and poured herself a glass. She undressed.

Manky, slender and sinewy, remarkably strong despite his slight frame, had been so extremely attractive to Hong Kong girls. She remembered the jealous stares of other women he knew when they had first started dating. And how she had revelled in that! Yet the only reason she had won him at all was that she was the first Hong Kong girl he had ever met who understood jazz.

And, she knew, she was the only Hong Kong girl he had ever met who would accept the independent, solitary life he demanded then, putting up with the temperament and moods he hid behind the mask of his friendly, flirtatious, social demeanor.

What was Manky doing this very moment, Rosemary wondered. He might be cruising the clubs, looking up old friends, and maybe, she considered jealously, even old girlfriends. Despite the reason for his trip home, she knew he was more than likely enjoying the reprieve from America, and her. She sank her body into the warm bubbles in the bathtub, feeling slightly giddy from the wine she had been drinking, feeling Manky's invisible fingers caress the loneliness out of her soul.

"What a most extraordinary thing!" Celia flung her papers and books on the desk as she entered the office. Her scarlet blouse, with a large, multi-colored macaw on the back, screamed out in contrast to her pale jeans. "Really most extraordinary," she repeated.

"What is?" Rosemary watched Celia's entrance, amused, relishing as she always did the musical quality of her accent and her customary flamboyance.

"Well this woman. In my class. She's from China and is giving Mandarin lessons to some young American kid half her age. He's asked her to marry him! And here's the best part - she's seriously considering it."

Rosemary felt a sudden stab. Surely it couldn't be . . . but, she reminded herself, there were many Mandarin tutors and students at UMASS. "Do you know him?" she asked as casually as she could.

"No, never met him. An-Mei's beautiful though - that's the woman in my class - so it wouldn't surprise me if some guy did fall in love with her. You know the kind I mean? The ones on some intent Tibetan quest who keep asking if their Mandarin pronunciation is correct?" Celia laughed, and her voice filled the room.

Rosemary couldn't help smiling. At any other time she'd have laughed along with Celia, who always made scathingly amusing comments about what she called "those other China watchers". Celia claimed to know only a "smidgin of pidgin Chinese", was more Jamaican than anything else, and loved to startle Americans out of their assumptions when they met her by answering their polite "about Chinese people" queries with "but darlings, why ask me? I'm Black."

"What's the matter Rosa-M? You're going all quiet on me."

It was difficult to hide anything from Celia. With her, everything was out front, no holds barred.

Celia shook her head. "Oh boy. I think it's coffee time."

Embarrassed, she half managed to tell Celia, as she knew she would, about Danny, of his unnerving presence and her physical attraction to him, especially in Man-Kit's absence. But she left out the part about how he pulled at something inside her, the jealousy she was feeling of An-Mei. That she couldn't explain to anyone, not even Manky.

"So you're wanting some," Celia said. "That's no crime. Hard man's good to find, you know."

"Oh Celia," Rosemary began to laugh.

"That's my girl, Rosa-M. You're taking all this way too seriously."

"But who wants to marry whom?"

"Who gives a shit? You know how these entanglements get

confused, especially when you're dealing with a Mainland Chinese! The point is, what are you going to do about it?"

"About what?"

"About . . . your 'problem'?"

"Oh that." Rosemary blushed.

"Cold showers," they said together.

Rosemary knew that Celia was, despite her stoic manner, someone with great empathy for the plight of others. Celia's had come to UMASS as a graduate student where she met and married a Black Jamaican poet. When she was pregnant, he had an affair with the wife of an English professor, a Swift scholar, a "classic case of misogyny derailed and Oreo cookie fantasy fulfilled, in one fell swoop - swift, eh?" In short, they eloped to Boston University where he got himself a poet-in-residency, and Celia was left to raise Jaimie on her own. No alimony. "Darling, a poet's money is like his sperm, ejected into the first available sewer."

Now, she worked as a teaching assistant and part time department administrator while finishing up her PhD. Celia did not waste unnecessary sympathy on herself.

Driving home, Rosemary reflected on everything Celia said. Her real "problem" was that she felt silly, because she had gotten caught up in Danny's little head game for lack of anything better to do.

But what had surprised her was Celia's reaction to the whole "marriage" thing between Danny and An-Mei.

"Do you know how many of my female students ask me about gay and straight men who have offered to marry them, some for a fee, some out of the goodness of their hearts? Or how many of my male students ask me if I think it's okay if some American girl who has fallen in love with them wants to marry them?"

Rosemary knew that none of her students had ever come to her about such things. Her students came crying about emotional longings, deep seated sadness, depressions brought on by the vagaries of fate, bitter sweet sorrows of homesickness. And she would let them cry, sure that the outburst of complaints was a sort of catharsis.

Celia's students, it seemed, came with solutions.

"But what do you say to them?" Rosemary had asked.

"The same thing. Don't ask the question unless you actually want to deal with the answer. Why ask? Immigration hasn't."

"And what do your students reply?"

"Oh, some go on about family honor, guys usually. Others waffle on about being caught. Some just want to know how to raise the money. And you know something else, not a single one of these foreign nationals, in my four years around this ESL program, has ever demonstrated a sign of suffering from some personal, ethical dilemma the way your friend seems to be suffering. You know what I've decided, Rosa-M? It's just simply not a question of ethics when the green card is the issue, at least, not if you're foreign."

Did ethics, like people, adapt to a foreign culture, Rosemary wondered as she pulled into her driveway.

At home, she put aside her dissertation and whirled into a frenzy of housecleaning. She plunged into every mundane chore she could find, any work that was Zen enough to free her from the confusion of thoughts and feelings.

It was two-and-a-half weeks since Man-Kit had left.

Any day now, she thought, as she dusted the baseboards, he would call and say that his father had died and that he would be home in a matter of days. And then when her Manky was back, everything would be right again.

They could even try to have the child they talked so much about.

She began to sweat. How good it felt to be able to sweat in cold New England. Manky was always incredulous that she never seemed to sweat, even in summer. To her, summers here were like winters compared to tropical Penang.

The phone rang. It was Man-Kit.

"Isn't it three in the morning?" she exclaimed.

"I know, couldn't sleep. Too damned humid and sticky."

He would not use air-conditioning. The perpetual air-conditioned indoor climate was something he detested about summers in Hong Kong.

"I'm listening to the one jazz program," he continued.

Any minute now, she thought, he would begin extemporizing, improvising. He had woken her often enough at three in the morning after a gig. Just to talk. He never expected her to respond.

"Surprising thing," he said, "I've realized how much I miss home. Hong Kong, I mean. Remember that house Ricky and Anna lived in, hidden by trees, right along the railroad track in Shatin?"

They were friends of Man-Kit, a Portuguese couple. Ricky had been a rock disk jockey on Radio Hong Kong's English language station. Anna was the personal secretary to some bigwig at the Hong Kong and Shanghai Bank.

"Anyway, that house didn't cost them much in rent, probably because it was so inconvenient to get to by public transport. And hell was it noisy! Remember those dinners during which the train would rumble past? Anna said she set her alarm by the train."

"We were always too stoned around them to notice," Rosemary reminded him.

"We could live in a house like that, you and I, Rosa-M. We could. We wouldn't have any trouble working in Hong Kong. It wouldn't be like in the States. The hell with 1997. We'll take our chances with our own kind."

He was silent for a moment. Rosemary could hear him brood, could hear his private voice warning him that it was too late to turn back. Games were necessary.

He started speaking again as suddenly as he had stopped.

"By the way, I ran into Anna. She's eight months pregnant, and looks absolutely wonderful. They still live in that house. She says hi.

You know, I played with Sonny during one of his rehearsals. Felt good to pick up the sticks again, even if it was rock. I stopped into the Jazz Club last weekend. You'd like the place. Thought about sitting in, but I chickened out. Pretty bad huh? God, I played better than any of those clowns. Maybe I just need to haul out the drum set again. I mean, that's why I had to go to America in the first place. Too little jazz in Hong Kong.

"And you know what? Why wait any longer, about children, I mean. I'll get that job, and we'll both be able to work legally. So we go to NYU, where that professor would love to have you part time, which is what you'd like, especially with a baby. Besides, if we had had a kid before, all our immigration problems could be solved because he or she would automatically be a citizen!"

Despite all the contradictions, all the dissonance of Man-Kit's solo, Rosemary felt the anxiety and tension that had plagued her melt away as she absorbed his words.

"Oh Manky, do you really think so?"

"Sure I do. We make life difficult for ourselves, don't we? Americans always talk about taking control of their lives. Well, that's what we need to do. Be Yankee."

Her exhilaration swelled as he continued to talk. It was this rapturous sensation, this overwhelming joy that made her feel Man-Kit owned her. Although the past year had been unusually difficult, their life together constantly swung in this pattern of highs and lows. Always, always, Man-Kit would break the tension that would build between the two extremes. He made her imagine all possibilities.

His drum set, each piece neatly locked away in its case in the hall closet, conjured itself up in her mind.

"And you know what else? The hell with this family of mine. If they can't see that there's no future in Hong Kong - I don't care if they're too scared to admit it or what, I'm tired of always being ragged on as a pessimist - we do what we want. That's always pulled us through before."

She could imagine him, stretched out on his family's sofa with the phone to his ear, his forehead damp with perspiration. Round about now, he would take off his glasses, rub the lenses against his shorts, cursing out his myopic condition. If he were here, he'd comment on her twenty twenty vision, either saying she was lucky to have been born in Malaysia instead of Hong Kong where everyone wore glasses, or simply placing his hand over her eyes and whispering, look, no fog.

"Of course it has," she assented. "It always has, ever since we rented that first, unbearably small room in that bitchy old woman's flat. Remember that?"

She heard him chuckle on the other end and wished she could see him, be with him, touch him. His shoulders were probably all tensed up, the way they always got when he was excited or under stress, and she wasn't there to massage them into relaxing.

"Hey Rosa-M, I don't really want to live in Hong Kong anymore. You know that was just talk, don't you? Everyone's scared here. Even Sonny admitted to me that he'd leave tomorrow if he could. Imagine! You know, Sonny doesn't have a passport, just a C.I. He was born in China.

"But dad said something in private to me. There's some talk, apparently, of Britain letting in a limited number of Hong Kong British subjects, which means civil servants like dad might have a way out. But you'll never believe what he said. He said that the British wouldn't do shit for the Chinese.

"So he tells me that if something happens to him, I'm to get mom and the girls out to America, since he's convinced that neither of my sisters will ever meet a man good enough for them to marry and maybe they'll meet someone "over there," as he puts it. He doesn't want them to go to Britain if we can help it, because, he claims, they'll be treated as badly as the Indians and Pakistanis. He made me promise. I did. Didn't know what else to say. I couldn't tell him what a long way off we still were from securing our own position."

Before he hung up, he added that his father's condition was worse, and that he loved her very much.

For the rest of the afternoon and into the early evening, she worked quite happily on her dissertation and forgot the housework. She did not think about Miss Chan and her father, or even about Danny. She did not eat dinner till almost ten o'clock. By the time she went to bed, she experienced a voluptuous sense of fatigue that she had not felt in a long time.

That night, she dreamt Danny's snake was slithering up her leg, and awoke suddenly, startled by the urgency of her dream.

6

But Danny did not go away. On Sunday, she went to the Midnite Lite with Celia.

Celia had not wanted to go at first, saying she had too much work to do, and that it would be difficult finding a sitter. But she had given in to Rosemary's cajoling. As she drove to meet Celia at the club, Rosemary wondered why she had been so insistent on doing this. It was as if she wanted Celia to anchor her.

As she drove to meet Celia at the club, Rosemary strained to see through the light drizzle of rain that blurred her windscreen. The hazy headlight glare captured the alternating darkness and light of the oncoming traffic.

The club was quiet. Summer kept the audience away. Rosemary bought herself and Celia beers and sat down at a table. Joel came over.

"I don't see you for over a year, and bang, you're here twice in a month."

She smiled. "It's like that. Improvising, I mean."

"Who's your friend?"

Celia extended her hand. "Celia Wong. I hope you guys are good. Rosa-M drags me down here when I should be home working."

Joel laughed. "We're slippery as a snake." He glanced slyly at Rosemary as he spoke.

He was not going to let her forget this, for all his own reasons. "Hey, Manky sends his love."

"Tell him to come home quick. You look lost without him." Joel stood up. "See you ladies later."

Rosemary began to feel hungry. It was a good sign, because it meant she had also begun to relax. She thought about french fries and onion rings. The band started their first set.

"How did you come to like jazz?" Celia continued. "I would hardly have thought of it as a Hong Kong thing."

"Oh, I suppose because of insomnia. This DJ, Tony da Costa, would come on at eleven or midnight and play jazz on Saturday nights. I started listening to his program when I was fourteen and never stopped." She swallowed a mouthful of beer and added, "Besides, it was music to masturbate by."

Celia laughed. It was a deep belly laugh. Rosemary had never laughed like that in her life, but she could feel it resonate. Everything was was going to be okay.

This was fun. This was like the old days when she hung out at jazz clubs with friends while Manky jammed. Back then, they never worried about regular meals or having to get up in the morning. They improvised. Life had an easy, natural flow. When Manky stopped playing, all that life ended, and, suddenly, they were almost as bad as their already professional friends back home who lived and breathed a clockwork regularity.

Celia nudged her out of her thoughts. "I think this is a friend of yours." Her head tilted towards a figure beside their table.

"Hello, Rosemary," said Danny. He had a beer in his hand.

She looked at him, and then at Celia. He was waiting to be asked to join them. When he was not, he pulled out a chair and sat down without being asked. Games.

"Hi, I'm Danny." He stuck out his hand to Celia, who shook it and introduced herself.

He turned to Rosemary. "So you girls out for a good time tonight?" It was a different pose. His voice was hard, edgy, aggressive. His face was unusually flushed. She thought perhaps he had drunk a lot.

"Where's your axe?" she asked.

"Didn't bring it. Nor the snake. Aren't you going to buy me a drink tonight, Rosemary?"

Rosemary disliked the agitation he created, but recognized the strong, if temporary, power this stranger exerted over her.

Celia sensed it too. She cleared her throat and said, "Anything going on here I ought to know about?"

"We're old friends, aren't we, Rosemary?"

Rosemary felt herself despairing. Why couldn't she think of something to say, something to ease the tension? She did that easily, automatically, with Manky, who owned her and had real power over her.

Her stomach muscles tightened. Suddenly, she wasn't hungry anymore. She looked at Celia, begging to be rescued.

"Aren't you An-Mei's friend?" Out of nowhere, it seemed, into the river of Joel's cool saxophone sound, Celia had dropped a stone.

"Why yes, how do you know her?" Danny's voice softened. Rosemary noticed he had smiled at the mention of An-Mei's name.

Celia continued. "She's in my class, and asked me to edit a translation for her. I remember seeing you with her when she came to pick up the piece."

"What was the translation?" Rosemary asked.

"The snake story." Danny and Celia chimed in together. They paused, and laughed as if sharing a private joke.

"Actually," Celia offered, "it was a dragon story, or rather a snake that became a dragon and created a gorge, called 'the gorge opened up by mistake.' It's an old Chinese tale."

"So tell. Jin tian wan shang women dou shih jong guo ren. We're all Chinese enough here tonight." Rosemary knew Celia understood more Chinese than she let on. Under the table,

Danny's knee brushed hers, stayed a moment, and moved away.

Celia complied. "It's the legend about the snake that became a dragon by drinking some magic waters. When he grew his scales and tail, he became very vain and wanted to head for the ocean where all dragons go. Every creature he met told him to go east along the river to the ocean, but he wouldn't listen because he thought the fish and tortoise who gave him advice too lowly for him. So he banged and crashed his way through the mountains, instead of following the river's path to the ocean. In this way, he opened up a gorge in the mountain-side."

"What happens to him?" Rosemary asked.

Danny interjected. "The gods punish the dragon for the destruction he causes, and execute him."

"And the gorge?"

"It remains for eternity.

"Later," Celia added, "the people in the nearby mountain village called the execution point the 'subdued dragon pillar'."

Rosemary reflected a moment. "Typical," she remarked at last, "Chinese don't like individuality. I mean, after all, the dragon was just asserting a little of his own identity, wasn't he?"

The music swelled. "Maybe, maybe not. The net result is a gorge and a story," Celia said.

"Don't you like the dragon, Rosemary?"

Danny's words, uttered in a low, lazy drawl, made Rosemary shiver. She looked at him, and saw his sly smile of complicity, urging her to bend to him, or was it only her imagination, fueled by desire?

"She's not the dragon type," Celia interposed, "are you Rosa-M?"

Rosemary knocked back the rest of her drink, excused herself, went to the bar and bought another. Joel was still at it. His solo wrapped itself tightly around her; the sax head forced its stare deep into her, Manky's stare.

She heard Danny saying to Celia as she returned, "So what year were you born?" and Celia replying, "Dragon. A good, fertile year," and both of them laughing. Perhaps this was just good fun, something she wished she understood. Had her marriage to Manky really changed her to the point that she couldn't just have fun?

Celia stood up as Rosemary returned. Listen, I've enjoyed this but I've got to go. The baby-sitter will be getting impatient by now."

Rosemary almost rose too, but changed her mind when she saw Celia's face.

"Don't leave on account of me," Celia said. She leaned over and hugged Rosemary. "I didn't say when to take the cold shower," she whispered.

She watched, a little reluctantly, as Celia left, a grin in her wake.

"So," Danny leaned closer, "now that your friend has left us alone."

"But we're not." She edged away.

"What do you mean?" he demanded, staying his ground.

"There's An-Mei." As she said this, she suddenly understood the hold she had on him, which lessened his power over her.

He pulled back abruptly, his expression cautious. She knew he was trying to figure out how much she knew.

"What do you want to do, Danny?"

"Right now? Guess?"

She averted her eyes, embarrassed.

Manky's lips, on her ear, caressed her memory. Damn

Danny and jazz and the beer she'd drunk! It wasn't fair. Life shouldn't insist on her making such choices.

Danny didn't move.

The music stopped. A feeble round of applause filled the club.

Joel walked towards her table.

"You weren't paying much attention to the music tonight." Joel challenged her, barely acknowledging Danny. "It's not like you Rosa-M."

"Blame it on the friends," she replied as lightheartedly as possible. But for just a moment, she heard Manky's voice, accusatory, from sometime in the past after one of his gigs, saying, "why weren't you paying attention tonight?"

"Friends?" Joel glanced sideways at Danny and walked away.

"Come on," Danny took her hand as he stood up. "Let's get some fresh air."

They walked outside to the back of the club which faced onto a parking lot. The humid heat permeated her body. She and Manky had stood there often, smoking pot in between sets. Sometimes, she hadn't gone when Manky hung out with the other musicians, and remained inside the club.

Danny held onto her hand.

"Look," she began, pulling back, even though she wanted to follow him, wanted to yield.

"It's okay, Rosemary, don't say anything."

They stopped behind the club in the shadows, the glare of the street lamp missing them by inches. She was more than a little giddy now, the effects of the beer tingling urgently through her body. Danny's eyes laughed into hers, and his rich, resonant voice caressed her. Right now, this moment, she could take him anywhere, quite unafraid. It was a delicious sensation.

He gently positioned her against a wall, his long fingers on her waist. She felt his hands move slowly down the side of her body, sliding down her back. The thin jersey dress she wore crumpled easily to the sensation as his fingers pressed gently into her thighs. He leaned closer to her, his head bent forward. She felt his breath down the front of her dress.

She was inundated by his closeness, his delectably slow persistence. It was almost what she wanted. All she had to do was lean towards him and acquiesce to this tenacious desire that now threatened to overwhelm her. She parted her lips.

He suddenly pulled away from her, and stepped backwards into the spotlight of the street lamp.

Before he could say anything, she said, "Let's go back to my place."

Then, he stretched out his long arms, and took both her hands in his. He raised her hands in the air and kissed them lightly. "I'll go collect my stuff," he said.

Rosemary leaned against the cool, brick wall for several minutes after he left. Had he wanted to, he could have had her right there, unresistant, against the building. A sudden flood of memories and voices assailed her - the encounters of the past fortnight with the still surreal Miss Chan, Danny and even Celia; the realization that her father was real, no matter how distant, as was her love and hatred for him; the persistence of her mother, so long buried from who she was and had become, evoked by Danny and his goddamned snake; Manky's absence, gnawing away at her, almost destroying her, despite the love that held them. She turned her face towards the wall and wept silently, unable to scream, unable to protest the horrible, empty feeling of abandonment that now engulfed her.

Her entire being was charged to a point she had never

before felt with anyone except Manky. "Games," she murmured, to the summer's night air.

Speeding along the highway. Eighty miles an hour.

Rosemary had passed her apartment about an hour ago and was near Hartford. The cooler air earlier that night had degenerated into a stubborn, humid warmth.

Her body murmured an angry protest.

Damn Manky! Where was he?

She was coming up to an exit.

Get off, she thought.

She braked, too suddenly, and sent the car careening in an unmanageable swerve down the ramp. A chilling flash of isolation brought her to her senses, and she steadied the car at the bottom of the ramp, but not without hitting the stop sign at an intersection, jolting her forward against the wheel.

For a long five minutes, she sat in the stopped vehicle, unable and unwilling to move, shaking.

A spotlight startled her into calm.

The police officer aimed a flashlight into her face. Rosemary grimaced.

"You want to step out, Miss?"

She complied.

He trained the beam towards the stop sign. Rosemary saw that there was no visible trace of damage on the sign. She must have slowed down more than she realized, she thought, relieved that her natural coordination had taken over.

"Are you okay?"

She kept her eyes level with his chin. "Just a little scared."

"You must have come down that ramp pretty fast."

For a second, she felt the familiar anger rise within her as she heard Manky chiding her about her reckless speeding. But the feeling faded almost as rapidly as it emerged at the concerned tone in the officer's voice. She instantly felt immensely foolish and contrite.

He continued. "Have you been drinking?"

"Just a couple of beers."

He studied her face. Rosemary took a deep gulp of the damp air.

"I'm sober, honest," she insisted, her confidence returning.

He looked down at her wedding ring.

"What's the matter? Have a fight with your husband?"

"Yes, kind of."

He smiled. "Go on. Go home now. You don't want to be out here at this hour."

Rosemary slid gratefully back behind the wheel. She drove the speed limit the entire way home.

Danny was waiting at her doorstep.

"Are you okay? I've been here a couple of hours." The concern in his voice was sincere, kind. "When I came out of the club and you weren't there . . ., oh, it doesn't matter anymore. Do you want me to go now?"

She touched his arm lightly. "No, come on in."

He followed her into the kitchen. She gave him a glass of water. It was a little past five and the sky was just beginning to lose its blackness.

Danny looked up from the glass. "You have the same last name as her. Well almost. You know, *gui xing Xu*."

His Mandarin accent was quite good. Because of the slightly sheepish expression on his face, he looked even younger than before, no older than one of her freshmen students.

She sat down opposite him. "You mean your Mandarin tutor, don't you?"

He nodded. Looking away from her, he said "An-Mei's from Beijing. She's asked me to marry her." His eyes turned tentatively towards her. "We're not lovers or anything . . . though we could be if she'd let me," the last part rushed, as if an afterthought. And then, "You do look a little like her."

We all look alike, Rosemary almost said, but bit her tongue. She was using the phrase too much. She heard the boy speaking, vulnerable yet appealing. Annoyingly so, she realized, unable, even now, to stem the rising jealousy against this other object of his dreamy attention.

He continued speaking, seemingly unaware of the effect he had on her. "But she wants to stay here and I can help if I marry her. All the more reason now since June 4. She's twice as old I am, and I very much want to help her. I don't know if I should do this or not.

He seemed in such a pained state. Rosemary believed him felt an anger welling in her at the unfairness of the situation An-Mei was in, at the unfairness of what she was asking Danny, and also at the passion this woman seemed to inspire in him.

"In China, she was a student of Chinese literature. For a long time after she graduated from Beijing Normal, she worked on a commune in Northern China. She doesn't talk about those days much. Do you know what she's studying at UMASS now? Engineering. Can you believe that? She said it was the easiest way for her to get into the exchange program. But she loves literature and language. It's easy to see that.

"She has an illegitimate child, you know, a little boy. She left him behind with the father. Since they're not married, she could marry me and get away with it. Once she gets her green card, or better yet, her American citizenship, she can divorce me, go back to Beijing and marry him, and then she can bring her whole family here. She has it all worked out."

He spoke with such a longing to ease the tension he had harbored within himself. Rosemary found herself wanting to take him in her arms, to comfort him, to love him passionately so that he could forget this pain, to forget this other Hui woman, this northern Chinese lover he so desired who probably was only manipulating him for her own ends.

"Should I do it?" he asked, and his large eyes, liquid and beautiful, held her like a deer captured in a headlight, frozen for a moment before its frightened flight.

"How long have you known her?" she asked.

"Three months."

Rosemary did not immediately respond. Three months! But she had to be fair. He was young, and appealing to her for help. Her thoughts shifted momentarily to her own situation. She and Man-Kit had entered the country on student visas to study for their Masters. He had since converted to a temporary H-1 work visa which he was hoping to use as a basis for his permanent residency, and she was still on F-1 student status as a doctoral candidate, although her time in the program was starting to run out. In fact, she sometimes believed that the only reason she was in a Phd program was to extend her visa in the easiest possible way, leaving the more complicated resolution of their long term status to Man-Kit. They had been too legal for Reagan's amnesty program, but not legal enough to become permanent residents. Man-Kit was still working out details with a potential employer in New York who had agreed to sponsor him. She knew that they were, in many ways, more fortunate than thousands of other legal and illegal immigrants in the country. And of course, they were from Hong Kong, not China, which made a world of difference.

But the uncertainty! She knew how awful it was, not knowing for sure whether or not a piece of paper would come through, a piece of paper that could change your whole life. And all the time, there were the stories of immigration raids in the middle of the night, nightmares of deportation, visions of having to leave and never being allowed to return.

She wanted to tell Danny, of course you must do this! You're empowered. You save her, so that one person, and maybe three persons in this case, could be freed from oppression, or at least, from unnecessary further anxiety.

But he was begging her judgment. She had to be fair, to him, and not to this unknown woman, this unknown "countrywoman" with whom he was obviously smitten. But Danny was smitten, or at least, vaguely in love with her too, the way he probably would be with any Chinese woman right now. It was the idea of a lover he wanted, one that would bring to life the jumbled learning in his head. Since he didn't even know the difference between China and Tibet, Rosemary suspected any Asian, not necessarily Chinese, woman would suffice. Manky's Vietnamese jazz singer flickered briefly across her mind.

"Three months is not a very long time," she said at last.

He stood up and began pacing her kitchen floor.

Why was he asking her? Because she looked like An-Mei? Rosemary found herself disliking this rival for Danny's attentions. Because he did not reply, she asked, "Are you in love with her?"

He stopped pacing and stood very still in the middle of the kitchen. "Yes. No. Oh, who knows? Have I fallen in love? Is that what this is about? She cried to me, you know, after she told me about her lover and child, and I comforted her and put her to sleep. I'd never seen anyone cry like that. It was as if she were crying for herself and the whole universe. She frightened me. And yet the next morning, it's like we're strangers, like it never happened."

He sat down again, as if exhausted by his speech. Rosemary poured him a glass of wine. Life was moving too rapidly for her, at an almost manic pace.

She had seen some of her female students cry like that. She had listened to some of her male students pour out confessions of loneliness and need just like Danny. Her students came from all over the world to face the isolation of a less-than-fertile promised land. She knew why Danny was asking her judgment.

He swallowed a mouthful of wine. "Is this fair, Rosemary? Is this right? I've only ever wanted to do the right thing."

The right thing! How American. A luxury in a world where people measured their lives in terms of green cards, acquired by lies and deception, even marriage. Danny's handsome face was drawn and tired, though the pallor of his complexion now had a rosy tinge of excitement. His forehead was creased with a frown, setting his large, Caucasian eyes even deeper into his face. Against his dark brown, almost black hair, the green of his eyes was startling, even a little surreal.

He had been gazing distractedly around him. Now, he looked directly at her, and caught her gaze. He smiled. She looked down into her glass, embarrassed, and sipped the wine to distract herself.

"When did you find all this out?" she asked.

He gulped down more wine. "Last night."

"I don't know you, Danny, " she replied, looking up at him. "I can't tell you what's right for you. It's a difficult thing she's asking of you, and an even more difficult thing you're asking of yourself."

His eyes lightened. There was a tenderness and openness about him she liked. It wasn't just pity or lust he elicited.

"Thanks," he said, calmer now. He reached across the table and touched her hand lightly. "I owe you."

The effect of his touch on her senses was powerful. She wanted to push his hand away, frightened by her desire for him. Yet all she would show him was a calm and composed face. "No you don't. That's what friends are for."

Danny stood up. He was remarkably lithe and tall, over six feet. The hairs on his legs and arms were a soft brown, not nearly as dark as the hair on his head, and they covered his skin like an airy layer of down. She could imagine his long arms encircling her entire body, and his legs between hers, the hairs caressing her skin. So different from Manky and his smooth, hairless skin.

"I've got to go," he said. He left, a few minutes later, his wine glass almost empty.

If only she could bring back the calm! Danny, it seemed, stirred up a lot more than the mere memory of a snake temple in Penang.

"It's late," she said, her classroom demeanor returning to save her. "I think I'll go to bed."

"Goodnight, Rosemary. Thank you for not being too angry with me."

Why, she wondered, was he so apologetic? It was almost six a.m.. Time for Celia's cold shower, and then she would call Manky. And then perhaps she might be able to sleep.

She wanted to call Manky after Danny left, but didn't dare because it would only be six in the morning in Hong Kong. Manky wouldn't mind; he could be awakened from the deepest sleep and be alert in a matter of seconds. But her sisters-in-law, whose bedroom was closest to the living room phone, would assail her in their rapid Cantonese and ask if she were chi sin crazy to call so early. Since they each could no longer have their own bedroom with Man-Kit's return, they would be even less sympathetic to an early morning phone call for no apparent emergency.

How could they, single as they still were, understand the bond and necessary communication between husband and wife?

In Hong Kong, she could have lorded her married status over them. She would have given them "lucky money" laisee packets at Chinese New Year, a gift given only by married persons and received only by single persons and children. And even her in-laws would have sided with her against their own daughters in any important family squabble. In Hong Kong, she would have been the adult as a married woman.

Here in the States, she felt more adult when she had been single, and more like a child as a married woman.

She rinsed out the wine glasses and dried them. The sky was only just beginning to lose its glow. Rosemary liked the long afternoons of summer. From the kitchen window, she could see across a field to the hills of the Pioneer Valley. Soon, it would be the season when all the trees ignited vales and hillsides with the fire of fall.

Autumn in New England was terribly soothing.

When she and Manky had first arrived at the University, they had lived in Amherst during their first two semesters. She had found that first fall semester a wonderfully calming time. Oh there had been the energy of new places, people, students, classes. But what she remembered most was the sense of freedom, of leaving behind the pervasive sense of restraint and disapproval that surrounded her affair with Man-Kit in Hong

Kong. Neither his family nor her family ever expressed anger, or ever were outwardly rude to them. Yet she knew, as he did, that because they had been unmarried in Hong Kong, their families, and even some of their friends, would never fully accept their being together.

Even their marriage, celebrated with neither family nor friends present - they hadn't told either family about the wedding - had taken place because at the time, Manky had gambled on obtaining a J-1 visa from his H-1, which meant she could get a J-2 as his spouse, both of which simplified their eventual applications for green cards.

Love, somehow, had nothing to do with anything.

But the phone rang again, insistent and loud.

"Rosa-M? I'm not waking you, am I?"

She almost cried in relief. Before she knew it, she was pouring out the whole, incomprehensible tale, about Danny, the Midnite Lite, her drive to nowhere and most of all, the horrible feeling of abandonment at being alone and needing him so badly that her life was completely off center. As she spoke, she felt the customary surge of comfort brought about by Manky's soothing presence. Quiet now, he was saying, as the words tumbled out through her tears. It's okay.

I won't leave you again, she heard him say, and she calmed down, her emotions more firmly in check. As she dried her eyes with the back of her hand, she began to wonder why in fact he had called.

"Is your father . . .?"

"He passed away this afternoon."

In that moment, she heard in his voice all the pain and bottled up sadness that demanded release. Yet there he was, calm, competent Manky, doing everything sensibly as always, comforting her instead, exhibiting no jealousy or anger, shouldering the responsibility of making their life continue.

The shock of reality calmed her like a spring rain, prodding her center into wakefulness, ensuring her survival.

"Oh Manky, I am sorry." She was more than sorry, feeling that she had let him down, that she had managed, as she often did, to grab center stage when what he was going through was so much more important. That her dependency and neediness hung heavily on him, preventing his necessary expression and release, until, too late, he would rage in anger at his inability to share his sorrow.

When he came home, she thought. Manky could explode when he came home. It was the only safe place for him too, she knew, picturing him calm, collected, while the rest of his family grieved.

"It's not your fault," he said. After a pause, he added, "I'm almost done with what I have to do Rosa-M. I'm coming home."

He told her he would take care of the funeral arrangements, and fly back to Massachusetts next Saturday.

7

On Wednesday morning, Rosemary saw Danny again.

He was in the corridor of Bartlett Hall by the classroom where she taught. He was carrying his bari sax case, but no snake. She knew at once that he had been waiting for her.

"I've decided about An-Mei," he said, as soon as he saw her.

The expectation in his voice! He was once again her student, begging her approval.

He didn't wait for her to ask. "I'm the dragon, aren't I? That's what she's been telling me all along. I have to sacrifice myself for her by taking the way I know is wrong."

How terribly idealistic he seemed. Yet his intensity persuaded her of the sincerity of his intentions. She wanted to ask him, and what about the music, or for that matter, the snake? Each of the faces he showed her seemed to disappear, as if her presence dissolved all these parts of him into nothingness.

Instead, she said, "Are you sure it's 'wrong'? Isn't the world full of dragons?"

They began walking towards her office.

"I'm selling my bari sax, by the way. To pay for my trip to China."

"When do you plan to go?"

"Soon. Once things are settled about An Mei. I'm going to Beijing to tell him, the father of her child I mean."

"And your snake?"

"Oh that." He gestured vaguely. "I guess I'll figure something out before I leave."

She wanted to tell him that none of his "sacrifice" would be worth much if he didn't somehow come closer to the meaning of his existence. And that all the passion, all the desire, all the heroism of his shouldering this white man's burden would dissipate.

But he wasn't looking for advice.

He stopped short. "I've bungled everything, haven't I, with you I mean. That's typical though." He looked petulant and unhappy.

His voice had a virginal quality that made Rosemary instantly realize how ridiculously young he was. It had been up to her to seduce Danny if that had been what she really wanted. Of course he would bungle it; his intent had never been to seduce, merely to experiment with a feeling he liked but didn't understand. She remembered Manky, the night she had caught the Vietnamese girl kissing him at a party. How he had pushed the girl away as Rosemary came into sight, and run after her saying, "please Rosa-M, it wasn't me." This wasn't the same. This had been her.

She put her hand on his arm. No tingling, no sensation. "Leyland," she said quietly. "Halfway through the alphabet."

His smile was all she needed. "You remembered."

"Someone once told me Rosemary means remembrance."

He walked her to her office door.

She touched his elbow. "Take care of yourself, Danny."

"I will," he said. Then, leaning forward, he kissed her cheek, and she whispered in his ear, *"Zai jian."*

Celia's infectiously warm grin greeted her. "Hey Rosa-M, what was that all about?"

"Oh, snakes and dragons, I guess," she replied, smiling a little dreamily. "Even dragons have to come down to earth in time. But we do say 'see you again', not goodbye, in Chinese."

Celia shook her head. "You're just too Chinese, darling," she said, a wry smile on her face.

Rosemary tried to stack her pile of papers on the desk. They slid into an untidy heap on the surface.

"You know," Celia observed after a short silence, "you're altogether too much in love with Man-Kit."

"It helps me feel invulnerable."

"There's nothing wrong with being vulnerable."

Rosemary riffled through her papers. "Isn't there?" she demanded.

"But you're too hot blooded, Rosa-M."

"So is he."

"Then maybe you both just need to cool down, or something."

Rosemary grinned. "Come on, Celia. It's just summer."

On her way home that afternoon, she listened to the China news reports on her car radio. The fear had subsided, and a certain amount of resignation had set in. But, said the announcer, among the students, there still was hope. She did not switch off the radio. At least, she decided, the worst was probably over, although the tremors would prevail for a long time to come.

That evening, Man-Kit called. His father's funeral arrangements had all been made and would take place on Thursday. He would fly back on Friday instead.

That night she had a dream. She was sitting naked, except for an orchid between her legs, at the bar in The Midnite Lite. Man-Kit was jamming with Joel and the band. Danny was playing a solo, coaxing long, languid notes out of his bari sax, playing even better than he really did. Danny's snake, which was in its cage at her feet, slithered out and up along the barstool around her legs. It coiled around her waist, its head brushing the petals of the orchid. Its unblinking eyes held hers as it slid further up along her arm, and stopped at her left elbow.

And then, the snake glided off in a single, rapid motion, and writhed away across the floor towards the bandstand, towards its master.

Rosemary woke up. Her covers were in disarray. She got out of bed and stood naked by the window, sipping the glass of water she kept each night on her nightstand.

In two days, Manky would be home.

They would make love silently as they always did. And then,

he would talk about his father. He would grieve at last, the way he hadn't been able to in Hong Kong, and cry like a child in her arms.

Then when the grief eventually passed, he would talk, with his usual impatience, about the rest of the trip and their life. He might complain about the company and the bureaucratic delay surrounding his visa. He might worry about his mother and sisters who, she knew, had no desire to move to America no matter what his father had said. He might say he wished they could take a vacation, and she might stifle her inclination to say not in the middle of the summer semester. He might tell her about all their old friends in Hong Kong, making her nostalgic, and say that he wished there were a realistic way for them to live there, at least for awhile.

They would even have a little fight, brought about by the tension of their time apart, after which they could make up and make love, perhaps without her diaphragm.

And Manky might actually take up his sticks again.

Hillsides and gorges opening up. Dragons in China.

It was starting to be light now.

The Pioneer Valley glimmered in the distance, green and lush. Rosemary pushed the window completely open. If only autumn would come. Autumn, with its crisp red falling leaves, meant a return to something sure and definite, something less shrill and edgy than the symphony of summer. Pieces fell into place during a New England autumn, as solid and firm as the pumpkins and gourds that crowded the vegetable stands along Route 9.

By autumn, China and June 4 in Tiananmen Square and its impact on Hong Kong and Chinese people everywhere would already have begun to fade into the recesses of remembrance, dulling the pain of a fresh wound.

By autumn, Manky could begin to put behind him the memories of Hong Kong and his father's death.

No, nothing would change when Manky returned, not in any perceivable way. The echoes of all that had happened would continue to resound for a long time. Now, the echoes of future feelings and words tumbled rapidly around her.

Through this jumble, their joint destiny together slowly emerged before her as a winding river full of strange and yet undiscovered life forms. Shadows and sunlight zigzagged this way and that, obscuring the banks and waters, concealing the flow from her. Rosemary listened hard in the distance, trying to hear the murmuring message of the water, hearing only the sounds of a solo, long forgotten, a remembrance of an earlier jazz life. Merging sight and sound, she knew the meaning of harmony, the meaning of all those musical terms Manky had tried to teach her. Why he always insisted that music had to be experienced live, so that you could see, smell, taste and feel what you were hearing with all your senses. And then she saw it, the end of that river, glimpsed through a thin veil of uncertain mist which might, as long she kept her eyes trained on it, eventually lift and lead, one day, to the ocean

LOVING GRAHAM

Short Story

Why is Boston always so cold?

Sixty Minutes . . . oh, what the hell does *Sixty Minutes* know? They're saying it's almost the year of the ram in Hong Kong, a city on the verge of 1997 which is when China can reclaim sovereignty, and that people are now wary, mistrustful and running away. Take it from me - being Hong Kong Chinese was always about being wary, mistrustful and running away.

When will the heat in this apartment come on?

I'm tired. Alan can keep his house, his trust fund, his best friend and his ego. I don't care if he thinks that I seduced Norman or that I'm sick and amoral. You know, adultery with his "best" friend wasn't the worst thing I could have done. What did he expect? He was never around, and Norman was. I can't stomach any more of his New England moral and intellectual vigor. I miss Hong Kong. I want to go back.

Mother can cry her eyes out, but Alan will be there to commiserate, the way Philip was there to commiserate when he divorced me way back when marriage mattered even more in my life. My parents and my ex-husbands: the happier families.

Where is that divorce lawyer?

I just want something that feels a bit like love, if not marriage.

Like loving Graham.

I met Graham Maitland in Hong Kong in the April of '79, exactly thirteen months after my divorce from Philip.

Alan and I were at a concert, Rachmaninoff, I think. Free tickets, of course, because the pianist was a rising young Vietnamese-Chinese star from Julliard, and the American embassy would want Alan Berman, one of the first American foreign correspondents in China, to be among the guests of honor.

I spent pre-curtain, intermission and post-curtain tagging along while Alan said hello to everyone.

Graham came along during intermission.

He was escorting an American client's wife, the client being in Tokyo that evening. She knew Alan and cornered him, and, after introductions - Alan's standard one for me being, by the way, she's Hui Man Ming's daughter - the two of them chattered away about the importance of Alan's upcoming assignment to Beijing, although I could see it wasn't his assignment she was really interested in.

Graham stared at me with his amazing grey eyes. I couldn't help staring back. He was tall - taller than Alan - and slender, almost thin, with wildly curly hair.

Long in Hong Kong what do you do? - I asked.

Half a year merchant banking - and he named a small, British firm which I knew.

I handed him my card in exchange for his.

He glanced at it and smiled - Chase Manhattan? Why?

Wharton, MBA - I told him, never taking my eyes off him.

How American of you.

Then I'll take it one step further. Let's do business, I said.

Yes, let's, Ms. Hui, he replied.

I was wearing a short, off-one-shoulder, crimson silk dress, and three inch heels - the kind of outfit Alan complained was too showy. But I saw how he relished the jealous glances of other men when we appeared together in public. Philip was the same way. The slut factor.

Graham's eyes traveled all over me. Blatantly.

My body blushed.

And will you go to China with your friend? - His eyes whispered the insinuation of his undertone.

You know I won't - I replied, and as soon as I said it he smiled in a way that told me he knew, saying - Then give me a call, sometime.

How could Alan have missed all that?

But then, Alan always missed things. Eight years of marriage and all his traipsing round the globe - surely he didn't think his catching me with Norman that once was the only time. I don't know what Norman told him. I tried with Alan, honestly I did. Once we moved to the States I stopped having affairs. Until Norman. What I don't understand is how I screwed up in almost exactly the same way twice. First Philip and his dear friend William, and now Alan and Norman. But best friends get reinstated with my husbands in a way that I can't.

Graham wouldn't have divorced me.

Where is that lawyer?

I might not have called Graham if Alan hadn't slighted him as a "pretty boy." Well, maybe that's not true. I probably was going to call Graham regardless. I still remember the sneer in Alan's voice, saying, poor Jane (or whatever the woman's name was), stuck with pretty boy when what she really needs is intelligent conversation.

How fortunate for her you were there then, I remarked, Yes it was, he replied in total earnestness, she really is an intelligent woman.

That did it.

The day I called Graham, Alan was preparing for his fling with celibacy, which was what he called his pending assignment to Beijing. Alan was flurrying, which is his second favorite state, the first being flurrying in the midst of any major political crisis that would ensure a front page byline.

How marvellous that you did call, I'd been thinking of you, Graham said, Is your friend away?

I smiled into the phone and replied, Almost.

Although, he continued - and there was the slightest hesitation in his voice - I hear he's more than just a friend?

But that isn't what matters to you, is it? - I replied.

I can't say why I knew, but clearly he knew I knew, because I heard that smile in his voice, the same callous, ice-cold smile I've seen on my face and heard in my voice whenever I'm about to do something that I'll apologize for, if I'm caught.

I think that was when I first had an inkling I could fall in love with Graham.

In fairness to Alan, Graham was something of a pretty boy. He could have been a fashion model, with his bedroom eyes and gigolo looks (I knew he had to be a good dancer, and he was). Even when he spoke seriously, he managed to sound frivolous.

Like about Anne, his ex-wife. An earl's daughter. Their marriage broke up when he was found dipping into clients' funds to expand his own portfolio. The real reason was that he had been sleeping with the wives of two of the partners at the London merchant banking firm where he worked. Which is how he ended up - in his words - banished to the colonies.

Graham told me this over wine and lunch the first time we met.

Mother was awfully upset - he said, a wry smile on his lips. She said she was glad Father wasn't alive to see it, since he adored Anne.

Everyone adored Anne, didn't they? - I asked and then I saw that smile, and the pretty boy face vanished.

Maybe I'm wrong, since Graham was so long ago, but I think we fell in love with each other at our first meal. I remembered I giggled first, and then Graham chortled and finally broke into laughter. And then he said, your turn, and I told him about Philip Shen and the adultery with William Cheung but the public excuse was my announcing at a joint family function that I did not plan to have children, which I later followed up by sterilizing myself.

Well, I don't like loose ends, and I knew I'd make a lousy mother - I said - and I was fed up of mucking with birth control. Of course, neither his family nor mine saw things my way, and Philip is a family man.

Graham dipped his finger in the wine, anointed my lips and whispered - the silence of the damned.

Oh I know we were drunk and behaving shamefully. It was exhilarating. Somehow, in our silent pact, I knew he understood the really bad part of me, the part that could never love a Philip, or, as I know now, an Alan.

We were at that French place at the top of the Mandarin Hotel, the one where the menus don't even list prices, and I knew without being told that Graham was writing the whole thing off on his company's expense, as he would all those expensive meals to follow, although he personally paid for the trip we took together to Bali. It was so refreshingly different from Alan, who was a tightwad, just like my father.

After all, I'm the kind of woman husbands love to be ashamed of.

Funny thing, my knowing this now. Must be age. I was twenty five, and Graham twenty nine. Alan knew he was wiser at thirty three. Back then, I think I had an idea, but didn't know for certain.

I remember the day Alan fell in love with me. We had just had sex on a Sunday afternoon when nothing was happening in China, during one of his trips to Hong Kong. I had been dating him for about eight months. He had met my parents who adored him, because he considered my dad famous, spoke Chinese fluently, had done Chinese literature and studies at Harvard and pretended that he and I were not engaging in pre-marital sex. The first time I stayed at his parents' house in New England, we slept in separate bedrooms.

Anyway, I was lying there thinking of Graham when Alan started tracing his fingers over my lips. Why do men always want to touch my mouth?

You have a sensuous mouth, he said. The first time I saw it, I knew it could, well, you know. And then, he told me he thought he could spend his life with me.

My first husband Philip was a lot less subtle - he was a press relations officer for the Trade Development Council. You'd make a great prostitute, he told me on our wedding night. And he meant that, sincerely, as a compliment.

The slut factor. That's what both my husbands wanted in marriage. They looked the other way when it suited them as long as I was discreet and they got what they wanted in bed.

And I knew how to give them what they wanted. It was the same deal their so-called best buddies, and all those others in between, expected from me, as long as the boundaries of marriage remained. It's as old as the great wall: keeping civilization in check and the barbarians at bay. I guess I understand.

Why the hell doesn't the heat come on properly in this apartment?

Loving Graham is the one sane thing I've done in all my thirty six years. He was the only man who pulled me up for air.

Graham and I didn't have sex more than three times in our eighteen month love affair. And I think we did only because . . . .

Round about our fourth date - although being with Graham wasn't really like dating except in a teenage sort of way - he finally popped the question.

So why Alan?

My parents adore him. Dad especially.

Your father's a pretty famous intellectual, isn't he?

He was in China, once. He's something of an expert on modern Chinese literature before the Cultural Revolution. But you know how fame is - only as good as those who acknowledge it.

And your mother?

I let her down once with Philip. She's still not over it, especially the way it ended. I've told her Alan doesn't want children. But all she says is I didn't have to cut off my womanhood, and that I'm unnatural, and she didn't raise me to be a bad woman, and what kind of mother would people think she was? Besides, Alan's American.

Is America where your parents want to go?

Yes. That's why they sent me to the U.S. to study.

They loathe the British, don't they?

No. They're pragmatic. Big pictures matter to them when it's expedient to do so.

And they left China . . . .?

With difficulty and hardship, of course. My mother and I came to Hong Kong first, and Dad did time being "reformed." He made a big sacrifice to ensure my liberty.

So what about Philip? Isn't he a British lackey?

He's Chinese. Racism isn't an exclusively Western thing. Besides, I've known him since I was twelve, and he did at least do graduate work in the U.S.

What about you?

What about me?

Poor baby, he said, and anointed my lips with wine again, only this time, he wasn't laughing at all.

Graham understood. His father, a consummate Royalist, had ensured his eldest son's Harrow-Cambridge career ending in marriage to an earl's daughter. He showed me a picture of Anne once. She looked like Princess Di with longer hair.

My mother would give you tea, he said, a little wistfully.

But only as a passing visitor, right?

She means well, he replied.

They always do.

There's never been anyone like Graham in my life before him or since.

I'm not trying to blame my parents, honestly I'm not. They're good people, decent people, full of ordinary human fears. They just wanted the best life for their only child, and themselves. It's being my father's daughter that's difficult. Hui Man Ming didn't think much of statistics, finance and my MBA, which weren't "genuine intellectual pursuits". I'd be a better person to him if I were a poet and a scholar. But then,

I wouldn't be in the position to take care of him and mother in case I didn't marry, and I am only a girl. My parents wanted a son, but Dad dried up after me.

I have looked after them though - I've always given them forty percent of my more than adequate salary as long as I've been working. Filial piety. Very Chinese, which is what my parents, and even I will always be, despite our Western-style lives. Alan understood.

Graham simply wouldn't have cut it in the parental scheme of things.

He said I had a great body and great legs which should be flaunted, at least on weekends. I'm tall for a Hong Kong Chinese woman, almost five feet seven, and I'm all legs. I would wear skin tight mini dresses with nothing underneath and do the round of parties with him. And he'd wear an off white suit with a turquoise or orange silk shirt that practically glowed in the dark. On Graham's boat parties, I'd wait till everyone was drunk enough and lead the women in taking off bikini tops. People talked. I told Alan that people liked to talk and that Graham and I had a business relationship. Alan believed me, because he wanted to, because he wouldn't be caught dead with Graham's crowd anyway, because I said the right things to the right people about him, because I was a convenient fuck when he got time off from China. As long as I was there when he wanted me. And I was there, at Graham's expense, which was a big mistake.

The bottom line is that I really wasn't having an affair with Graham.

I was just in love with him.

It's crazy, I know, but Graham and I didn't care about the hallowed sex act. We just liked to tease. We'd drive out to the villages in the New Territories or to the beaches on the south side of the island at two in the morning, and feel each other up in the back seat of his Prelude. And he thought nothing of running his hand under my blouse or up my skirt in any semi private corner at a party. Once, at a dinner, he kept his hand up my thigh all during dessert. The very proper gentleman on the other side of me, who pretended not to see us, spent a rather long time in the bathroom afterwards.

Loving Graham is like plunging into the South China Sea at the height of the worst typhoon.

Alan was posted to Beijing for a year and a half. He came to Hong Kong every other month for a week, and wanted it badly when he arrived. He didn't want to get engaged while he was still in China, which was fine by me, although my mother found this distressing. I don't know why. She and my father were separated for seven years but remained true to each other, my mother never giving up hope and helping to engineer Dad's release. My father the victim of history, and my mother the worshipping wife. The perfect love. Alan was almost in tears when they told him their story.

My parents are a hard act to follow.

What Alan didn't know, or pretended not to know about were all the men I did sleep with behind his back. It was easy having affairs in Hong Kong, and I couldn't seem to help myself. After all, no one got hurt since no marriages broke up except mine, and that was only because . . . oh who knows why for sure? I guess Alan's right. I'm not cut out for marriage.

Graham helped matters. He and I procured for each other. I introduced him to a slender, almost anorexic English girl who waterskiied beautifully and was married to the dullest Scottish auditor. Graham is as graceful on skis as he is on a dance floor.

Graham introduced me to his client, Jane's husband (I call

her Jane because I never can remember her name). He met me in Tokyo during a conveniently arranged joint business trip. I felt a strange vindication screwing him while his wife's lust for Alan remained unfulfilled.

I liked procuring and enjoyed liaisons that required discretion. So did Graham. After all, that's more or less what we both did for a living. We introduced people, made money for people, found money for people - discreetly, without any fuss or bother, without asking difficult questions of morality - for a price.

But ultimately, I'll pay, or so Alan says, just like I'll pay for being promiscuous.

I don't deny I was promiscuous. Jane's husband wasn't the only one. Alan probably knew but pretended not to. Oh, Alan knew. The day he told my father he wanted to marry me, my father approved saying, good, maybe you can settle her down, and they both laughed knowingly, while my mother simply looked puzzled.

With Alan and Philip in Hong Kong, there didn't seem to be any other way to be. Life was one constant race, like the horses at Happy Valley racetrack, and my husbands had to win or place. I was the long shot. Then there were their confirmed bachelor "best friends," whom they asked to take care of me while they scurried through their frenzied, successful careers. Norman hung around me with hungry eyes in Alan's absence, having spent his life in Alan's shadow. And William? William said he and Philip went to their first prostitutes together, and that they shared all their women.

I wish that lawyer would get here with those divorce papers so that I can get this marriage over with.

I should switch this TV off. Norman used to come over for dinner and watch *Sixty Minutes* with me when Alan was away, and what with the wine and the fact that I was bored and lonely and homesick for Hong Kong, Norman did the trick.

Sixty Minutes is such a joke. They go to Hong Kong once and do this great in-depth story on the psychology of the Hong Kong Chinese *vis à vis* the 1997 changeover in political rule. They should interview my father in California - he would love that. Oh yes, Alan did a great job stage managing their immigration. Pulled all the right strings at the Consulate to speed things up, even got Dad a part time position teaching Chinese at Berkeley - to make him feel important again. Philip, dear boy, is taking advantage of the Canadian government's immigration point system to qualify for his visa. Hong Kong British though he is, he wouldn't be caught dead in Britain.

I think England would be rather nice.

I wish my father had sent me to Cambridge instead of Penn, although he'd sooner disown me than have done that. Besides, he had to pull strings through the U.S.-China Cultural Exchange, where he worked as an assistant administrator, to get me scholarships for which I am grateful, since I otherwise couldn't have afforded college abroad.

I like tea. Boston's weather is no better than London's, which is where, I imagine Graham probably is now. Oh Alan tried. He made sure I'd settle right in here with a decent job at First Boston and all, but the only reason I came is because of him, because somehow, marriage was still important then even if monogamy was a bore, because at least my parents approved of me for a little while.

Now that things are clearly over between me and Alan, I should go back. Everyone's leaving, so there are plenty of jobs. I don't need to run away from Hong Kong. Communists, colonialists, capitalists - what's the difference? It's not the system that counts but surviving the system. The desperation *Sixty Minutes* keeps associating with Hong Kong people and our political future . . . isn't desperation most of what life's all about?

But all this politics and sex stuff has nothing to do with anything. I've listened to endless debates and discussions by the likes of Alan and my father about politics. And I've endured as many of Alan's lectures about sex and morality as I can possibly stand. With Alan, it was always imperative to work towards mutual satisfaction during lovemaking. Once he got over the novelty of being married to a bad girl, he wanted sex to be some ultimate expression of love, and dragged me to three different sex therapists to sort out my "problem." I think that was when I began to come apart.

Boston has not been the liberating experience Alan assured me it would be. You see, Alan didn't accuse me of frigidity until we moved to Boston.

Graham knew from the start I was frigid, just like I knew he was impotent. He could only get excited enough to have sex after hours of foreplay, which made him a great one night stand with other men's wives. I hardly feel a thing during sex. Which was why he could turn me on with his teasing and games, while Philip and Alan and the slew of others couldn't do a thing with me. He didn't put much store in the sex act itself, just in all the trappings around it. It was the way I liked it, the way I truly experienced the physical pleasure that Alan couldn't coax out of me, despite all his forays into Freud, Jung and the *Kama Sutra.*

Besides, Graham wasn't impotent around me.

He told me Anne told all their friends that three doctors had said the reason she didn't get pregnant had nothing to do with her. He didn't blame her though, anymore than I blame Alan or Philip.

Alan wasn't completely deceived. He asked me once how I kept myself amused in his absence. I told him I had friends, but said I waited for him. He liked that. The funny thing was that Alan liked me to be independent, especially in having a lucrative job and knowing lots of people. But he was horribly jealous of Graham. I suppose he was right to be jealous. I could have left him for Graham.

But the fact is Alan preempted me. We almost didn't get married because of Graham. This was shortly before his stint in China ended in '81, after which he was going to be based in Hong Kong.

He said he had serious doubts about our future together because we were too different. He pointed to Graham as the prime example of that difference. I simply wasn't sufficiently serious which, he was quick to point out, he couldn't understand since my parents were the most cultured, intelligent and wonderful people he knew. Why I persisted in adolescent outrages with the likes of Graham was beyond him. It wasn't proper, especially in Hong Kong - couldn't I see that I was even beginning to suffer professionally? Graham was a poor business relationship to cultivate. Why couldn't I consort with the likes of Jane and her husband? As president of the Association of American University Women, Jane knew all the right people.

I chose not to point out Jane's husband's idea of consorting.

So, Alan concluded, it was best if we cooled off for awhile - of course we'd be free to see other people - and see how things worked out.

He told me this right after the evening I was late for a dinner with several of his important friends, Jane and husband included, because I'd been out that afternoon on another of

Graham's boat parties.

I didn't stay with Alan that night.

Instead, I hailed a taxi and went straight to Graham's flat.

It's over, I told him.

He stared at me with his amazing grey eyes, almost, it seemed, in disbelief.

But your parents?

They don't know yet.

He smiled that smile and said, then let's go to Bali before they find out.

The first time Graham and I had sex was in Bali. It was like Eden there. The beaches stretch out along miles of blackish sand, and at sunset, the skies scream with scarlet fire. Graham found us these huts right on the beach, away from all the resort hotels. And then he bought us magic mushrooms, the natural LSD kind, and after a bowl of magic mushroom soup I was flying along the nudist beach where only the European tourists go.

Sex was an afterthought.

All through my psychedelic high, Graham laughed and called me his Alice, his pretty girl. It was a comforting feeling, being in Wonderland. We were naked on the beach, and all that sex stuff was as faraway and remote as the North Pole. I couldn't imagine doing anything like that with Alan or Philip. Alan meant being serious and sensual and real, all of which weighed on me like an albatross rotting in the sunshine.

I can't even remember whether or not I had an orgasm.

Coming back to Hong Kong was a downer. My mother cried for days, saying that I was ruining my life all over again and wasn't once with Philip enough? She said I was stupid and worthless despite all my advantages, advantages she never had, and how could I let a wonderful man like Alan go?

My father was stern and silent. He's a lot like Alan, stoic to a fault, with a strong sense of moral outrage when it suits him. It was his years of suffering in China as the uncompromising intellectual that did it, separated from my mother and me in Hong Kong, that he's held over my head all my life as if I were to blame. When he lashed out at me, it was about Graham. My father had heard, from Alan of course, about Graham's financial misstep that brought him to Hong Kong in the first place.

I could tell they would not be open to the idea of meeting Graham.

Graham was wonderful to me during the aftermath of my break up with Alan. He spent all his free time with me. I remember he bought me a deep green silk dress with a low back. It cheered me up marvelously when I tried it on at his flat. Alan didn't believe in indulging my wardrobe. Graham also sent me a dozen orchids every week for three months. I know it was silly and extravagant and frivolous. But he made me feel good for who I was, not for who I was supposed to be in my career track MBA position, or as the socially responsible future wife of Alan Berman, or as the daughter of Hui Man Ming.

Those were the happiest months of my life.

Why did marrying Alan matter so much to me?

You need him, don't you? Graham said.

To immigrate you mean? My father could set it up if he tried.

But he wants you to do it, doesn't he?

I could try through my job.

You and how many others? Besides, you need him for more than that, don't you?

We were sitting on his roof in our swimsuits eating raw,

sliced tomatoes. He was right of course, the way he always was. I couldn't really arrange anything through my job. I didn't have the wherewithal. I've always gotten by because I cater to just enough of the right people, not because I have any strength of character and certainly not because I have the courage of any convictions, the way Alan or my father have. Besides, I knew, although my parents didn't, that I was beginning to slide off track professionally. I could probably coast for a long time, especially if I continued to cater to my base of clients, the ones who needed a veneer of respectability to shelter the profits of their questionable activities. The bank didn't care, as long as their end was legal. I couldn't take my job seriously, investing all that money for people who had too much of it to begin with. What did it really matter if the market was going up, down or collapsing?

You're on the verge, Graham said.

I wish I weren't.

Graham was silent for a long time, over an hour. Finally - Make up with him.

But that means . . . .

He took both my hands in his and kissed them. Don't cry my love. We've had our honeymoon, he said.

We stared at each other for a long time, and his grey eyes were warmly liquid like the hot springs of Java. Just him and me, with me on the verge.

He finally made love to me at around five in the morning. He was gentle and considerate, almost as earnest as Alan. It was different with Graham, though. Better. I didn't have to work for his approval.

So I gave Graham up. It took more than half a year to bring Alan around. What I had to go through! He "reformed" my wardrobe - by this time, he called my clothes indecent, not just showy - and dragged me to every serious lecture and cultural event he could find. I had to promise not to see Graham anymore, a promise I broke only once. But Alan came round in the end because he couldn't stay away. The slut factor. Works every time.

Why did Graham let me go?

Graham was eons ago. He married the waterskiier who left the Scottish auditor. His marriage didn't last either; his fault, naturally. He got caught with a client's wife while staying at the man's home in Singapore. The story flew to Hong Kong's financial community since the man was well known, and his wife liked to kiss and tell. Alan delighted in telling me all about it. This was about two years ago. I don't know what happened to him after that.

What's so damned important about marriage? About family? They haven't anything to do with love.

If that attorney doesn't get here soon, or the heat come on properly, I'm going straight to Logan International and getting on board the next flight to Hong Kong.

The last time I saw Graham, it was purely by chance. We were at the Equatorial Hotel in Kuala Lumpur on business. It was shortly before I was to move to Boston.

I've missed you, he said.

Me too.

Will you like Boston?

I doubt it, I replied.

It's awfully far away, from everything you're used to, I mean.

I'll have to be good then, won't I?

Will you be good for long?

I don't know. How about you?

I doubt I'll have the courage, he said.

Alan has tons of courage. He won a Pulitzer for his outspoken reports on the conditions in China. These days, he's interviewing my parents and all their friends who left China and Hong Kong and are safe in America. The ones who now want to "speak out." He'll probably be acclaimed, at least by the American press, for reporting the outrage that the British government is perpetrating on Hong Kong as 1997 approaches. My parents are proud of him and ashamed of me. I've apologized to no avail.

The last night I spent with Graham, he said - let's go for a swim, Ms. Hui.

It was around four in the morning. We had hours ago called our spouses to say we were turning in early. We had also finished two bottles of wine over the sexiest dinner I'd had in a long time.

The air was about eighty five degrees, and the water in the pool wasn't a whole lot cooler. I stripped completely and dove in. Graham followed. And there under the water, minutes before the security guards scurried out with their flashlights, Graham entered me and made me burst with the pleasure that Alan could never make me feel.

So maybe I don't know about marriage and never will. Alan said so. But he also said I couldn't love, because I was shallow and amoral and didn't have the courage or selflessness to know what truly matters in life.

He's wrong, you know. At least about the love part.

THE STONE WINDOW

A Story in Four Parts

1
The Benefactor

The second week of his holiday in Greece, Ralph Carder saw her sketching at the port of Kea.

She looked curiously out of place: a young, Oriental woman - Japanese, mused Ralph - among the fishermen. Ralph noticed her early in the morning as he set off to explore the island. At noon, when he returned to the port, she was still there at the cafe, sketch pad and pencil in hand. He wondered whether she had sketched all morning.

In the evening, after a swim and shower, Ralph did not see her at the port. Sunset was resplendent. The division between sea and sand, so ordinary by day, was sharply delineated by the red glow. Ralph walked along the beach till nightfall. Kea *was* perfect, a haven compared to London, an island treasure to which he must return.

The next day, he saw her talking to an American couple at the taverna. As before, her long, black hair was tied tightly in a ponytail. He thought of joining them - they were among the few visitors who dribbled into the autumn off season - but hesitated. He was not yet so bored as to need the company of Americans. Of course, the Oriental woman might not be American. He glanced at her again. No, not American. Her gestures, small and contained, were decidedly Oriental (perhaps Korean, he reconsidered). But he shied away, preferring his English reserve.

By evening, the solitude had become oppressive. Athens and Crete, where he had spent the previous week, were livelier. More - how he hated to admit it - touristy. It was all very well sniffing the freshly baked bread, exalting at the scenery, contemplating the silence. But it did get horribly dull. At dinner in the taverna, he struck up a conversation with the American couple.

The husband was an architect, as was Ralph. They were retired, unpretentious Midwesterners who had sailed in on their yacht.

"This is real near the mainland," explained the man. "Makes navigation easy."

Their yacht was quite luxurious. Ralph joined them on board for a brandy after dinner.

"There's Philomena," said the woman, peering towards the shore.

"Who?" asked Ralph.

"That artist from Hong Kong. You've seen her - the only Chinese around here. She's always got a sketch pad with her."

"Oh, yes," Ralph muttered, straining to see.

"Wonder what she sees in him," the wife said.

Her tone, acid and almost angry, struck Ralph. He saw the offending man: a middle aged, white haired, pot bellied man. Philomena and he were with a group of men.

"Why do you think she's with him?" Ralph asked.

"She said she lived with a Greek man. Her - what was it she called him - her benefactor. I don't know what she meant."

"How odd," said Ralph.

The conversation shifted to another topic. Ralph had a vision of Philomena in an orgy with all those Greeks. Artists, he thought, they were like that. Later, back in his *pension*, he found it hard to sleep.

The American couple sailed out the next day, and he was again at loose ends. Perhaps Kea was a mistake. He had expected an idyllic spot, away from the usual crowds, where he might meet a different sort of traveler. But everyone, it seemed, sailed in on their private yachts, and stayed around the port. Only he ventured inland, testing his limited Greek, waiting for the ferry scheduled three days hence to take him back to Athens.

He had been walking uphill for almost an hour when he came across Philomena perched on a rock. She was wearing black shorts and a black cotton blouse, and looked young, perhaps in her early twenties.

"Hello," he said.

She glanced up, shielding her eyes, but did not respond. Suddenly, like a cat, she twisted her body and slid onto the ground. Her lean, brown legs stretched out under his gaze. He sat down next to her. "What are you sketching?"

She stared straight ahead and snapped her sketchbook shut. "Why do you want to know?"

Ralph felt the sting of her rebuff. I'd like to slap her across the mouth, he thought. The violence of his reaction startled him. He was normally a calm person. "I'm just being sociable."

"Is that what you call it?"

There was a slight British inflection in her accent. She didn't move, and did not look at him. Ralph found his gaze fixated on her bare legs. Her skin was smooth and completely unmarked. Even her feet, clad only in sandals, seemed delicate and untouched by the roughness of the landscape around her. Like a child's.

He decided to try a different tack. "You're an artist, aren't you?"

"Yes."

"Oils, watercolors, charcoal . . .?"

"Oils."

"And has life been good here with the benefactor, Philomena?"

That got her attention. She looked directly at him instead of straight ahead. "You disapprove?"

"Should that matter?"

She jumped to her feet in a single, swift, easy movement. "No." She began to walk away.

"Then will you come out with me?" he called after her.

She gave him a quick backward glance, but continued walking. "Come to my studio," she said. "Your body's not ideal, but it will do for posing." And she disappeared down the hill and around a corner, out of his sight.

He felt rather silly over the whole experience. What had possessed him to call after her like that? That had been a waste of time. He stood up, and brushed off the seat of his pants.

In the evening, he walked along the beach and noticed the house for the first time. It stood atop a hill at the southern end of the beach, and had a stone window. He moved closer to make sure. It was a stone window. Odd, what good was a window one couldn't see out of?

He remained at the foot of the hill, puzzled.

A shout startled him. The doors of the house flung open, and people streamed out onto the patio. It was then he noticed another odd thing. The entire house was made of stone, of large, roughly hewn blocks. It was the only one which did not have the smoothly whitewashed walls of all the other houses around it.

"Ralph! Come up here and join us," Philomena called from the patio. Next to her, leaning against the railing, was the fat Greek.

Her whole demeanor had changed. She was wearing a bright yellow dress, and her long hair was loose.

He went towards the house, wondering how she knew his name.

Philomena took him by the arm and kissed both his cheeks in greeting. She looked older. Ralph realized it was probably her makeup. She introduced him to the fat Greek, whose name day party it was. Ralph quickly found himself surrounded by laughter, dancing, food, and *retsina.* It did not take him long to get drunk. A large woman in black danced up to him, tapped his cheek, and said "English!" to everyone's delight. He lost sight of Philomena for a couple of hours.

When next he saw her, it was in the room with the stone window at the back of the house. He found it hard to keep his eyes off her thighs, which flashed at him through the slit in her skirt.

She said, "This is where I paint."

"But there's no light in here." His words, he realized, were slurred by retsina.

"There's a window."

"A stone window," he said, and suddenly thought, how ridiculous I sound. And all he could think of was *I have to hold her, I have to touch her . . .*

They embraced, and the sensation of her bare arms against his was cold. Then they were back in the midst of the party, and she was dancing with her benefactor.

In the morning, he awoke alone on the patio. Someone had thrown a blanket over him. He was naked. His clothes were strewn on a chair beside him.

The benefactor was standing in the doorway of the house.

"*Kali mara,*" he greeted.

Ralph sat up, head reeling, and mumbled a reply. The Greek laughed. He continued speaking, too rapidly for Ralph to understand. But Ralph caught "Philomena" and "*kala!*" and wondered whether his reference to beauty was for her, her painting, or both. As Ralph got dressed, the benefactor held up both hands towards him as if he were holding an invisible blossom. Ralph thought he said something that sounded like, "Philomena, *kalaki-moo.*" Not till he returned to his *pension* did he realize that perhaps the man might have meant "Philomena, my little doll."

For the rest of his stay, he did not see Philomena alone again. The benefactor seemed to be around all the time. On the last morning, Ralph awoke with an erection, having dreamt he watched Philomena and the Greek fucking, while all the time the Greek laughed, and laughed.

Two years later, when autumn had made London's weather tolerable, Ralph was struck by some paintings in a gallery window off Upper Grosvenor Square. A watercolor, in particular, stopped him long enough to go in. The background had to be

Kea, nowhere else. But the foreground was a conglomerate of buildings and faces, buildings *with* faces, he realized, upon closer inspection. And the colors seemed limited to grey and scarlet, although he was sure some hint of green or blue washed the scene.

The proprietor approached him. "Would you care to look at that more closely, sir?"

"Yes, please. Who's the artist?"

"She Chinese, and signs herself by her surname Hui. A rather elusive middle aged woman who lives in Greece. It's the only piece of hers we've got."

Ralph continued to study it. It was surprisingly compressed, and the faces were Chinese. Philomena had said oils. But this painting had to be hers. It had to be.

He bought it, because the price was reasonable, and because it was just the right size for an empty wall in his flat where the painting hung, undisturbed, for several years.

2

A Gambler in Athens and a Girl from Hong Kong

Fall in Athens was infinitely better than fall in Boston, thought Hui Sai Yee, as she sipped a grainy Greek coffee on her first morning in Syntagma Square. It was early, before eight. The adjacent coffee shop had not yet opened for business. Or perhaps, she thought, it had closed for the season.

"Philomena? Philomena Hui?"

The voice, and the hovering figure, gave her a start. Hui was her surname. But Philomena? A virgin martyr's namesake in Athens, but Chinese? She shook her head.

"From Hong Kong?" the man continued. "You look just

like her."

He was Greek, middle aged, and pot bellied. His face could have been handsome, but was badly scarred by pockmarks. It was a good pick up line, she mused, as he sat down, uninvited.

"I am Constantin," he declared.

"I am American," she replied, "from Boston. Philomena and I are not related."

He ordered two cups of coffee. She did not protest. It was amazing, she thought, how readily people sometimes made themselves at home around her. Her Grandma who raised her in America often complained that too little bothered her.

"You look just like her," he repeated. "The same long, black hair, and those sloped eyes. You are small too, like her."

She resisted the temptation to say all we Chinese look alike, and waited to see what he would say. He continued talking, quite unrestrainedly, as if he had known her for a long time.

In a minute, she decided, she would leave him to see the Acropolis. After all, she wasn't here to be picked up.

"What do you do?" Constantin asked.

It felt like an omen, at least Grandma would have described it as such, that a stranger could inject into his commonplace question the problem of her existence. A year ago, she would have replied quite casually, I'm a stringer for UPI. Yet here she was, thirty, living off savings, of no fixed abode or profession, by her own choice.

"I'm a writer," she replied. What the heck, she'd have to begin saying it sometime. Grandma's voice cackled in her memory: You want to write stories? I'll tell you about my life in China. Why go to Greece to write? What's in Greece?

Constantin's eyes lit up. "Very good, very good. Our country is good for writers. Listen, I'm not a bad camaki boy. I'll buy you coffee, and tell you the story about Philomena, and then," he struck his hands together twice in a gesture of dismissal, "that's all. I don't ask for nothing."

His English was remarkably good. No harm in listening, she decided. The Acropolis was probably still closed. She was sure he was doing *camaki*, though with more imagination than most. But then, this was Syntagma. Adapting was part of her style.

"First, I must show you something." He pulled out his wallet, removed and unfolded a sheet of paper. It was a sketch of a house on a hill.

She glanced at the picture. "What about it?"

"Look at the window."

At first, it had looked like the side of an ordinary stone house with a window. But now, as she scrutinized it, she saw that the window pane was shaded to match the markings of the stones. The effect was disquieting.

"It looks," she said, "like a window made of stone."

"Exactly!" He folded up the sheet. "It took me a long time to realize what she meant when she said, 'Inside, I see light, but from the outside, it is dark.' Anyway, Philomena Hui is an artist from Hong Kong. And she lived in this house on one of the islands."

"How did you meet her?"

"Listen," he held up his finger dramatically, "do not interrupt me, and I'll tell you. She was a crazy, crazy woman. Like a little child. After she left the man who owned that house in the picture, she lived alone, on Hydra, I think. I told her she needed a man to look after her, and she got angry at me. Imagine! She got angry a lot."

She was about to ask him another question, but he signalled her to be silent.

"My wife divorced me seven years ago. Now, I am a gambler. Well, I am a souvenir shop owner, but I gamble away profits." He made a shrugging gesture with his hands. "For seven years now, I have been alone. It's a terrible thing for a man to be divorced in Greece with no wife to look after. But you wouldn't understand about these things. You are too young, like her. I would have stopped gambling for her."

As she listened to him, Sai Yee could hear Constantin saying to Philomena - you need me, you must need me, because I am a man. Was Philomena, if she ever existed, really crazy? She was dubious.

Constantin continued at full momentum. "Philomena came one day to my shop and bought some pottery. She wanted to send these to Hong Kong, to her parents, she said. From the beginning, I told myself, don't bother with this woman. Something about her was not quite right; she behaved like a bad woman, even though she wasn't."

"What do you mean?"

"I saw her many times alone, in the Plaka and Syntagma. Everyone talked about her, everyone knew she was a bad woman. Only I knew she wasn't."

"But why do you say she was 'bad'?"

"You know, too many people talk talk talk about her. Said she went with many men. Said she was crazy. She stayed in a little hotel in the Plaka by herself."

Perhaps, she thought, she had made a mistake listening to him. He seemed a little crazy, and Philomena sounded too mysterious to be real. But she persevered. "What happened between you?"

"I took her to a gambling house, but only because she insisted," he added quickly. "You understand, I'm a respectable man, even though I'm divorced and a gambler. I don't take ladies to bad places. You wouldn't go to one, would you?"

"I don't gamble."

"As I said, you wouldn't go to one."

What was it he objected to in this Philomena that made him say such curious things, she wondered. He obviously didn't seem to expect much response from her, as if her questions interrupted something that didn't warrant questioning.

He continued without pause. "And she gambled crazy. Put all her money in - they played blackjack there. Didn't even wait for me to introduce her, to explain that she was just a tourist who wanted to see the place. She spoke Greek too, which I didn't expect, and won plenty. Then she stopped, just when I would have continued playing. I asked her later why she stopped, and she said, 'I have a fixed amount in mind that I can win or lose. I am not interested in gains or losses, just in maintaining a balance. It is important for my *wa*.'"

The way he said it sounded more like "*hwa*" and she wondered if he meant the Chinese for harmony or peace.

"Philomena stayed in Athens for a couple of weeks. I offered her my home, tried to make friends with her. But she was unfriendly. Only one time, we went to dinner together, and then she insisted on paying. Here is the strangest part: she paid for the meal with a gold American Express card."

He waited, clearly expecting a reaction.

Perhaps he was mad, she thought. "Many people have credit cards."

"But Philomena was from Hong Kong. She was just a girl. In Hong Kong, the Chinese people live in huts on hillsides. I know. I saw it for myself in pictures."

What pictures had he seen, she wondered. She pictured the bustling, modern city she had visited just two years ago, when she first discovered her parents were alive there. But it struck her that he would not be interested in the truth. Finally, she asked, "How old was Philomena?"

"How old?" He looked at her as if the question were absurd. "How would I know?"

"Then what makes you think she was a girl?"

He finished off his coffee and stood up. "You do not believe me. But I tell you: this was true, this happened. I can't tell you how old she was, but she was a girl. Believe me, I know." He wrote down his shop address, invited her to visit, and, as abruptly as he had appeared, he walked away.

During her stay in Greece, Hui Sai Yee met many people who told her stories. Many of these she soon forgot. But Constantin's she remembered, although it was impossible to write anything about him. Once, she tried a portrait of a gambler, but found, after several drafts, that she had learnt nothing about gambling from him. The story of Philomena disturbed her, but she couldn't quite say why.

The day in January that her first novel was rejected she wandered around Upper Grosvenor Square, wondering how writers made a living if they didn't have other jobs or were independently wealthy. Grandma never complained, but Sai Yee didn't like asking for money from her to subsidize what little she could make doing pick up work. UPI had already asked her to work for them in London. But writing a novel about her immigrant grandmother in Boston, was not linked, in her mind, to working for UPI.

It was then that she saw Constantin's portrait in the window of a gallery.

The Chinese artist stamp in the left corner read "Hui." Sai Yee asked the proprietor if by chance this was a Philomena Hui.

"Philomela Hui?" he repeated.

"No, Philomena," she said. "The saint, not the nightingale."

He smiled at her. Sai Yee could tell he liked the way she turned his slip of the tongue around. She thought he had a kind face. For the next fifteen minutes, he searched through papers on his desk and in his files, emerging at last with a triumphant "aha, you're right."

Yes, he said, as he riffled through a file he'd found, her name was indeed Philomena with an "n", and she was from Hong Kong.

"Have you met her?" Sai Yee wanted to know. "I mean, how did you acquire this portrait?"

He frowned, trying to recall. "It must have been about a year ago, yes, that's right. She came in with some oils. Normally, I don't buy anything from someone who walks in off the street, but she seemed desperate for money. Some of her work was really quite good. On an impulse, I gave her a little something for a couple of the oils and this charcoal, which is the only piece I have left."

"What was she like?" And, to explain her curiosity, she added, "this may sound strange, but I think she might be a relative of mine whom I've never met. You see, we have the same surname, and I'm also from Hong Kong."

He was even more forthcoming after that. Yes, he remembered now, that she was a small woman, not particularly attractive, but rather able to command one's attention. Quiet though. Spoke as little as possible. How old? Oh, he couldn't say for sure but mid forties or fifty perhaps? A bit eccentric, but no more so than most artists. As an afterthought, he remarked that if she and Philomena were related, he couldn't see much family resemblance, and that of course the artist was much older than her.

Sai Yee bought the charcoal portrait - it startled her how exactly ugly Philomena had made him. She contemplated sending it to Constantin's shop. But, in the end, she kept the drawing. It was some time before she returned to Greece again, and when she did, Constantin had long been filed away as notes for a story that remained unwritten. The picture, however, she framed and hung over the bureau in her room in Grandma's Boston apartment, the one place she still called "home."

3
An Agean Box

On the second morning of their honeymoon, Ralph Carder and Hui Sai Yee stood on a ledge of Hydra's coast, and stared at the large chest washed up by the Aegean onto the rocks below. It was fall . He climbed down to take a closer look. She followed.

"It's just like a Philomena Hui," said Sai Yee.

"You're right, you know," Ralph agreed. "But why?"

"Because you see it but can't see into it."

Ralph bent over the box and touched the damp, purplish tatters that covered it. Shreds of the rotted fabric came loose in his hand. He pushed it with his foot, but the box wouldn't budge.

"How long do you suppose it's been here?" she asked.

He knelt down and felt the base of the box. Sharp barnacles had formed which connected its base to the rocks. "Here, feel that," he said. "But watch your fingers."

She knelt close to him, and caressed the sharp roughness.

Ralph said, "It's sort of crusted, isn't it?"

Sai Yee pulled at the latch, but it wouldn't give. Rust flakes tinted her fingers a dirty orange.

"So what do you think of our treasure chest, darling?" He nestled his chin against her cheek.

"Is that what it is? Are you sure it isn't Pandora's box?"

He laughed. "Could be. Want to open it?"

She said, "Let's leave it alone."

He meant to say, I met Philomena once, you know, but didn't. At that same moment, she was thinking of Constantin, and wanted to tell Ralph that she felt a kinship with the mysterious Philomena, which was partly due to her supposed resemblance, but also didn't. A moment later, he was pushing her against the box in a playful tumble, and she, in answer, pulled his body tightly against hers, and they kissed, for awhile, on the rocks.

Later that day, they showered together. Sai Yee soaped the back of his neck, and he closed his eyes against the spray.

Only three months ago, this naked person behind him had bumped into him at an exhibit of Philomena Hui's "Stone Window And Other Works" on a London's summer evening, and had had the audacity to say, "Do you always meet women this way?" before introducing herself. And then to discover that she was from Boston, to which he was going to be transferred, and that she was planning to go home, and that she shared his love for Greece and more importantly, Greek mythology, and . . .

"We're on her island, you know," Sai Yee shouted over the jet of water. "Maybe we'll meet her."

Ralph stepped out of the shower and began drying himself. "I don't want to," he said.

"Why not?"

"We have better things to do on our honeymoon than track down iconoclastic painters from Hong Kong."

He regretted his lie immediately, and covered his face with the towel to avoid looking at her. He never wanted to see Philomena again! Often enough, he had wanted to tell Sai Yee about meeting Philomena. But he was too embarrassed by the whole incident. It made him look foolish.

The water gurgled down the drain in the shower as Sai Yee finished rinsing off. He felt her hand reach out from behind the curtain to rub his neck, and Philomena vanished from his thoughts.

At noon the next day, they sunbathed on a secluded rock plateau off the eastern coast of the island. Sai Yee watched Ralph dive into the Aegean. He was slender and graceful, like a seagull.

"The water's delicious," he shouted. "Join me?"

"Later. I want to read."

She watched Ralph swim away, disappearing behind a wall of rocks to the west. He had told her once that he could swim for hours.

For the next ten minutes, she tried to read, but her thoughts wandered to the new novel she had begun writing. An October honeymoon in Greece: what could be further away from life begun first in China, and then with Grandma in Boston? Hadn't she told Ralph, when they first talked of marriage, that they were agreeably suited to each other because neither had relatives or friends to object? Ralph was an only child whose parents had both passed away. As for her, what did she really know about parents now in Hong Kong whom she had separated from in China when she was eight? And her grandmother had passed away earlier this year, just after the Chinese New Year.

A twig snapped behind her.

She turned around. "Ralph?"

There was no reply.

"Is someone there?"

The silence frightened her. There was, as Grandma would say, a ghost.

"*Taai do gwai gu,*" she murmured. Too many ghost stories. Her momentary lapse into Cantonese startled her. She had a sudden remembrance of Constantin's face staring at her from the portrait in the London gallery.

Her imagination was over excited, she decided; she returned to her reading. A rustle of leaves sounded behind her. She turned quickly, and thought she saw a flag of long black hair disappear further up the slope.

After they had made love, they lay together in the early morning hours. Sai Yee said, "Do you think Philomena has long hair?"

"Like yours, you mean?" he replied, stroking and coiling her thick strands.

She almost said, I'm told I look like her, but stopped herself. That presence, that "ghost" she had sensed earlier, had returned. She sat up.

"Darling, what's the matter?"

She did not reply, but got out of bed and proceeded to get dressed.

"What do you think you're doing, Sai Yee? It's four in the morning."

"Come on, let's go out."

"Where to?"

"The box by the sea. The one we found the other morning. You know, Pandora's."

He followed her, wondering, is my wife a little mad? As they headed towards the Aegean coast in the dark, he thought that Sai Yee did, in a way, remind him of Philomena.

Over her shoulder, Sai Yee said, "In Pandora's box, hope remained. The way the story goes, it isn't clear whether it was a barrel or a box. Nor is it clear who really opened the box, because in one version, it's Epimetheus her husband who opens it, although most accounts say Pandora opened it out of curiosity and accidentally unleashed evil in the world."

Ralph picked up her train. "Then there's the other Pandora story, of the original most beautiful woman created by Zeus as revenge upon mankind for the theft of fire by Prometheus. You know, woman as evil sent to destroy man, with or without the box. Sometimes, I think that version has more validity even though the other one's better known. Accidental curiosity seems too ungod-like an incident for the creation of evil."

They arrived at the box, and she felt the top.

"It's warm. Someone's been sitting on this," she declared.

"What on earth do you mean?"

"Philomena's been here. I'm sure of it. She's trying to tell me something."

"Perhaps you're to write her story."

She embraced him, thinking, Ralph's easy acceptance completes me, is a part of me. Anyone else would have thought her mad. When he'd proposed, he said, "you won't have to work anymore for UPI. I'll support you. I want you to be free to write." How angry she had been at first! How they had fought as she tried to explain why she couldn't have some man support her. And he, uncomprehending, had said, "but don't you want to write?"

She stroked his hair, which was soft like a baby's. "You're probably right," she said, "perhaps I do have to write something about her." And then, feeling a wave of emotion overcome her, she exclaimed, "You're my benefactor. You want to save my artistic life, and I love you for it."

Her words held an uncomfortable ring for him, but he smiled and said, "Yes, you're right."

"When we get back to London, I'll quit my job. I won't work for them in Boston."

"All right," he said. And then, "I do love you, you know."

They left Hydra the next day.

"Let's go inland," she suggested. "Perhaps to Thessaloniki."

"Let's," he agreed.

They watched the port disappear as they sailed off. A pretty island, Ralph thought, but not terribly real. No cars allowed. A historically preserved sanctuary for visiting tourists to enthuse over. Overpriced rooms. Somewhere in the hills of Hydra, Philomena painted pictures that London's art buying public celebrated.

Sai Yee said, "You know, I lived in Hong Kong for a short while with an aunt before I went to America. She lived in a building along Chatham Road in Kowloon. I could look across the harbor and see the hills of Hong Kong. There are buildings dotted all over the hills there, just like here."

"And that's why she paints here. Is that what you mean?"

"I don't know."

They remained on deck in silence. It was a clear, crisp autumn morning. How complicated it was, thought Ralph, this whole business of knowing another person. Sai Yee smiled at him, and he wondered whether or not she read his thoughts.

"Do you suppose her stone window is on Hydra?" she asked.

"No." He had answered too quickly, he realized, seeing Sai Yee's puzzled look.

"How do you know?"

"She painted it before she moved here. Remember? It was in the notes for the exhibit."

"Was it?" She smiled. "Of course, I did have my mind on something else that day."

They kissed. The boat chugged its way back to Athens. They passed the eastern coast of the island where Aegean waves broke against a crusted old box on the rocks. Had the lovers looked up, they might have caught a last glimpse of it. But they were too engrossed in their embrace to notice.

4
Philomena

At dusk, the man on Hydra known only as "Roach" sat at the waterfront cafe table farthest away from the pier. Ralph sat at his table. A crowd began to gather around them.

Roach scratched his pockmarked cheek, lit his pipe, spat, and took a sip of coffee. After a pause, he began the story he often told to locals and tourists alike, always beginning his tale at any point that suited him at the time of telling. His English was good. People said he used to live in Athens years ago and learned his English from tourists.

"She used to recite a poem by Li Po, the famous Chinese poet" he began, "to maintain her *wa. Wa* means harmony. It was important to her. She told me this translation:

From bedside moon is bright,
Lights up ground below.
Raise head to see moonglow,
Lower head to recall village.

"She could not recall, she said, her city-village. And she would cry and cry, as if to remember were the most important thing. I told her to forget.

"Sometimes, she tried to paint. But she couldn't any longer; her hands shook too much."

"Was she alcoholic?" Ralph asked. "People said that about her."

Roach waved his hand in a gesture of dismissal. "No, no, you don't understand. I'm a simple man. I can't explain these things well. But she wasn't an alcoholic. She was a very frightened little girl, and I had to take care of her.

"There was a man, Demetrius. He was young and tall, and very handsome, not ugly and fat like me. He loved her, and wanted her to marry him and take him to China. But he was a bad man, very lazy and shiftless. He preyed on women who visit our island, and made love to them. She despised him, but kept him around her.

"You see, I tell you she was lonely. She wanted this man to take care of her, but he couldn't. In the end, Demetrius went away one summer to Hollywood with an American woman who was very fat, but very rich. She was a hairdresser for the movie stars. She came to the port to see them sail away. Her eyes were angry and jealous. I watched her that day; I'd always watched her, even in the days when she still painted and was friendly towards foreigners. I knew that one day she would need me."

Roach coughed, and stopped to refill his pipe. He was thin

and bony, and his gnarled hands were brown as the wings of a roach. It was hard for him to talk about her now that she was gone. And the cancer in his throat caused him pain. But he did talk, each week as he waited for her boat from Athens, to anyone who would listen. Now, he had been waiting for years.

"Philomela had bad parents," he began suddenly. "They gambled. Her mother never suckled her, never taught her to be a woman. This was why she seemed to be a bad woman even though she wasn't."

"Why do you call her 'Philomela'? Why do you say she was 'bad'?" Ralph interrupted.

"Philomela is her name. Why do you need to ask? It is not I who call her bad, but people did. Because she gambles."

"In Athens? What does she play?"

"No, no." Roach gestured impatiently. "I only said she gambles. It is what she does with her life. I'm not talking about playing for money." He paused, and tapped his pipe which had gone out.

"Please," he continued, "let me go on and you listen. One night, after her screams, she told me about her life. I must tell you about the screams. Many many months passed before I could get her to stop. I was tired, always looking after her. I caught very few fish during that time.

"It was about four or four thirty one morning. I was walking along the path to Kamini, where the road is high above the water. I heard her screams. It was a series of screams, unending. At first, I couldn't see where she was. All I knew was that those screams came from below, from near the sea.

"I began to climb down the rocks towards the source of the sound. When I found her, she was sitting like a bird on a big old box with her hands between her thighs. Just screaming."

"Like a nightingale," Ralph interrupted. "Or a swallow." He

gazed into the distance with a faraway look in his eyes. "The daughters of the king of Athens."

Roach gestured impatiently. "You mix up my story. She wouldn't like that. Listen," he waved his hand at the audience, "she looked like a bird. That's all you need to know. So I continue.

"'Chinese woman,' I said to her, 'stop screaming.'

"She did not stop. It was as if she had not heard me. I said again, louder this time, 'Chinese woman, you must stop screaming.' But she carried right on.

"I was afraid that people would wake up and bring the police. I knew she must be ill - she had not been to the port for weeks. Perhaps, I thought, she had a fever. So I picked her up and threw her into the sea.

"Well, the screaming stopped at last, and I waited a few minutes to see if she could swim. When she looked like she was drowning, I jumped in and pulled her back to the rocks."

He stopped, and a satisfied smile appeared. His coarse, reddened, contorted features did not improve with his smile. He removed his cap, and scratched his slick, black hair.

Ralph asked, "Did she have a nervous breakdown? Is that why she stopped painting?"

Roach shook his head vigorously. "No, no. I tell you I'm a simple man. Those are fancy words for doctors and educated people. I only tell what I see, nothing more. She needed to scream. She had needed to for a long time, and I let her. I tell you, although you too probably won't believe me: she was lonely, she needed someone to take care of her. Is that so hard to understand?

"I took her to her home, undressed her, and put her to bed like a baby. She looked at me as if she did not know me, but I'm sure she recognized me. I've known her for a long, long time, but she was famous and I was not. I sat by her bed, and watched her sleep. From that night on, I began to live with her.

"After that, I would try to follow her to the rocks. She rarely spoke to me, hardly acknowledged my presence. She was very sly. When she wanted to scream she would sneak out without my knowing, and I would find her, perched like a bird on the box, screaming.

"Some mornings, she would mumble to herself in Chinese. It was important to her to remember her past. After all, she was not young even thought she looked like a girl. When she noticed me, she would say, in Greek, 'Ghosts, ghosts. I won't let them have me. I will paint the insides of my mind.' You know, she spoke Greek beautifully. More beautifully than me. She even knew classical Greek. I wanted to get her off the rocks to hear her speak. On those mornings by the sea, she was bewitched by the Aegean and the dawn. She had no place for me."

Ralph continued to interrogate Roach. "Did she have a friend?" he asked. "Another Chinese woman? The one she called her sister?"

"She had many many friends. People came to see her from all over the world. Artists came to learn from her. And buyers came because her paintings were worth a lot of money, yet everyone had heard that on Hydra, she would give away her half finished or even finished canvases."

Roach belched, and took another sip of coffee. Some of the crowd around him dispersed, and he collected the drachmas they left. Ralph stayed, and ordered Roach an ouzo. He gulped it down, and the waiter brought him a second glass which he held but did not drink.

A boat sailed into the harbor, and Roach stood up, squinted against the setting sun, his hand shading his eyes. As the boat neared, he sat down again.

"She's not coming back today," he declared, and gulped down the second ouzo. He relit his pipe, got up, and walked away.

Ralph sat until the sky was dark. His head hurt. The pain was getting worse. How long had he been coming here, to this island, in his search for the woman he loved? He used to know, used to count off each year he missed her. Now, he no longer counted.

Philomela and Procne, daughters of Pandion, king of Athens. Tereus violated them both, marrying Procne and imprisoning Philomela after severing her tongue, all without Procne's knowledge.

He began walking towards Kamini, towards his room. It was spring. Boston's spring air was bracing. The breeze was gentler here. And the island was covered with poppies and daffodils. Ralph climbed up a ridge overlooking the sea and stopped to watch the waves. Almost Easter. Almost time to crack blood red eggs at midnight after a feast of roasted lamb.

Procne got her revenge. She sacrificed her son, Tereus' child, and served his flesh to Tereus.

Ralph gazed at the sea for an hour, maybe longer. Sometimes, the sound of the waves eased the pain. At other times, the incessant pounding of the water frightened him, and he would run back to the hills, away from the shores. At Faneuil Hall one day, Sai Yee had said something like that. Or perhaps it was the day they walked around Chinatown and she saw her grandma's ghost. He couldn't remember.

Did Tereus enjoy the feast of his child Itys?

He continued along the path towards Kamini, his eyes

trained on the rocks below. He hadn't seen the box, it seemed, for quite awhile. It was there somewhere. He knew it. Sai Yee had wanted to bring what she called the Philomena Hui box back to Boston. Ralph stopped in his tracks, startled by the clarity of this memory. There were moments he could remember exactly, the way things used to be, the way he once was. But the moments would pass, and he would lapse into an easy forgetfulness, recalling only an image of her.

Of whom? Procne became a swallow and Philomela the nightingale. That's what the English poets say. Originally, it was the other way around because Philomela became the swallow that twitters but can't sing. Nightingales sing. They need their tongues.

The box was rusted shut. If Philomena had ever sat on that box, she only kept it further shut. Ralph stopped searching the rocks and continued walking, his eyes on the path ahead. Philomena's body was small, like a girl's, the night they made love. It had to have been Philomena that night. He couldn't remember another woman there at the party who was as small. But he wasn't sure, couldn't ever be sure.

His head hurt.

Ralph climbed the stairs to his room on the second floor. He opened the unlocked door. Cooking smells emanated from his landlady's home below. She welcomed him back to Hydra each spring when he returned, and asked if he had enjoyed his autumn in Kea. It had been easy at the beginning. This year though, she seemed uneasy, almost a little unwilling to take him back. In the end, everything worked out fine. He paid her extra and explained his weight loss on his illness. His appearance had frightened her, he knew.

Philomela wove a tapestry depicting the story of her imprisonment and sent it to Procne. Sisters find a way to talk, even without a tongue.

Opposite his bed hung the Philomena Hui watercolor. A few years back, he had it verified as one of hers. It was valuable, one of the few known watercolors in existence. Ralph kept it on Hydra. When he was away, his landlady stored it for him.

He poured himself an ouzo and added water.

When Sai Yee had disappeared, suddenly one night . . . the pain became unbearable. Ralph lay down in bed, hoping it would go away. Memory increased the pain. He had to stop remembering, had to rid himself completely of the past. Only then would the agony end.

He stared at the picture. Chinese faces on buildings. The skyline of Hong Kong, of Philomena's city village. The scarlet and grey swath of color captured him long before the buildings and faces. Sai Yee asked, the first time she saw it, is that perhaps her face on the center building, it's the only woman . . . what else had Sai Yee said? Ralph thought his head would burst.

Something someone said - it was the buildings, that drove her out, and the hordes of people, increasing all the time. Yet, in the stillness of Hydra, she claimed to find no peace. No Chinese in Greece, she said, except lonely cooks in Chinese restaurants. Who said? Philomena? Sai Yee?

He watched the picture change in hue from scarlet and grey to blue and green. It changed quickly today, like an automatic remote flicking between television channels. Soon, the moving colors would settle into a mixture of oils thick on the canvas. Like a stone window.

Eventually, he knew, sleep would come. He waited for that moment, the time when all voices were stilled, except for her tongue-less murmurings, soothing his body to slumber.

VALEDICTION

Short Story

"So let us melt, and make no noise
No tear-floods, nor sigh-tempests move,
'Twere profanation of our joys
To tell the laity our love."

"Valediction: Forbidding Mourning"
John Donne

London, 1989. Winter. Note in my *ga je's* hotel room.

Dear muihmuih,
Until we meet again.
Love.

Hong Kong, 1995. Fall. My fortieth birthday. Letter to my elder sister.

Dear *ga je,*

Do you remember that day, twenty or so years ago, in your *appartement* in Rouen, that modern if sterile place in a tower in the town you were going to leave once your husband got a job back in Paris . . . do you remember how you designed my sanctuary, the one I would some day have as a published, income earning novelist (yes I can hear you breathing an enormous sigh of relief — at last, about time)? You sketched every room for me — the monk's cell for my rough wooden writing desk; a cushioned reading space where the dumbwaiter led "downstairs" to an invisible kitchen and a cook who would cater to my every appetite; the library filled with shelves of books . . . and you promised you would one day commission an architect to build what you had drawn. When I saw Elvis' Graceland two years ago, and all those special rooms he designed, I remembered. But I don't want a Graceland; the imagined sanctuary of your charcoal sketches is all I need to survive my writing life.

And now, after the years have disappeared, vanished with my *gwailo* foreign devil husbands and insignificant others who no longer employ my life (thank god for US laws and alimony, however meager and late the payments), I finally found that space, albeit smaller and less grand than you originally imagined, and not a stone house in some coastal town along the eastern seaboard of the United States as you promised. It's taken me, oh a lifetime, or at least a few decades, moving and looking and striking out on new paths with such regularity that I am no longer surprising to any member of our internationally over-extended *wah kiu* family. When my first novel appeared in 1990, the Vancouver branch disowned me, you know, so there goes the last of the inheritance aspiration; the Singapore-singers-of-karaoke cousins refuse to keep my books at home as they consider them poison to the minds of their children; the clan in Java, that fried-in-peanut-oil-seriously-overcholesteralized horde of doctors, lawyers and pussy-whipped chiefs have told me I will never have the services of any of their chauffeured vehicles ever again (twice I was driven from Jakarta to Bandung and back to visit grandma's grave — for this I should be prostrate with gratitude); and the ones in Hong Kong are hugely thankful I write under a name that cannot be linked to theirs, since they must suffer me here in their city.

But what would amuse you most is our grandfather's reaction, issued edict-like from his haven in Perth — he said that what literary talents I had came from his branch of the family, but that it was a shame I chose to prostitute my talents in novels with "too much sex" instead of marrying a nice Chinese man (meaning Jen-Wei, his partner's grandson, who has more mistresses than condoms, but will inherit the fortune his father has amassed) the way he always told me I ought to, which would then free me to write about his life and the heritage of our family, a much "nobler" subject. Shades of *Red Chamber* nightmares! I must descend from a different lineage.

Dear *ga je* – Just what is family anyway? Bloodlines tie us. And for me, marriage and relationships created even more "families" which I couldn't avoid or disavow, unless, like *Mission Impossible*, a disintegrating tape could disavow all knowledge once each episodic week — How I used to love that show; how you used to tease me about it.

Family aside, it's also this "overseas Chinese" *wah kiu* business that gets in the way. Grandpop never fails to remind us of our heritage as he updates the genealogical chart each year for the family and all its branches. (His latest thing, you know, is proving the purity of our Chinese blood, despite the Indonesian, Caucasian and even Latino bloods that have seeped their infectious way into the generations). What kind of *dongxi* are we? How English fails me, despite all my English language novels! And *ga je*, how the Western World fails us for our most intimate expressions, our sense of family, our understanding of love.

Yet *c'est la vie*, isn't it, for this daughter of Hui.

Ga je, you'd probably like this flat I found back home in Hong Kong. Even by Paris standards, it's very large, over 1,500 square feet — 150 square meters to you. (I remember how you taught me that easy, approximate conversion. Helpful, as your teachings always turn out to be, because Hong Kong will be going more than merely metric in 1997). But large it is, larger than your Paris apartment and a lot more expensive, though not a walk up of six flights (how did you endure it with baby Jean-Pierre on your hip, the shopping in your bag, and your briefcase of work . . . I always admired your energy, your stamina to get a Ph.D. and married both in the same year while I struggled to finish my Bachelor's over six years, and then still didn't, during which you kept me going by the example of your life) — so my flat is enormous compared to our old home, and, well, luxurious. Yes, I hear you chiding me — *Muihmuih!* Ever my spoilt girl.

But *ga je*, she's happy. You don't have to come and save her here.

Actually, you'd like it. It's in Mid-Levels, "miles away" from home in Hillwood Road. How faraway it seems to *ma mi* and *da di*, way across the harbor, even though it's only fifteen minutes from where they are in Tsimshatsui to Central by the

MTR. You know, there's an escalator now that snakes from Central up to Mid Levels, which stops at several roads. The Hakka women coolies of our girlhood would have appreciated this moving staircase cut into the hillside, even if it does go against the grain of the dragon. In fact, some evenings I almost see one of them around Staunton Street standing still on an escalator step, rising to the heavens, and dropping, for just a moment, the load of bricks balanced on two bamboo baskets hanging from a pole across her shoulder.

But the parents! We were always too "faraway" for them, weren't we? Sometimes, I think of them as frozen into a past tense of safety. The first time, at college, was at least invisibly faraway. I almost made it you know. The blood from my wrists was difficult to stanch, the nurse told you. But what I want to say is that I remember how you came to me when I called in the middle of the night, the night he asked you to marry him. Eight or nine hours on a Greyhound it must have taken from New York to my petty, little, Boston college world. How I must have terrified you. And perhaps, if I'd made it, you could have had a life.

This flat though. It's in an old, pre-war building, just like home. I bought some high wooden screens to separate the living and dining room, like the kind in Uncle Bian Lee's place in Mongkok, the ones in pawn shops *ma mi* used to take us to when she didn't want to show her face anymore at Uncle's place, entreating him for yet another loan, pretending she was pawning her family's jewelry because she didn't care for them. The ceilings are, oh, twelve feet I'd say. Two lengths of my current lover would almost fit to the top — no, I know you don't want to hear about yet another one so I'll spare you the details, but at least he isn't a husband, no, don't roll your eyes at me — he's a Northern Chinese dissident poet from Beijing, they're the best kind, dissidents, that is.

But you! Living your almost perfect life. Married to an almost acceptable husband. You're the only woman I know of in this day and age who married the man who took her virginity — even Hong Kong women don't do that anymore. Even though he was French-American, at least he spoke beautiful Mandarin. *Da di* never had the grace to compliment him, but at least you could see how pleased he was to be able to converse in Mandarin with his son-in-law, after years of suffering the indignity of Hong Kong's Cantonese speaking populace who made fun of his accent. Yes, he was hopeless, wasn't he! And still is, despite all his years of Chinese school in Indonesia and his fluent Mandarin. But he gets his own back. A Cantonese trying to speak Mandarin is worse than an Australian speaking English — that's what he still says.

There's a tree outside my flat. A sprawling banyan. A pair of white cockatoos and a squirrel live in it. It reminds me of the tree we used to climb in the park near our school, the one out of which I fell and suffered a huge bruise on my forehead. You took care of me, took me to the hospital, and then rung the parents to summon them to fetch us because you didn't have enough money for a taxi. How old were you then? Only twelve at most I think.

But those cockatoos. They're not supposed to be there. Escaped from the Botanical Gardens, I think, or some such story. Who knows? All I know is that they shouldn't be in my banyan tree, no more than I should be in this city, this supposed home city of ours. I'm not like the squirrel; he belongs. He's got the right reflexes.

But here I am. It's a third floor flat, an easy walk up. The parents haven't seen it yet, haven't displayed even the slightest curiosity, but then again you know how they are. Did you know that they never visited my other place either, the one which my news-anchor lover rented when I lived here previously, and that was in Kowloon, albeit "miles" away on Broadcast Drive . . . Why am I complaining? Because they made it to your wedding halfway round the world, and gave you a dowry of jewelry and money fit for the queen that you are?

Why am I so sure you'd like my sanctuary?

When we were young, do you remember how I hated the sea, because, I said, it was always like taking a lukewarm bath. You were the queen who called me princess, and told me stories about my special *petit prince* on a flying black horse who would steal me away to another planet. Our new world had fields of poppies and daffodils, lots of them all over the hillsides, surrounded by an ocean of icy cold water into which I could dive and swim for miles. And it was quiet; there were no cars.

Remember the second time you rescued me? I had plunged into the Charles River in winter, and the nurses were trying to thaw me out. When you arrived by plane from New York, I was still hallucinating from the mushrooms and babbling about planetary horses. The nurse's aide said to you that I thought I was *le petit prince*, to which you replied, I was. How we laughed over that afterwards when you held me and welcomed me back! And I begged you not to tell our parents and you promised me you wouldn't. You kept that promise, too, didn't you?

Ga je! How did you love me so long?

Did I remember to say I moved into this flat in summer, at the beginning of summer? I missed the rains the day the movers arrived with all my things from New York. The very next day, it poured. Nothing could be worse than wet boxes brought into an old flat where damp rises, the way it does here. The ceiling in my study is streaking through the new coat of paint. The landlord did paint, and cleaned after a fashion. But he's off in Canada somewhere, and leaves these details to his sister who manages his property. No children. He refused to rent to anyone with children. The flat stood empty for awhile. A three-bedroom 1,500 square foot flat simply doesn't get snapped up by couples with no children. It is a flat for a Hong Kong family.

You would know how to make a home of it, with your children and your Shanghainese man.

Don't you understand how much *da di* and *ma mi* would have liked him? Oh I know he spoke accented Mandarin, which *da di* would have commented on, but at least his English was good enough for *ma mi*. And you and he could have jabbered with the children in French. Funny but for all your intelligence, without a doubt superior to mine, you just never understood about bloodlines. All you had to do was leave that husband, show up with your man and children in tow on the parental doorstep, and they would never have turned you away.

You don't believe me? No, I guess you would have a hard time believing me, divorced twice over the way I was, having affairs with local Hong Kong painters who exhibited my naked body across canvases in Hong Kong's art galleries with a distinctly clear representation of my face —poor *ma mi*, she couldn't face any of her friends for weeks when that happened. But I did it all here, not "faraway" in New York. It was we who were far, not they. Homage is paid to the Middle Kingdom — that is, to every Chinese parent that ever existed — not the other way around. I know each of my many returns was fraught with scandal, or the possibility of yet another familial loss of face. But I came home, like a dutiful daughter, for ma mi to weep over in shame. I didn't deny her that pleasure.

When Amelia was born, the parents diligently studied the photos you sent. How fortunate she came after Jean-Pierre. Don't you remember how all your baby things were embroidered with W for William, since they were convinced of your masculinity? *Ah non!* you say, our parents were not that Chinese, being as they were *wah kiu*, and never threading into Hong Kong society completely. Why do you think they waited so long before having me? Not to risk another disappointment? Or was I an accident? They'll never say, and we'll never know. So it's the guessing game, the favorite pastime of Chinese life.

But when Amelia was born . . . they studied those photos for a long time. Finally, *da di* looked up at both *ma mi* and me and declared, "She looks Chinese, thank goodness."

It was just before I took the trip to New York and OD'd on speed and Jim Beam. Remember that trip? That was my watershed attempt; you began your talking cure with me after that, once a week at great telephone expense to yourself and your family. And you stayed with me, sometimes for weeks at a time, or had me stay with you. Do you wonder that my brother-in-law found himself a few girlfriends?

Stoic sister, you should be in this flat of mine with your wonderful Shanghainese man. He truly loved you, perhaps even more than your husband did. The only reason I can afford it is because I'm the "right profile". The landlord said he would rent it to me because his sister was my schoolmate and vouched for me, actually told him he had enough money and should see his way clear to supporting a penniless writer who was after all, "one of us"? So yes, I live in luxury for a song because the schoolmate was once my lover and this way she knows there's less chance (though not no chance) that I'll keep our affair out of my novels and away from her very wealthy and socially prominent husband's eyes. I'm not immune to bribery.

You haven't always liked my "right" profile, have you? I can't say I blame you. Being right the way it worked for me was about being wrong, but taking that wrongness to such extreme heights (call it selfishness, license, self-indulgence — whatever it was, it worked, and, unlike Miller, I didn't even have to prostitute my lover for my daily bread) that it became the only way to be, the way everyone expected me to be. It was my *libération*, my *jie fang*. I didn't always like your responsible nature, your willingness to accept the roles dished out by Confucius and other tyrants. The charm of my irrepressible irresponsibility, backed by just enough talent, squeaked me by, especially in our shallow home city where a little melodrama goes a long way for lack of anything deeper to observe. Besides, I was good gossip for the party circuit. You chastised me, scolded me mercilessly as all good *ga je's* are supposed to do. But you never blamed my writing, the way the family did, because they couldn't understand, could they, why I had to do what I did instead of getting a job or married properly, the way I was supposed to.

I know now I was born to write. In your own way, you tried to tell me, without placing the pressure of being accepted on me, without expectation of a livelihood or success (how I've appreciated your many bailout loans for my extravagances over the years), without condemning the myriad wrong turns I took in pursuit of what I thought the artistic life should be. You painted my real dream, made me think, despite all proof to the contrary, that it was possible. Things only came true if you said they would. I am about so much fiction and always have been. You are about fact, about facing life the way it is, the way it has to be.

So why has this farewell taken so long to say, since that departure on your fortieth birthday?

You told me once you would not live past forty. It was in Paris, at the worst point of your marriage. I was young and "recuperating" from my most recent attempt. Have you forgiven me for not really knowing what you meant? Oh what am I saying? Of course you've forgiven me. You've always forgiven me.

But I should have known what you meant!

I think I understand. We were close in time and space. You changed my diapers; we fought on our parents' bed. I went after you with a knife and fork once when we were little, angry over some imagined hurt. So how could I not understand?

If nothing else, we could have lived in this flat together with your children. It's big and beautiful and spacious. I don't have the married lover anymore. He comes to Hong Kong often, which is ironic because, now that I've moved here where it would be much easier to see him because he travels out this way all the time, I've dumped him back in New York along with the husband. You know, the one you never thought much of, but didn't have the heart to say so? I know. You were right. You looked upon my husbands and lovers with disdain, and rightly so. Men let you down, you always said.

So why did you believe in love and romance and promises of forever? (You were dreadful that way — despite my multiple lovers I didn't really fall in love the way you did). I think it helped you survive adolescence, and, for a time in Paris, your marriage. And then your Shanghainese came along. A

Chinese doctor! And the son of a respectable businessman. What a perfect *wah kiu* son-in-law he would have made for the parents. He even wanted to come live in Hong Kong. You should at least have had an affair with him. But no, it was only love you wanted, and love you got. He called me once, to see if I could convince you to leave your husband. You wouldn't listen. And in the end he married, and that was the end of your second chance at love and happiness.

Of course your husband shouldn't have left you, despite the fact that we all knew it wasn't a marriage worth saving by then. Of course *you* shouldn't have disappeared to England that day the way you did, so that he could complain about how you just "upped and left your children" (what a hypocrite, he left you after all, and it's not like Amelia and Jean Pierre were left alone for any length of time since your mother-in-law was coming to visit that evening).

But it's too many years now to blame my brother-in-law any longer. He could *almost* be forgiven his flings with mistresses. After all, you were busy with the children, and me. Even I couldn't expect him to understand your devotion to such a prodigal, profligate and ungrateful sister. You never even told him about your own love affair, such as it was. What absolute fidelity your marriage inspired in you! As long as you could be in love, and if not that, as long as the marriage held, you could remain with me, with all of us.

Your children do remarkably well you know — I've been going to see them at least twice a year, and they still ask me to tell them stories every time. So I tell them about all the worlds beyond their own. It's the least I can do for my family.

You gave up on romance, didn't you? Perhaps if you had held onto the magic of falling in love . . . but for what happened in London afterwards I blame myself — for not going there when you called, for not being there on the one occasion you asked for help. Which is why I am no longer married to the man who stopped me, who whined his jealousy, even though you had never, in all those years, ever asked for a favor. Why didn't you shout? Why didn't you scream? Why didn't you din into my stupid head the real reason for your call, instead of coating your pain, the way you always do, because who I was, what I was, had to dominate the space between us? In the end, even that husband of mine wasn't to blame – he always whined.

Who wasn't he, the man who killed you? Why *wasn't* he there for you to fall in love with, to become starry-eyed over, like the heroines of all those romance novels you loved to read as a girl? Why didn't he materialize just one more time, to offer a bit of hope for surviving your divorce, your life?

Just like all your romance novelists, I let you down, didn't I? Me and the man who wasn't.

What triggered it that day? Why that day? I've turned it over and over again in my mind, to no answer, no lightening of the mystery. But it's not a mystery, is it? I can almost hear what you'd say — Death needs no pride, no *raison d'être*. It's life that demands our devotion and love.

I only know how to write my kind of novels now. Writing's the one promise I made to anyone that I've kept and will keep — when you told me that last time on the phone to write, always write no matter what, how could I know that my promise was what you needed to hear, to know you'd completed the last of your family obligations? I imagine you calling, first our parents, then your ex, then your children. And finally your *muihmuih*. "Little sister," how softly you said it.

Even when you asked me to come, it was less a plea than a request, understated, the way you always are in life, and in death.

You didn't even leave a mess. How like you to be so neat, to leave no blood, to have slept into your overdose in the bathtub so that cleaning up would be no problem. Just a body in a hotel room, with the exact cash payment on the dresser next to the hotel bill you had the foresight to ask for the night before. And my phone number on the envelope of that three-line note.

I keep it, along with your sketches of my sanctuary.

Dear ga je.
Until we meet.
All my love.
Muihmui.